Second Chance Town

Karly Lane lives on the mid north coast of New South Wales. Proud mum to four beautiful children and wife of one very patient mechanic, she is lucky enough to spend her day doing the two things she loves most—being a mum and writing stories set in beautiful rural Australia.

Also by Karly Lane

North Star

Morgan's Law

Bridie's Choice

Poppy's Dilemma

Gemma's Bluff

Tallowood Bound

Karly

LANE

Second Chance Town

ARENA
ALLEN&UNWIN

First published in 2016

Arena Books, an imprint of
Allen & Unwin
83 Alexander Street
Crows Nest NSW 2065
Australia
Phone: (61 2) 8425 0100
Email: info@allenandunwin.com
Web: www.allenandunwin.com

Cataloguing-in-Publication details are available
from the National Library of Australia
www.trove.nla.gov.au

ISBN 978 1 76029 181 5

Set in 12.4/17.6 pt Sabon LT Pro by Bookhouse, Sydney
Printed and bound in China by Hang Tai Printing Company Limited

10 9 8 7 6 5

FSC
www.fsc.org
MIX
Paper from
responsible sources
FSC® C023121

To everyone who has ever fallen off the horse, made mistakes, strayed from the path, or lost the plot; dust yourself off, say you're sorry, get your bearings, and plot a new course.

Today is your second chance.

One

Lucy Parker stared out of the smudged window. The road leading into Bundah stretched away as far as the eye could see. Baxter's Fuel Depot, the service station where she'd worked most of her adult life, was either the last business you passed or the first, depending on which direction you were headed. For most people it was the last as they headed out of town, never to be seen again. Traffic *into* Bundah was rare.

A dusty four-wheel drive went past and Lucy recognised it as belonging to Ken Baxter, the local chamber of commerce president, real estate and livestock agent, and owner of Baxter's Fuel Depot. If Ken had his way, Bundah's days of quiet streets would be over for good. All week Lucy had been hearing the mixed opinions about his latest scheme.

Ken's ideas for boosting tourism regularly sparked good-natured debate, until they were dismissed as too ambitious or far-fetched, but this time was different. This time his idea had the potential to really work and that seemed to have sent a ripple of unease through the small community.

Bundah had been a booming timber town until the early 1980s when the industry had been shut down. Like other small rural towns across the country which had been founded on timber, it had begun to shrivel and die.

Not much had changed about the little town over the years. It still had its shady verandah front shops and wide streets—a leftover relic from the days when bullock teams needed room to turn around their massive loads of logs in the main street. Lucy personally thought the main street was the town's best asset. The architecture remained virtually unchanged from the way it looked back in the 1800s. Unlike other towns in the district which over the years had tacked on bits and pieces to their main street, the result looking like a dog's breakfast, Bundah still had charm. If only they could get more tourists to take the road less travelled—literally—and explore the area, Lucy felt sure they would be captivated.

For years Ken had claimed he'd return Bundah to its thriving self again, but after so many failed attempts people had stopped taking him seriously. The town couldn't take another flop like the cowpat-throwing festival. Ken had been positive the festival would draw a large crowd from surrounding districts and become an annual feature on the local calendar . . . and it may have done had more people than cattle actually turned up on the day!

This time, however, Ken had outdone himself. Already there'd been a few enquiries about the ad he'd convinced the chamber of commerce and the Bundah Progress Committee to place in some of the city newspapers. And now, weeks later, a few new faces had started arriving in town.

Lucy pushed away from the counter to go in search of window cleaner. It was time to tackle the dusty streaks that had been driving her crazy for the past few days.

As she wiped the last of the water drops from the now sparkling window, Lucy turned to see a sleek, dangerous-looking road bike ease to a stop in front of the bowser.

The rider, dressed in full riding gear complete with leather jacket, pants and dark-tinted helmet, looked the part of the intimidating, faceless biker. For a moment Lucy experienced something weird, almost like a warning, before she shook off the notion and set aside the bucket of water to make her way across the service driveway.

'Nice day for a ride. How much would you like?' she asked, unhooking the nozzle from the pump and waiting for the helmeted rider to unlock the cap on his fuel tank, high on the uppermost part of the machine.

The rider slid off the big black bike with a slow, practised ease, before removing his helmet and sitting it on the seat. He took his time taking off his leather gloves before he turned to face her. 'I'll do it.'

Lucy held back her impatience as she waited for the man to practically undress before her. His haughty tone only irritated her further and she held the man's level stare with a spark of resentment. 'We offer full driveway service here,' she said with an abrupt nod towards the front of the station.

She watched as he turned to the faded sign which stated just that. 'Well, that's nice and all, but no one touches my bike but me . . . so maybe we could make an exception just this once.'

His voice was deep and had a slight gravelly edge to it that for some insane reason reminded her of smooth malted Scotch . . . Insane because she didn't even drink Scotch; and, besides, she had no idea if a voice *could* sound like that! Lucy bit back an irritated sigh and began counting to ten. She had no idea why this stranger annoyed her so much, but a recent quote she'd read on Facebook came to mind—*She may not be a sex therapist, but she could spot a wanker when she saw one.* A small grin hovered on her lips as she relinquished the pump and turned away to head back inside.

Lucy tried to concentrate on the spreadsheet on her computer screen but her gaze continued to stray to the man fussing about his motorbike outside. Arrogant or not, the guy sure did know how to fill out a pair of leather bike pants. With a shake of her head, she cleared away the wayward thoughts and tried to focus on the accounts.

Numbers. That's what she needed to focus on. Numbers made sense. They were logical and rational and rarely gave you nasty surprises. They were what she needed to be thinking about, not sexy male butts in tight black leather

. . . With a sigh of frustration she turned away from the window and took a sip of water from the bottle on the desk. 'Focus Lucy!' she muttered.

A few minutes later she looked up when the bell above the door rang and Mr Sex-on-Legs walked inside. She took his money, giving him his change without a word, and returned to the spreadsheet. Damned if she was going to wish him a good day after his brisk dismissal earlier.

'Do you know where I can find Ken Baxter?'

'He's probably in his office.' She pointed towards the stock and station office about a third of the way down the main street, surprised he'd come to Bundah for a reason.

'Thanks. Have a good day.'

'You too,' she replied automatically then frowned when she realised she was supposed to be ignoring him. 'Well, that's what you get for cutting off your nose to spite your face,' she knew her mum would have said if she'd been here.

The bike pulled out of the driveway with a low throbbing roar and she chided herself for not finding out more about this guy so she had some interesting information to report. She baulked at calling it gossip. After all, *gossip* was best left to the older generation around here. It was a skill that needed to be honed and perfected over time to know how to apply precisely the right quantities of curiosity and concern in order to extract maximum information. She should know, she'd experienced the lethal extraction on a number of occasions.

A car pulled into the driveway and Lucy headed out to the petrol pump. A few seconds later two more cars pulled in, both of which she'd filled only the day before and would in no way be in need of fuel this soon. With a small shake of her head, she knew she was about to be grilled for information about the leather-clad biker who was probably, at this very moment, inside Ken's office talking business.

Hugh Thompson stared at the tall man in the old felt hat and tried not to let his neutral expression slip. So far, he'd only spoken to the guy over the phone, but this wasn't the image of a real estate agent he'd had in his mind. Where were the slick suit and polished shoes? This guy was wearing faded jeans and a checked work shirt, with a hat that looked to be about a century old and in desperate need of a good wash.

As Hugh had ridden up the mountain range earlier, his excitement had begun to grow. He knew this venture was a winner. The tight corners and breathtaking views of the mountain road were a bike enthusiast's dream. He'd done his research, he knew that a place like Bundah, tucked away at the top of the range, would be the perfect base for bike riders exploring the different rides the area offered. They had a choice of narrow, twisty roads winding through rainforest, or wide-open highways that went for miles, as well as everything in between. He'd offer a top-notch pub as a destination with excellent food and accommodation and, down the track, maybe even guided road trips for riders who didn't want to explore alone.

'It's a good deal. You won't find a better pub for this price anywhere,' Ken said, interrupting his thoughts.

Hugh didn't bother arguing. He'd already been up to inspect the old pub, which was apparently called the 'top pub' as opposed to the 'bottom pub' at the other end of town. It had been sadly neglected for the last decade or so, and empty for the last five years after the publican had passed away and his family hadn't been able to afford its upkeep.

Hugh knew he was in a position to negotiate a good price and, even though the place needed an extensive facelift, he was pretty sure that after three years of getting the place up and running, he'd be able to sell for a big profit. *If* he managed to get the place up and running, that was. Although God knows, he'd overcome bigger trials in his life.

To say the past few years had been a struggle would be an understatement, but that was all behind him now. This would be a fresh start, a clean slate. Here he might just have a chance to build a future.

He'd done his homework—he *always* did his homework. Hugh Thompson was not a man to jump feet first into something this big . . . Well, not any more anyway. He liked to be prepared. Even though in his previous life he'd often had to think on his feet, he was never one to rush into anything unprepared and he prided himself on professionalism.

Sadness crept into his chest cavity, unexpected and painful in its intensity as he thought about his old job. He'd been careful not to let his thoughts drift back there too often for this very reason. It took some effort but he pushed away that train of thought, remembering where he was.

'So? What do you think?' The real estate agent waited expectantly for some kind of sign.

Hugh could have put the poor guy out of his misery if he really wanted to, but that damn hat was annoying the living Jesus out of him so he decided to let him stew for a bit longer. 'I'll think about it. Can you recommend anywhere decent to stay the night?'

If all went according to his carefully thought-out plans, he should be able to double his money and maybe set up somewhere else. Maybe some place on the coast. Yep, three years was doable. How hard could it be?

The bottom pub, or the Emperor if the faded engraving set into the brickwork high above the front door was to be believed, was the only accommodation in town. Hugh booked himself a room and climbed the solid timber staircase wearily. It had been a long ride, but his spirits rose when he recalled the steady climb up the mountain range. There was nothing better than long sweeping curves and tight bends for an exhilarating bike ride. The blood had been hammering through his veins, adrenaline pumping, and nothing else had mattered but feeling the road beneath his tyres and hearing the roar of the engine under him. He'd felt . . . *alive*.

Hugh unlocked the door of the room and tossed his bag on the saggy-looking bed he'd just paid for. The curtains were a burnt orange colour, probably the seventies originals, and they matched the orange velour bedspread. If he ignored the musty smell, he could almost pretend he was in a swanky overpriced inner city motel. It was all *very* retro. He particularly liked the authentic cigarette burns in the threadbare bedspread; they just oozed class.

If this was his only competition in town, he might achieve his goal more easily than he'd anticipated. His pub was going to be nothing like this crappy place. He knew his clientele; he'd spent the last two years working odd jobs, saving as much cash as he could to complete the final step of his plan, and in doing so had travelled around the country on his bike, so he knew exactly what bike enthusiasts wanted. The bar would serve cocktails and stock an impressive cellar. He was going to provide clean, not too pricey accommodation with outdoor dining and quality food. After a long day on the bike, these riders wanted somewhere to relax. Yep, he knew exactly what he was doing.

The unknown part was whether he could rely on the clientele to come through for him once the pub was completed. He didn't want to think what would happen if that part of the plan fell through. If he had to, there were a few favours he could call in, but he hoped he wouldn't have to. Instead the PR work he intended to invest in would produce results.

With a sigh, he changed out of his riding gear and into jeans and a T-shirt to head downstairs for a meal. He ordered a beer and wandered across to a pair of frosted glass doors marked *Restaurant.* Walking in and giving the room a quick once-over, he noticed the bold swirling patterns of the carpet and formica-topped tables. The room was old-fashioned—and not in a good way.

Noticing a few of the other patrons glancing over at him, he realised this was another thing he'd have to get used to. It'd been a long time since he'd lived in a town where someone new stuck out. It was something he'd forgotten about, having lived in the city for too many years to count. He gave a small nod of greeting to a couple seated across from him but then lowered his gaze—he didn't feel like making conversation tonight and he knew it wouldn't take much encouragement to start up a friendly chat around here.

An image of the woman at the service station flashed before his eyes. Lucy Parker. Ken had been kind enough to provide her name earlier today and he'd tucked it away safely to think about later. He bit back a smile as he remembered their brief encounter. She'd worn her dark hair pulled up in a ponytail which had swung jauntily in time with her hips as she'd marched back towards the service station. She hadn't been too happy about handing over the petrol pump and he'd watched her abrupt departure, admiring the roundness of her backside covered by faded denim jeans. Part of him had twitched in appreciation, reminding him of what that had been sadly lacking from his life for too long.

Sex had been the last thing on his mind over the past few months. His whole world had almost come crashing down around him and it had taken every ounce of strength to keep it all together. Maybe now that he'd put it all behind him he could afford to blow off a bit of steam if he found a willing woman. Somehow, though, he didn't think Ms Parker was going to be all that willing, which was a pity. She had a sassy mouth and a body he found all too distracting.

He hadn't meant to act like a jerk, but she was pretty damn cute when she was pissed off and he couldn't help stirring her up. Maybe he'd try some of the old Thompson charm on her next time and see what happened. Now if he could just dig around and try to remember where he'd left said charm . . . Judging by how long ago he'd last used it, he was going to need a while to scrape off all the rust and knock out some of the dints before he tried it again.

'What can I get you, love?'

Hugh looked up to see a thin, middle-aged woman with grey hair piled on top of her head standing beside him with a notepad. Her nicotine-stained fingers held a pen ready to jot down his order.

'Think I'll grab the special of the day, thanks.'

'No worries. Is that it?' she asked, waiting for him to hand back the laminated menu he'd picked up from the table.

He nodded and watched her hurry back to the kitchen to give his order to the chef. He would have liked to quiz her on a few things, like how busy they got, but decided not to on the off chance that the chef took exception to the upcoming competition and spat in his meal . . . or worse! No, best to play his cards close to his chest, he thought, easing back in his chair as he sipped his beer and surveyed the room.

Two

Lucy finished loading the last of the groceries into the back of the ute and secured the cover, stretching the loops over hooks to cover the rear of the utility and keep her food from flying out while she drove.

The drive home took barely a few minutes, nothing was very far away in Bundah—it was one of the things she liked about the place; that and the beautiful mountains that surrounded their small town. They were situated on top of the range, flanked below by dense rainforest and national parks. She'd moved here at fifteen with her family. Her father had been transferred to Bundah to manage the small bank, but within three years the bank had been restructured and small branches like Bundah were no longer deemed viable. It didn't seem to matter that the bank was the only one within a ninety-kilometre radius and that, back then, internet banking had never been heard of. Big business didn't worry about little things like that.

She turned into her street and parked in the driveway of her modest cottage, a leftover from when Bundah had provided workers' housing for the timber cutters and their families. Lucy loved her little home. It still had a lot of its original fixtures and so much character that she could almost hear the walls telling her their secrets as she lay in bed at night.

It was small, but it suited Lucy and her daughter, Isabella, just fine. They'd moved in when Belle had been a toddler, marking a turning point in Lucy's life. This was where everything had changed for the better. She'd made her fair share of mistakes and bad choices—and paid a heavy price. Losing her sister and then discovering she was about to become a mother had been the wake-up call she'd needed to get her act together.

The smell of the simmering stew in the slow cooker greeted Lucy as she opened the front door, carrying the groceries from the car. 'Belle, I'm home,' she called, then swore quietly as she kicked her toe on the corner of the coffee table.

Unpacking the bags, she frowned as she realised there'd been no answer to her greeting. She left the groceries on the bench to go in search of her daughter.

There was no sign of seventeen-year-old Belle and a quick check of her bedroom showed she hadn't been home since school finished either, judging by the lack of the usual schoolbag or uniform strewn across the floor.

In the kitchen Lucy searched through her handbag for her mobile. The sound of the front door opening and a muted ringtone signalled Belle's arrival, and she disconnected the call as her daughter walked into the kitchen. 'That was well timed. Where have you been?'

Belle gave her mother a guarded look before dropping her backpack on the kitchen floor and opening the fridge. 'I went to Casey's to hang out for a while. I didn't realise how late it was. Sorry.'

'You know you're supposed to call me at work and let me know if you're going anywhere other than straight home from school,' Lucy said.

'Yeah, I know. I forgot. Sorry. What's for tea?'

Lucy frowned, annoyed that Belle could so easily shrug off something this important, but the phone rang and the opportunity to continue the conversation was lost. By the time she'd dealt with the change of time for the next P&C meeting, Belle had already finished her meal and was heading to her bedroom to do her homework.

Stifling an irritated sigh, Lucy served out her own meal and sat down at the small kitchen table to eat. As far as teenage girls went, Lucy knew she'd had it relatively easy with Belle. She'd silently shuddered many times as she listened to other friends complaining about their latest run-ins with their kids. But recently there had been some worrying incidences of drug use amongst local high school kids, and this only added to the list of possible dangers for bored teenagers in a small country town. Only this morning Nicole had mentioned that two kids had been rushed down the mountain to Armidale Hospital the previous night, both in a critical condition after taking an unknown substance. The news had sent a ripple of fear through Lucy and she had an irrational urge to protect Belle by locking her away from all the dangers lurking out there in the real world.

She stood up and took her plate to the sink.

Belle was an easy child to love, happy and outgoing, but over the last few weeks Lucy had noticed a slight distance building between them. Something had changed. She wasn't sure what exactly, but the fact Belle now preferred going into her room to read or to talk on the phone with friends instead of spending the evening watching TV together definitely wasn't helping. Lucy wiped her hands on the tea towel and looked pensively down the hallway to the closed door of her daughter's bedroom. There was nothing concrete Lucy could actually call her on—she was still doing her homework and chores—but there was definitely something going on and it was time to nip it in the bud.

Lucy set her shoulders as she made her way towards the bedroom and knocked on the door. 'Belle, I thought we might watch a movie together tonight before bed. I feel like watching something soppy. How about it?'

'I'm doing homework, Mum.'

'You can finish it off tomorrow, can't you?' said Lucy, opening the door to find her daughter sitting cross-legged on her bed, surrounded by open textbooks and folders.

'You know most parents wouldn't expect their kids to ditch their homework just to watch TV,' Belle said haughtily.

'Most parents don't have a child who has her homework done at least two weeks in advance. Come on, Belle. One slack night won't make any difference.'

'I'm not taking any chances. I won't get out of this godforsaken town if I don't get enough marks to get into uni, will I?'

Belle's tone of voice rendered Lucy speechless for a moment. She'd never heard her speak so vehemently about wanting to leave. 'What's brought this on?'

'I'm sick of being treated like a child! You control everything, even Stringybark, which is *mine*.'

Lucy held back a moan of frustration at the mention of the property Belle's late grandfather had put in trust for Belle.

'When you're twenty-five you can do whatever you like with it.'

'When I'm twenty-five it'll be probably be worth nothing. I heard the other day that Mr Baxter made a fortune selling a place to that German family. It's half the size of Stringybark. We need to sell it now, while it's worth something. Come on, Mum. If we sell it I can use the money for uni. I can travel overseas for a year, anything I want.'

'Which is exactly why your grandfather put it in trust,' said Lucy, conjuring up an image of the old man sitting on his sunny verandah. Fred Monroe hadn't always been an easy man to love. He'd been grumpy and gruff and set in his stubborn ways, but they'd forged a bond over mutual loss and she missed him every day.

'I don't see what the big deal is. You've been working and saving for me to go to uni for years. Sell Stringybark and I can pay my own way. You wouldn't have to skimp and save any more.'

'Trust me. You'll be thanking me later when the money hasn't been blown on university, holidays and shopping sprees. By twenty-five you'll have a clearer idea of where it is you want to be in life, which is something you can't possibly know at eighteen.'

'See? There you go, assuming that I don't know what I want to do with my life!'

'Okay? What do you want to do with your life?'

'You know what? Don't even bother. I don't care any more. I just want to finish school and get as far away from this stupid town so I can live my own life.'

'Where is this resentment coming from all of a sudden?' asked Lucy, taken aback.

'I've always felt this way. You've just never wanted to hear it before.'

'What are you talking about?' Lucy asked, moving further into the room to stand by her daughter's bed.

'Nothing. Don't worry about it, Mum. Let's just not discuss it as usual and pretend it doesn't matter.'

'Belle, for goodness sake, what's gotten into you? Tell me what's wrong?'

'You *do* realise that at the end of this year I'll be gone, don't you?' said Belle, frowning up at her.

'Yes. I realise that,' said Lucy.

'Really? So you acknowledge that by then I'll be an adult?'

'Yes, once you turn eighteen you'll be an adult.'

'But until then I'm supposed to stay on a leash around here where you can keep an eye on me?'

'You're hardly on a leash, Belle.'

'Oh please! *Where have you been? Why didn't you call me? Come straight home from school. No, you can't go to that party this weekend,*' Belle mimicked.

'What was I thinking, being a concerned parent? Shame on me for wanting to make sure you're safe,' said Lucy, shaking her head.

'It's not a joke, Mother.'

Lucy raised an eyebrow. *Mother?*

'I'm not a child and yet you keep treating me like one. Do you know what they all say about me at school?' She barely gave Lucy a second to answer. 'They call me Princess Belle, because I'm never allowed to go to parties or hang out with anyone from school. Like I'm too good for everyone around here!'

'Oh, for goodness sake—'

'See! You're doing it again—brushing me off like I'm a two-year-old kid throwing a tantrum.'

'What's brought this on?'

'It doesn't matter,' Belle snapped, dropping her gaze back to the books on her bed.

'Clearly it does.'

'Marty Andrews is having his eighteenth birthday party and everyone else got an invite but me . . . He didn't bother inviting me because *everyone knows* I'm not allowed to go anywhere.'

Lucy winced a little at that. Was she really that much of an ogre? It was true she didn't let Belle go to parties when she knew they weren't going to be supervised. She knew many of the parents around town *did* let their kids go to these impromptu parties which were often held out on a property around a bonfire and always involved utes, lots of alcohol and more teenage hormones on the rampage than mossies in a swap.

She also knew the kinds of young girls who went along to these events and she knew their parents. It made her blood boil that because some parents had absolutely no rules the parents who did were considered tyrants.

'I'm not going to apologise for that, Belle. We've been through this before. There's no way on God's green earth I'm letting you run wild to do whatever you like. You don't need to be out at all hours of the night with older kids who are drinking alcohol. You're seventeen and you're underage.'

'You are *so* old-fashioned, Mum,' Belle snapped back.

Lucy shrugged before turning to leave the bedroom. 'You've only got to put up with it for the rest of the year. If you change your mind, Meg Ryan and I will be out in the lounge room.'

Lucy thought she heard a mumbled reply but chose to let it slide. So far they'd managed to keep their disagreements civil, but tonight seemed to mark a turning point. Was she going to lose her happy, carefree child to teenage mutiny this close to the finish line?

Just as Lucy was about to sit down at last, a silver Audi pulled up at the bowser. She muttered crossly under her breath. She'd been trying to get the business activity statement finished all morning without success. Pushing away from the desk, she went outside with a smile on her face and a cheery wave. 'Hi guys, how much would you like?' she asked the man who had opened his door.

'Oh my goodness. Would you look at this, Russell? They even fill up your car for you here.'

Lucy paused as she unscrewed the cap, eyeing warily the man who had just climbed out of the driver seat. Was he making fun of her? She couldn't tell; he was too busy waving his hands around excitedly at the other man seated in the passenger side.

'Is there a loo around here?' he asked, jumping a little from one foot to the other. 'I'm about to explode if I don't get to a toot right now.'

Lucy pointed towards the side of the building.

The passenger, who she assumed was Russell, opened his door and climbed out. 'Just fill her up thanks, doll.'

Doll? Was this guy serious? Lucy watched the large man do some stretches, and had to bite her lip to stop giggling as he completed his little exercise routine with a few high-knee steps. 'Been travelling a while, I take it,' she said.

'Feels like *forever*. Who knew how far this little place was from anywhere. Just between you and me, sweet pea, I haven't been able to feel my butt since yesterday afternoon.'

Lucy gave a sympathetic chuckle. 'How much further do you have to go?'

'Thankfully, no further. We're here to inspect a premises for rent,' the driver announced, catching the question as he returned to the car.

Lucy looked at the men uncertainly just as the nozzle clicked off to indicate the tank was full. Securing the petrol cap, she allowed Russell to lead the way into the service station to pay.

'So you're here because of the ad in the paper?' Lucy asked.

'That's right. We own a coffee shop in Melbourne, but we've been thinking about doing something different for a while now. Then last weekend we came across your chamber of commerce's ad to take a tree change. It sounded exactly what we were after, so here we are on a road trip to check it out.'

'Well,' said Lucy, handing over his receipt, 'I hope you like what you find.'

Lucy looked out the window as the man who'd been driving appeared to be trying to get his passenger's attention. For a moment she was confused, until Nate Pearce, the local police officer, walked in.

Russell gave a dramatic sigh. 'Steve's always been a pushover for a man in uniform.'

Lucy suppressed a smile at the startled expression which crossed Nate's face as he overheard the comment.

'Officer.' Russell nodded politely as he walked out the door.

'Who the hell was that?' Nate asked, seeming a little stunned by the whole encounter.

'I think *that* was our new café owners . . . or will be if they like the rest of town as much as they liked *you*,' she teased.

'I hope Bundah's ready for *them*,' he said with a chuckle.

'What can I do for you?' Lucy liked Nate. He was a nice guy. He'd moved to Bundah about ten years ago with his wife but she hadn't liked it out here and had gone to visit her parents not long after they'd arrived . . . and never come back. Maybe because they seemed to share a similar past, in which for whatever reasons their dreams had never quite turned out the way they'd supposed to, Lucy had always had a soft spot for him. But early on she had made it clear she wasn't interested in a relationship and Nate had never pushed the issue. They'd remained good friends over the years.

Nate turned his attention back to Lucy and leaned against the counter casually. 'Just wanted to have a word with you about Belle.'

'Why? What's happened?' asked Lucy, a hundred different scenarios running through her head at once.

'Nothing's happened; it's all right. I just wanted to give you a bit of a heads-up, that's all.'

Although her initial fears of accidents and her child lying in an emergency room were put at ease, something about his tone warned her not to let down her guard completely.

'Look, Belle's a good kid, but I've been spotting her after school hanging around with some kids who, let's say, I'm on a first name basis with, and not in a good way. I just thought you might want to know.'

'Yes, of course I do, but I can't believe she'd be sneaking around like that. She usually tells me what she's doing.'

Nate gave a tired chuckle. 'She's a teenager, Luce. Welcome to my world.'

What was happening to the well-behaved, quiet child she'd always known? 'Well, it won't be happening any more. Is it still illegal to lock your teenager in a cupboard?'

Nate's deep laugh drew a smile from her, but she was only half joking. What were her options if her daughter suddenly decided to ignore the parental rules she'd so far been happy to obey? Lucy couldn't be there in the afternoons to play warden; she'd relied on her daughter being sensible enough to stay at home alone for the last two and a half years. Surely at seventeen she wasn't going to have to get her child a babysitter!

'I really don't think you need to be too concerned about Belle; she's just stretching her wings a bit. They all seem to go through it at some stage.'

'Thank you for letting me know. I really appreciate it.'

'No worries. All part of the service.'

'I'm pretty sure Bundah gets a lot more service than most places. We're lucky to have you looking out for us.'

'Ah well, it's not like I get run off my feet with crime around here, is it?'

'I hope it stays that way. What do you think about the chamber of commerce's new population push?'

The policeman looked up the road towards the main street with a pensive expression. 'Hard to say. Could be a good thing . . . depends what kinda people it brings our way, I guess.'

Briefly Lucy's thoughts went to the leather-clad stranger she'd met yesterday and she wondered if he was an example of what they had to look forward to . . . She couldn't make up her mind whether that was a good or a bad thing.

That afternoon, as soon as Lucy heard the front door open, she called her daughter into the kitchen.

'What are you doing home so early?' Belle asked, her gaze roaming the kitchen, spying the plate of pancakes and hot chocolate waiting at the breakfast bar for her.

'I took an early mark this afternoon.'

'Why?'

'Because I wanted to spend some time with you. Sit down and eat these pancakes before they go cold,' Lucy said, pushing the plate towards her daughter pointedly.

'Pancakes? But it's not raining.'

'It was a pancake kinda afternoon, I thought,' Lucy shrugged. It was their thing. When Belle had been younger, weekends and after school on rainy days they'd always made pancakes. Since Lucy had taken on the job of manager at the service station it'd been a while since she'd been home after school—and even longer since she'd made pancakes. It was the down side to securing a better income for her and Belle. She knew how lucky she was to have a full-time job in a small town. It was a luxury becoming scarce in small rural communities. Ken Baxter could be an obnoxious boss, and they had had their run-ins, but on the whole she enjoyed her job and the responsibility of managing a business.

She watched as her daughter poured golden syrup on her pancake.

'So why are you really home early?' Belle asked.

'I'm worried about you,' Lucy said.

'Why?'

'I had a visit from Nate today. He thought I should know about the kids you've been hanging around with lately.'

Belle stopped eating and stared at her mother. 'It's none of his business who I hang around with. What right does he have running off to tell you about everything I do?'

'Maybe because he knows you and actually cares about what happens to you?'

'You mean he's trying to score points with *you*.'

'Don't go down this track again, Belle, and don't change the topic.'

'It's true! He's always had a thing for you, Mum. It's just not fair. He's spying on me just to get in *your* good books.'

'Yes, I'm sure he has nothing better to do than spy on a seventeen year old and report back to me.'

'Well, it's none of his business. We weren't doing anything wrong.'

'If everything is so above board, how come you haven't mentioned that you've been hanging around town after school?'

'Because it's none of your business,' Belle snapped.

'I beg your pardon! Somewhere along the line you seem to have forgotten that I'm your *mother*. I'm *making* it my business to know what you're up to.'

'I'm not a baby!'

'Then stop acting like one.'

'You make me so mad! I can't talk to you any more,' Belle stood up and moved to pick up her backpack in the kitchen doorway.

'Sit back down. You don't need to talk to me, but I haven't finished talking to *you*,' Lucy said, feeling extremely proud of herself for not having raised her voice. Belle folded her arms across her chest and glared at her mother for a few moments until Lucy narrowed her eyes warningly, and then she stomped back to take a seat on the bar stool she'd just vacated.

'What's with all the attitude lately? Is this still about that party?'

'It's about everything! I'm old enough not to get the third degree about who I hang around with and where I go. I'm over it!'

'Well, tough. I'm not letting you throw your life away.'

'I'm not you! And I'm not Aunty Claire either.'

For a moment Lucy's throat contracted at the mention of her sister's name. She'd always been honest with her daughter, telling her about her older sister's addiction to drugs and alcohol as a teenager. She'd hoped that by not pretending it hadn't happened, she might be able to instil in Belle the dangers of drug use at a young age and stop any curiosity she might have to experiment as Claire had.

Her sister's overdose had almost destroyed her family. Her parents had been distraught, losing their child, and then, on top of that, a few months later Lucy had been forced to tell them she was pregnant. Her poor parents had gone through a hell of a year. She pushed away the threatening emotion and focused on her daughter. 'Until the end of the year, you're stuck with me, so you'll just have to put up with it.'

'You can't make me.'

Lucy knew her mouth had dropped open, but she couldn't do anything about it. She was absolutely horrified by the way her child was speaking to her. It was as though she'd been possessed by some kind of evil being—who was this kid? 'I *can* make you . . . and trust me, things *will* be different around here from now on.'

'This is so unfair! You're punishing me for *everyone else's* mistakes. Just because *you* went and got yourself pregnant at my age, and your sister was a drug addict, doesn't mean I'm going to do the same thing. I'm not that stupid.' Belle turned away and stormed off to her bedroom, slamming the door behind her for good measure.

Lucy let go of the back of the chair and straightened slowly. Her daughter's words had felt like a blow to her stomach. *Had* she been pushing too hard all these years? She certainly hadn't intended to make her child's life unbearable! Maybe she had been a lot more strict with her than some of her friends' parents were, but they had two parents to share the load when it came to discipline—she only had herself.

Lucy closed her eyes and let out a slow breath. *Help me out here, Claire. Am I doing the right thing? How else do*

I stop her from making the mistakes that we both made? Lucy opened her eyes and strived for a calmness she was far from feeling.

Belle was her responsibility until the end of the year when she turned eighteen and finished school. After that she'd be off to university and she'd be in charge of her own life. All Lucy could hope for then was that Belle would remember the values her mother had been trying to instil in her all these years and she'd know how to make good decisions. It was so hard to start loosening her grip, though. So much could go wrong in the blink of an eye.

Three

The Bundah Country Women's Association was as much a part of Bundah as the buildings and landscape. Lucy's own mother was a life member of the national heritage, as her grandmother had been in her day. It was a family tradition and Lucy loved being a part of something so worthwhile.

As in any organisation, there were times of conflict amongst the many different types of personalities but, on the whole, Bundah CWA was a close-knit, hard-working group of women. Lucy knew that if ever she were in trouble, every single one of them would be there to help her out.

'Oh good, Lucy dear, you're here . . . at last. Okay, let's get started,' Mavis announced loudly as Lucy tried to slip into the old hall unnoticed. She was running late again; she always seemed to be the last one to arrive.

Lucy took a seat next to her best friend, Nicole, exchanging a small grimace for being on the receiving end of Mavis's not so subtle rebuke.

'Firstly, ladies, I'd like to start off by addressing a few of the latest happenings around town. As a result of the chamber of commerce's ad campaign, we've had quite a bit of interest. In fact, as of today, I've been advised by Ken that we've had two firm offers for new businesses and he has sent out applications and prospectus kits to at least a dozen other people requesting more information. I think it's safe to say that Ken may have finally found a winner.'

There was a ripple of applause through the small hall and more than a few curious questions circulating the room. 'Now, now, ladies, let's have a bit of quiet and I'll go through the information Ken has kindly provided me.' She waited for the room to quieten and then continued. 'So, the top pub has been sold to a Mr Hugh Thompson. He's a newcomer from the city but apparently we don't have any further information about him.'

'I've seen him. Very handsome man. Was there any mention of a *Mrs* Thompson there, Mavis?' Stella Davies called out hopefully. Stella was the town cougar . . . or would have been had there been any eligible younger men for her to pounce on. At sixty-five she was still a firm believer in the old adage that if you've got it, flaunt it. She had a penchant for leopard-print clothing and high heels and was a frequent visitor to Mavis's hair salon for the regular upkeep of her bleach-blonde mane. Lucy had to hand it to her, she'd never once seen the woman with regrowth in the entire time she'd lived in Bundah.

'Not from what I can see here, Stella,' Mavis replied peering over the top of her reading glasses with a disapproving glare. 'Also, the old post office building has been rented and the premises is to be renovated and made into a coffee shop.'

'Do we know who's leased that property, Mavis?' a voice called out from the back of the hall.

Mavis shook her head. 'I believe it's two brothers, or so Ken thought, but I'm sure there will be more details to follow.'

There was a hum of conversation as the news was discussed and the newcomers' chances of success were weighed up.

'A coffee shop? Well, it's about time.' Nicole gave a small squeal.

Lucy gave a small chuckle.

'What?'

She tilted her head closer to her friend. 'If it's who I think it is, I reckon we're in for a treat!'

'How is it you always get to meet everyone before I do?'

Lucy gave a shrug. 'Everyone needs fuel.'

'So who are they, these brothers? Are they young? Single? Good-looking?'

'Let's just say, I'm pretty sure they're *not* brothers.'

'Now,' Mavis cut in after a few minutes, 'I think it would be nice to extend a welcome to these newcomers. I thought we could organise a supper in conjunction with the chamber of commerce and the progress committee.'

A chorus of nods accompanied the suggestion and it was tentatively noted to be put to the other two committees at their next meetings. Personally Lucy wondered why they even bothered with all the formalities—just about everyone in the room was a member or on the committee of the other two organisations anyway—but things were always done according to the rule book. They took their committees very seriously around here.

There was a flurry of offers to deliver the invitations to Hugh Thompson, but Mavis declared that she would be personally hand-delivering the invites. As president, she thought that would only be proper. Lucy and Nicole swapped an amused grin as Stella fluffed about in her chair like a disgruntled hen, her hopes of having an excuse to corner Hugh Thompson firmly squashed under the firm heel of Mavis Quillin's Homypeded foot.

'So is he as good-looking as everyone's saying he is?' Nicole asked as she and Lucy walked to their cars after the meeting.

'Who?'

'Oh, please!' Nicole rolled her eyes and shook her head at Lucy. 'Don't give me that. As if you don't know who I'm talking about! The mysterious Hugh Thompson.'

'Oh, him.'

'Yes. *Him*. Now spill; what's he like?'

'I saw him for all of five minutes. He barely said a word.'

'So how come you're acting all weird?'

'I am not!'

'Are too!'

'How old are you again?'

Nicole poked her in the ribs and laughed at Lucy's haughty tone. 'Old enough to know when you're all hot and bothered about something.'

She had to concede the woman had her on a technicality: if anyone knew her better than she knew herself, it was Nicole. Nicole had been her first friend ever since she'd moved to Bundah all those years ago.

Lucy had been to more than her fair share of new schools because her father's job transferred them on a three-yearly interval, but no matter how many times she'd done it, she'd never gotten used to that horrible first-day-in-a-new-school feeling. It had always been a scary, sickening ordeal, but moving to Bundah had been different. From the minute she'd been teamed up with Nicole as her 'buddy', the two girls had been inseparable. The down side of having a best friend who knew you so well was . . . that they knew you so well!

'He's egotistical and thinks he's better than everyone else.'

'Really? Why, what happened?'

'He wouldn't let me put the petrol in his stupid bike.'

'Oh, wow. What a jerk!' Nicole gushed sarcastically.

'It was his whole . . . attitude. Trust me, no matter how good-looking the guy is, he's not worth the trouble.'

'So he *is* good looking?'

Lucy gave a frustrated groan. The woman had missed her calling as a lawyer. She could twist and turn words like a pro. 'If you like your looks, with a bucket load of attitude.'

'Well, he certainly made an impression on you. This welcome shindig should be all kinds of fun.'

'What a shame I won't be attending.'

'Oh? You're going to tell Mavis you're not planning on going? Good luck with that then!'

Lucy's shoulders slumped at the thought. Mavis was not a person you wanted to get off side. Behind that gentile façade was a very savvy businesswoman who had run her own hairdressing business for over forty years and was behind just about every other major organisation in town. There was no doubt she loved her town and had a heart of gold, even if she could occasionally come across as a bit of a dragon.

'Cheer up. If it makes you feel any better, no man can remain high and mighty with Stella circling like a hungry wolf. If for nothing else, I'd go for the entertainment value.'

This lifted Lucy's spirits and she couldn't quite rein in the malicious grin that followed the thought.

'Thatta girl!' Nicole patted her arm sagely. 'Hey, can you ask Belle if she can babysit for me Saturday night? My darling husband is taking me out on the town to celebrate our anniversary.'

Nicole had married the son of the town doctor. The Fairbridge family had a long history in Bundah. Mrs Fairbridge took great pride in being the wife of the town doctor, and Lucy knew that in the early years of her marriage Nicole had struggled to adjust to her mother-in-law's high expectations. Mrs Fairbridge's lifestyle was very different to the life Lucy had led growing up as the daughter of a labourer employed by the local council.

Beverly Fairbridge spent a great deal of time travelling to and from Sydney; she was heavily into the arts and took great pride in being a patron for a number of state and national art galleries. It took quite a few years for Nicole and her mother-in-law to forge some kind of amicable relationship, but it was through art that they had formed a bond. Much of Nicole's time was now spent organising fundraising events to help support art galleries and provide scholarships to support the art community. But Nicole would always be Nicole, no matter how well she dressed or how big a house she lived in. She had never forgotten where she'd come from or who her friends had been and she could always be counted on to speak her mind, something that still occasionally managed to get her in trouble with her in-laws.

'Can you believe it's been fourteen years since the wedding? You get less than that for murder,' Nicole said.

Fourteen years. It did seem a long time. A familiar pang of regret hit her. Nicole's life had followed a very different path to her own. Nicole, unlike her, had finished high school and gone on to university. While Jackson studied medicine, she'd followed her own dream: working at the Art Galley of New South Wales. They'd eventually left the city and returned to Bundah so Jackson could join his father in the family practice. And thank goodness he had—he was the only doctor in town. With the old town hospital having closed down years ago, he was the only local medical help Bundah had.

Lucy loved her friend and was happy that she had a man she adored by her side, but a little part of her was envious too. She sometimes wished she had a husband by her side, who knew her the way Jackson knew Nicole, who was a good, loving father and could be depended on to stay by her side and grow old with her.

'You okay?'

Lucy forced a bright smile to her face and waved off her friend's concern. She had to get away from Nicole before she felt even sorrier for herself. She hated wishing for the impossible and, even worse, she hated that it was her own stupid fault for choosing the path she'd taken.

She said a hurried goodbye to Nicole and then slid behind the wheel of her car. The streetlights passed by her window in a blur. Thank goodness there was no other traffic on the road tonight. Walking inside, she dumped her handbag on the kitchen table and walked into her bedroom.

High up in the top of her wardrobe she removed a box and placed it on the bed. A ripple of sadness stirred in her chest as she slowly dug through the contents. This was her box of memories: the things she treasured and kept safe. There was Belle's first tooth, and all the Mother's Day cards she'd made over the years. Lucy touched the cards, lovingly before putting them aside and withdrawing a photo album. She carefully turned the pages, noticing they were beginning to turn a little bit brown with age.

She stopped at one photo and gently ran her fingers over the plastic. The photo of Claire and herself taken at Sea World on a family holiday just before they moved to Bundah.

Lucy had been fourteen and Claire sixteen. Claire's golden hair, long tanned legs and wide smile gave the impression of a young girl with a big future ahead of her. With their arms slung across each other's shoulders, it was a moment of sisterly love captured forever.

Another photo showed a bunch of kids at a party. In the background she saw the bonfire and, even now, she remembered the warmth of it on her back that night. She could still hear the music and smell the campfire smoke. Her gaze fell on the face of one the boys in the photo. A nineteen-year-old with a lopsided smile and bad-boy image that was irresistible to a seventeen year old with rampaging hormones. She remembered vividly hot, heavy kisses and stolen moments making out in the back of his ute. The heady feeling of his arms around her, showing the world she belonged to him. Mick was everything her parents had warned her to stay away from when she'd been growing up . . . and she hadn't listened.

She stared at the happy faces in the photograph and blinked back the sting of tears. She'd been so young. The girl in the photo could have been Belle. God, what a fool she'd been to believe so completely that she knew what love was back then.

'Mum?'

Lucy put the album back in the box and took a deep breath before calling out to her daughter. 'I'm home. Won't be a minute.' Returning the box back to its place on top of the wardrobe, she walked from her bedroom, gently closing the door on her memories.

Four

Lucy had been meaning to stop by and check on how the new café owners were doing. She'd seen them a number of times around town and each time they'd greeted her like some long-lost friend. Seeing their car out the front of the old post office building, she pulled over on a whim and parked her ute.

The front door was open but she still knocked on the old timber door to announce her arrival. When there was no response, Lucy gingerly pushed the door wider and stepped over boxes and tins of paint and stacks of timber, then called out a hello.

'Coming.' Russell's big head poked around the door to what had once been the mail-sorting room. 'Lucy! How are you?'

'I'm good. I just wanted to drop by to say hi. How's everything going?'

'Fabulously. Oh, I know it doesn't look like it, but we're making remarkable progress,' Steven told her with a proud smile, appearing from out the back. 'We didn't want to change anything structurally, so we've only really had superficial stuff to do to the place. We wanted to keep the old-world charm. These fixtures are magnificent.'

Lucy had to agree. 'It looks great.'

The front desk of the old post office had been turned into a counter with an industrial-sized coffee machine taking pride of place in the centre. Blackboards had been mounted on the wall behind the counter, ready for the menu to be written on, and a large glass display case sat ready to be filled with all sorts of delectable treats.

'I'm glad you're here, Luce. We need a victim to try out some of Steve's ideas for the menu.'

Russell had already informed her that Steve was a professional pastry chef and, judging from the smells of vanilla and chocolate swirling about the place, it seemed he'd been busy cooking up a storm. Lucy's mouth was already watering at the thought of having real coffee and fattening pastries for morning tea on a regular basis.

'We've got a few friends coming up this weekend to help put on the finishing touches before the opening,' Russell said as they seated themselves at the front counter, waiting for Steve to bring out some samples. 'Should be a fun weekend,' he said, wiggling his eyebrows comically. 'What do you reckon the good folk of Bundah will think of having more of us arriving on their doorstep?'

She was aware that there had been quite a lot of speculation about Steve and Russell. The few times she'd bumped into them in the supermarket, it had been impossible to ignore the pointed looks and hushed conversations happening around them. It infuriated Lucy, but neither Steve nor Russell seemed overly fazed about it.

'The majority of the town isn't as closed-minded as the few people you may have already dealt with.'

'Well, I hope you're right,' Steven said with a dramatic roll of his eyes. 'Anyway, let's celebrate our almost-ready-for-opening with a coffee. We've just set up this beauty and we were just about to give her a whirl. What do you say?'

'I wouldn't say no to coffee. Fire 'er up,' Lucy grinned.

There had been an undeniable buzz of activity around Bundah over the past few weeks. Contractors from surrounding towns were becoming a regular feature to work on various projects. The largest employer seemed to be the top pub. It was all very hush-hush, with the front of the pub being screened off from the main street and scaffolding covering the building.

More than one resident had had their nose put out of joint when they'd dropped by to get a peek at how things were progressing and had been politely but firmly turned away by the new owner. Lucy secretly wondered how he was going to operate in town once the renovations were complete if he continued to get the locals offside. Surely he realised he needed the patronage of the town, and getting their backs up now was not going to be beneficial to the future of his business.

All in all, though, there was an atmosphere of optimism running through Bundah nowadays, and the man wearing the biggest grin was Ken Baxter. Not only had he finally succeeded in getting one of his schemes to pay off, he was also experiencing a real estate boom. He'd sold the top pub, which had been a weight around his neck for too many years. On top of that, he'd rented out various houses to new business owners who'd made the move to town, and sold a property just out of Bundah to a German family who'd seen media reports about the town's new push for population.

Bundah itself was becoming somewhat of a celebrity as well. Two film crews had recently done stories on the incentives to move to the area and showcased the business opportunities on prime-time national television. It was all still a bit surreal. The town had gone from struggling to keep its head above water to being inundated with public interest.

Incentives to move to Bundah included subsidised rent. As in many regional areas, a lot of older farms had multiple residences on them, left over from a time when farmers could afford to employ outside workers. For the most part, these houses had been left unoccupied and had started to fall into disrepair. In exchange for free rent for the first six months, successful applicants were asked to do minor maintenance and general upkeep of these properties. This gave the property owners a future income from rental properties that would otherwise go to waste. Rent in the cities was reaching all-time highs, and it was apparent that the prospect of cheaper rent and living expenses was very attractive to a lot of families looking to make a lifestyle change.

However, it was no good attracting all these people into town if there was no work for them to come to, and so a new scheme had been launched to try to stimulate economic growth in the region. People applying for the scheme had to be willing to start a new business in town.

The chamber of commerce had already welcomed in three new businesses: a mechanical repair shop, a takeaway food store and an electrician. Having tradespeople in town was a welcome change. Over the past few years they'd had to be sourced from other towns and many charged travelling or call-out fees.

All this rapid change was having a very strange effect on the locals. The majority were happy that there was new life being breathed into town. The younger residents, in particular, were excited about the changes. A coffee shop opening in town, for instance, would be a luxury, after spending too many years without one. However, for many of the older residents, there was an undercurrent of unease. Today it might be a little coffee shop, but tomorrow, in their opinion, they might be building a huge shopping complex. The fact that Bundah, nestled in the mountains, was as far from a thriving metropolis as you could get didn't seem to ease their minds at all. Change, it seemed, was always going to meet with resistance.

Lucy was quietly tapping her fingernails on the desk as she waited for Ken to finish talking on his phone and sign the invoices she'd prepared for him. Suddenly the roar of a motorbike made her heart rate spike. She couldn't tell whether it was the loud noise or the prospect of it being Hugh Thompson that made her so jumpy. She looked up. It was him all right; she recognised the easy way he swung off the machine. Oh, for goodness sake! Why was she acting so stupid? He was just a customer.

She didn't bother going out—there was no chance he was going to let her anywhere near his precious bike. Lucy fought off the fluttery feeling in her stomach. Maybe there was something seriously wrong with her. She'd never had such an alarming reaction to a man before. She'd always been able to laugh off Nicole's warning about being in the prime of her life and becoming sexually frustrated—until now.

She watched as he tilted his head back and unclipped his helmet before removing it. Every movement was slow and unhurried. He sat his helmet on the seat of the bike as he unhooked the petrol pump. Lucy followed his movements almost against her will. He wasn't good-looking in a movie star kind of way, but he had a rough, edgy kind of appeal that caught her eye, and it was obvious he was in good shape beneath those denim jeans and leather jacket. Of course he chose *that* moment to glance up and catch her watching him through the office window.

She looked away, cursing beneath her breath, and searched for something to do so she could look busy. *Just stop it!* she told herself firmly. *You're a mature, confident woman . . . You're the mother of a teenager, for God's sake! Act your age!*

She finally heard Ken finishing his phone call and forced a smile, sliding the papers across the counter for him to sign.

'Is there something else I can get for you, Ken?' Lucy asked when he didn't immediately hand back the pen after signing.

'Actually, Luce, there *was* something. I have people coming up on the weekend to look at land and I immediately thought of Stringybark. It would be ideal for these buyers.' Lucy shook her head but Ken quickly continued, 'Why not just let me show these people around and see if they make an offer? What can it hurt?'

It was a conspiracy: first Belle and now Ken. 'I don't know how to put it any clearer, Ken: Stringybark is not for sale.'

'This could set you and Belle up for life. I just don't understand why you continue to hold on to that damn farm when it's doing nothing for you.'

'You know why I'm holding on to it.'

'It's a bloody waste if you ask me.'

He'd been trying to buy the land from her for years, but lately he'd begun really pushing her on it.

She'd had a perfectly fine agreement in place for the past ten years, leasing the land to an old school friend, Ross, who rented the house and ran his cattle on it. The regular money coming in went into a savings account for Belle's education, so it earned her an income until she came of age, and then, if she still wanted to, she could sell it for more than it had been worth fourteen years ago when Belle's grandfather had died and left it to her.

'Stringybark's not for sale,' Lucy repeated firmly. 'Please stop asking me about it.'

Ken let out a frustrated sigh and pushed himself away from the counter, mumbling under his breath as he went.

Lucy looked up and saw Hugh Thompson. Immediately she felt a warm glow creeping up her neck. How long had he been standing there? She hoped it hadn't been long. Taking a calming breath, she straightened and summoned a tight smile. 'Just the petrol today then?'

'Thanks, Lucy.'

She didn't dare look up again, concentrating on processing the payment through the register instead. Eventually, though, when he didn't move to pay her, she was forced to and was slightly disconcerted to find him simply watching her.

'That's twenty dollars even, thanks.'

'You're not eager to cash in on the property boom happening at the moment, I take it?'

Lucy was not amused. Who the hell went around sticking their nose in a complete stranger's business like that? Well, *aside* from just about everyone in Bundah. 'Privacy isn't one of Ken's stronger points.'

'Well, that's reassuring.' Handing across a twenty dollar note, he sounded anything but reassured and probably wondered just how much of his personal business Ken had been broadcasting to the local community.

As Lucy took the cash she felt his gaze resting on her and she tried not to squirm uncomfortably.

'For a quiet town there seems to be a lot of action going on.'

Lucy's gaze skittered across to his, surprised that he'd initiated a conversation. 'It's not normally like this.'

'This big push Baxter's making seems to be paying off.'

'Trust me, no one's more surprised by that fact than Ken himself.'

'Guess that can only be a good thing for the town—luring people to invest in the place,' he said.

'Weren't you also one of the lured?' Lucy asked somewhat sceptically as she pushed the till shut with her hip, handing over his docket.

'Nope. I've had this place set in my sights for a while now.'

'Really?'

'Yep. Had my eye on the pub for a good twelve months or so,' he said, leaning against the counter as though settling in for a chat.

'Online or something?'

'Yeah. I was looking around for an old pub to buy and I saw this one. Kept my eye on it until I was ready to make a bid and here I am.'

'Oh. Well, it's a beautiful old building. One of the first built in Bundah back in the late 1800s. I'm glad someone has finally bought it. It's been sad to see it neglected for so long.'

'You're a bit of a history buff then?'

His interest surprised her. 'Not really, I just like old buildings.'

'I found a bunch of photographs of the pub in some boxes under the staircase. I'm thinking of getting them framed.

Can you recommend anywhere around here where I could get them done?'

'Really? Wow, that's pretty cool. Mr Goodwin who runs the hardware and camping shop does framing as a bit of a hobby. You could try him.'

'Thanks. I will.' He straightened, taking his helmet from the counter. 'Ahh, by the way, this welcome committee thing I've been invited to . . .'

Lucy lifted her gaze to find him looking oddly uncomfortable, which didn't fit with his tough guy image at all. She waited for him to continue.

'I don't actually have to attend, do I?' he said.

'That *is* kind of the point of a welcome get-together, Hugh . . . to *welcome* you to town,' she explained slowly, as though he might have been hiding how dimwitted he really was.

'Well, yeah, but I mean how seriously do they take it all?'

'Seriously enough.' His attitude was beginning to annoy her. The town was trying to welcome him to the community and he was looking for a way to get out of it. 'You know, you could show a little more courtesy.'

'Excuse me?' he seemed taken aback by her comment.

'This Mr Antisocial thing you've got going on. There's been talk about how rude you've been over the renovation lockdown, and now you're going to throw a lovely welcome get-together back in the faces of the people who are going out of their way to be nice to you.'

'I didn't ask for anyone to throw a party. Besides, what's wrong with wanting to keep my business private?'

'Oh boy, did you pick the wrong kind of town to move to if that's what you hope to achieve,' she said.

'I don't have time to stop and chat to every person who decides to drop in and introduce themselves. I'm on a schedule.' He shook his head to ward off her disapproving frown. 'Look, once the renovations are done, I'll open the premises to the public but, until then, it's none of anyone else's business but mine.'

'Oh, *then* you'll have time to play Mr Sociable. When you expect everyone to come and support you!' She sincerely hoped her stupid libido was paying attention to this. How could she think this rude, insensitive jerk was worth lusting over?

'I hope to be drawing in a lot of business from outside the community so, in the long run, this town will be thanking me.'

'Not if you don't show a little community spirit, they won't,' she snapped. Honestly! The egotistical hide of this guy! 'You *better* show up at that meet and greet,' she warned.

'Well, if it means that much to you,' he finally said in a lazy, low drawl that had Lucy stubbornly ignoring the tingle in parts of her that had no business tingling.

'Believe me, *I* couldn't care less. But I know how much this means to a lot of people in town and they don't deserve to have it thrown back in their faces.'

'All right, easy tiger,' he said, holding up his hands. 'Jeez, if you wanted me to go so bad all you had to do was ask nicely.' He turned away but stopped at the door and threw over his shoulder, 'So I'll see you tonight, Lucy?'

'Oh, I'll be there, because I'm part of a community and *I* have community spirit,' she retorted.

'Yeah, I see that,' he said, then stepped outside.

Lucy followed his retreat from the shop and across the driveway pensively, stubbornly ignoring the little quiver of excitement her recalcitrant libido seemed to be experiencing at the prospect of seeing him later that night. 'Oh, go back to sleep,' she mumbled irritably. Just because he was the hottest thing to arrive in Bundah in a long time didn't mean he was worth losing her head over. She'd done that once and the consequences had been life-changing. She wasn't about to go back and do it all again a second time.

Five

It was turning cold at night now as autumn crept closer into winter and Lucy wondered what kind of turnout they'd get at tonight's welcome supper. An evening snuggled down in front of the TV was a much more attractive prospect than going back out into the chill of the evening. But, if this was what it took to be hospitable, then damn it, she'd grit her teeth and bear it. The other guests had better be more grateful than Hugh bloody Thompson, though, or there would be big trouble.

Lucy glanced around the CWA hall as she entered and breathed a sigh of relief that he was nowhere in sight. He probably wouldn't even come she huffed as she carried her chicken curry across the old timber floor to the long food table already groaning with offerings.

One thing the women of this town did well was cook. If anything was worth coming out for tonight, it was for the food. As usual, everyone had cooked up a storm. There was a smorgasbord of savoury dishes on the table and the aroma was mouth-watering. And the piled table didn't even include the cakes and desserts that Lucy knew would be waiting in the kitchen.

'Did I *have* to come to this thing, Mum?' Belle complained quietly.

'Yes. Now look happy.'

'Because this is *exactly* where a teenage girl in the prime of her social life wants to be caught dead . . . surrounded by old people and strangers.'

'Smile, or your social life as you know it will die a quick but painful death,' Lucy warned through a fake bright smile.

'Can't miss something I never had, I suppose,' Belle said, plastering something that looked more like a grimace than an actual smile on her face as she stalked across to the other side of the room.

'Ah, teenagers. Gotta love 'em.'

Lucy turned, startled by the low murmur from beside her, and discovered Hugh watching Belle as she slumped against a wall and looked sulky. 'You came.'

'Oh ye of little faith,' he said with a lazy smile.

What did she say to that? There was a good part of her that tended to reserve her faith in people until they proved they were worthy of believing in. Life experience could do that to a person.

This was the first time she'd seen him out of his leather jacket. Obviously he hadn't ridden here tonight. Although he'd been in jeans the last time she saw him, they were old working pants; tonight he'd made an effort and wore a clean set, with a black shirt, the sleeves rolled up. Lucy tried not to stare at his arms, but the tribal-looking tattoo on his forearm caught her attention. Of course he had tats. The bad-boy image was now complete: bike, leathers, tats.

'Impressive turnout.'

'I wouldn't expect anything less. If you hadn't shown up, Mavis would have dragged you here.'

'She doesn't give the impression of being a woman you say no to.'

'Exactly when is your grand opening date, anyway?'

'The long weekend in June.'

'That's not far off.' She looked up at him doubtfully. 'You really think you'll get that old place renovated in just seven weeks?'

'Hope so. I'm doing a lot of it myself, so I can work around the clock if I have to. As long as the tradies don't hold things up, I reckon I can do it.'

'Have you done this before? Fixed up old pubs?'

'Nope. First pub.'

'What did you do before?'

'I worked construction a long time ago, when I first left school, but more recently I've been working in the mining industry.'

'Nothing like a huge project to break your teeth on. Most people would probably start with something a little smaller, you know.'

'I'm not most people.'

Lucy felt trapped as his steady gaze clung to hers and a small grin settled on his lips. No, he wasn't like most people . . . he was like hot, gooey, melted chocolate on your fingers that you wanted to slowly and thoroughly lick clean . . . She swallowed hard as she dragged her eyes away from him and tried to rid the unexpectedly lurid images from her mind.

'Well, hello there handsome.'

Lucy jumped a little as the sultry voice interrupted the uncomfortably intimate moment. She saw Hugh's smile slip a little as his gaze slid across to the owner of the voice.

Lucy had never been more relieved to have Stella Davies intrude on a conversation in all her life. 'Oh, Stella, have you met Hugh Thompson yet? Hugh, Stella. If you'll excuse me, I'd better go and socialise. I'll leave you in Stella's capable hands, Hugh.'

She didn't dare look back. She could sense Hugh's dismay, but he was a big boy and more than capable of taking care of himself. She, on the other hand, was not capable of dealing with Hugh Thompson. He confused her. The few times they'd spoken, he'd managed to annoy her, but tonight it was obvious there was an underlying thing between them that she really didn't want to analyse. Obviously, he was under the mistaken impression that he could just flash that cocky grin and strut around looking all mysterious and dangerous and women would fall at his feet. Well, not this one. She didn't need a man to complicate her nice quiet existence. She'd worked hard to make a comfortable life for herself and Belle; the last thing she needed was to have some fella come along and mess it all up for her.

'I'm having serious doubts about you, woman.'

Lucy spun around and found Nicole standing behind her, watching Hugh trying to evade Stella and her enormous breasts as they threatened to overflow from the top of her dangerously low-cut mini dress.

'And why would that be?'

'That man is utterly gorgeous! Why didn't you tell me?'

'You're married, remember?'

'Yeah, but I'm not numb from the neck down.'

'Nicole!'

'What?'

Lucy caught that unrepentant mischievous gleam in her friend's eye and could only chuckle in dismay. '*You* are hopeless and should be ashamed of yourself.'

Shrugging off Lucy's accusation, Nicole turned away from the tall dark stranger and shook her head. 'Poor bugger, I feel sorry for him. I think I'd better go and rescue him from Stella.'

'Don't you dare.' Lucy panicked at the thought. 'He's fine. He's probably enjoying all the attention.'

'I don't think so,' Nicole murmured with a small grimace. 'You know, I never really understood the term "man-eater" before tonight. Stella Davies should act her damn age.'

'Lucy, dear, I need a word,' Mavis said, steering Lucy by the elbow through the crowd towards the kitchen.

'Is there something wrong?'

'Well, yes. Have you met the two gentlemen from the coffee shop yet?'

'Russell and Steven? Yes, why?'

Mavis's eyebrow lifted with an unimpressed tilt. 'You do realise they're . . . *homosexuals,* don't you?'

Lucy tried not to giggle at the older woman's hushed whisper. 'Umm, yes. I did pick up on that.'

'Well, it would have been nice to have been given some warning. Ken Baxter's been telling everyone they're brothers, silly old bugger! I looked like a right dill sprouting on about how close they must be to live and work together in a business.'

'I'm sure they understand. It probably happens to them all the time.' Inside, Lucy winced slightly and was glad she hadn't been present during the awkward exchange.

'You wait until I get my hands on Ken!'

Lucy hoped Ken wasn't planning on showing up tonight: the mood Mavis was in, he'd surely regret it. She was about to try to smooth the woman's ruffled feathers when Mavis called out to someone in the kitchen. 'Excuse me, dear,' she said to Lucy. 'I'd better go and stop these two putting out the dessert before we've even had supper. Honestly, must I do *everything* around here?'

As if anyone would be able to stop you, Lucy thought with an amused shake of her head as she watched Mavis dash off.

'That was not nice . . . In fact, I'd even go as far as to say that wasn't very *community spirited* of you,' Hugh's low voice raised hairs along her arms and almost made her choke on her apricot chicken. She wiped a napkin across her lips and forced down the mouthful of food before looking up. She was sitting on the top step of the stage and his eyes were level with hers. Up this close she could see they were deep blue with a darker shade of navy circling the iris and thick black lashes any woman would envy.

'I don't know what you're talking about,' she denied, but found herself mesmerised by the smile that spread across his face but didn't quite reach his eyes. In fact his expression was not relaxed and friendly, it was more the kind of look that promised all kinds of sinful retribution and turned her blood to fire.

Clearing her throat, Lucy was alarmed to realise she'd somehow leaned in close to Hugh and she drew back quickly in embarrassment. Thrusting her plastic plate into his hands, she scampered to her feet. 'I have to go.' She didn't look back, she didn't dare. She caught Belle's eye halfway across the floor and nodded towards the front door. She didn't have to do anything more: Belle was more than happy to cut the evening short. Lucy didn't even bother collecting her casserole dish; she just needed to get as far away from Hugh Thompson as she could before she made an even bigger fool of herself.

Six

'Did you hear, dear?' Mavis sounded outraged as she called to Lucy from the door of her salon.

Lucy swapped hands as the heavy grocery bags began to cut off her circulation. She was really trying to get home early tonight. She'd been at meetings for the past two evenings and had hardly had time to speak to Belle, and tonight she wanted to cook a special dinner to make up for it. Unfortunately, Mavis wasn't going to make it easy for her.

With a resigned sigh, Lucy placed the groceries on the ground at her feet. 'Hear what, Mavis?'

'That Thompson fella is planning on turning the pub into some kind of bikie retreat. Can you just imagine that! Here in Bundah, hundreds of long-haired, tattooed bikers.'

'Bikers?' Lucy said doubtfully.

'Bikers,' Mavis repeated firmly. 'And won't that just be lovely? There'll probably be fights and unsavoury types hanging around the place. It won't be safe to walk the streets. And to think that we welcomed him into our little community with open arms.'

'I can't really picture bikie gangs flooding into town, Mavis. We're a bit off the beaten track for that. I think they'd tend to stick more to the highway.'

'This would be the perfect place for them. They could go wild and there'd be no one here to stop them.'

'I'm sure Sergeant Pearce wouldn't let things get out of control.' Nate Pearce would have to be the most capable man she knew. Maybe she should go and ask him what the hell was going on around here? 'I'm sorry, Mavis, but I really have to keep moving. I've got to get home to Belle.' She picked up the heavy bags once more and smiled a farewell to her elderly friend.

Mavis wasn't offended, she'd already spied another unsuspecting citizen who was clearly in need of enlightenment, and she bustled off with a vague wave goodbye.

What had happened to her quiet uneventful town, Lucy wondered as she loaded the groceries into the back of the ute. The rumour mill had been working on overdrive since all the new faces had begun arriving in town. It seemed that every hour there was something new to be updated on. It was beginning to drive her a little bit crazy.

Lucy inserted the key into the front door but found that it wasn't locked. She staggered into the house with her fingers hooked through the plastic bag handles, going numb. 'Belle,' she called, almost tripping over the bags of groceries she'd just placed on the floor. 'Belle!' she yelled louder. There was no answer. Then she noticed the mess. Magazines and newspapers that were usually stacked neatly on the coffee table were all over the lounge room floor.

She marched to the end of the hall and opened the bedroom door. She found Belle, headphones on, lying across her bed reading, completely oblivious to her mother's calling. Lucy crossed to the bed and Belle looked up and yelped in surprise.

'I've been calling out to you.'

'I didn't hear,' Belle said, taking off her headphones.

'Don't have the music up so loud, then. Honestly, Belle, the house could be falling down around you and you'd be completely oblivious.'

'I'm studying.'

'Well, I need a hand unloading the shopping,' Lucy snapped, waiting for her daughter to get off the bed. 'And then you can tidy up the mess in the lounge room.'

'What mess?'

They walked back along the hall and Lucy pointed at the magazines on the floor.

'I didn't do it.'

'Just pick it up, Belle,' Lucy sighed wearily, heading outside to bring in another load of bags. 'And how many times have I told you to lock the door when you're home alone.'

'I did,' she said, dropping the bags she carried in with a huff. 'Why are you so grumpy?'

'Maybe because I've been working all day and then shopping. The least you can do is hear me when I call you, and not trash the house,' Lucy replied irritably.

'Jeez, calm down. Go take a bath or something and I'll pack this away.'

'Really?'

'Anything to stop you snapping my head off.'

Lucy stared at her daughter and her anger instantly deflated. 'Just keep one ear open when you have your headphones on, okay?'

'Okay. Whatever,' Belle sighed, turning away to unpack the groceries.

Lucy decided to take Belle up on her offer. Maybe a nice hot bath would put her in a better mood. She stopped by the coffee table and scooped up the magazines, putting them back in a neat pile.

'Was that really so hard?' she muttered under her breath as she headed back down the hall to her bedroom. Lucy kicked off her shoes and took off her watch, placing it on the dressing table as she walked past. As she went to get her pyjamas from under her pillow, she paused and stared at her wardrobe. Two of the drawers were partially opened. Lucy inched closer and pulled the top one open, frowning as she discovered the contents, which were usually neatly folded, looked as though they'd been rummaged through.

'Belle,' she called out through the door. 'Have you been in my room today?'

'No. Why?'

A strange prickling sensation ran through her body as her gaze flitted about the bedroom. Nothing else seemed to be disturbed. Lucy took her jewellery box from the wardrobe and was relieved to see her grandmother's two rings were still inside, as well as the set of pearls her parents had given her for her twenty-first birthday. She rubbed her hands along her arms, then collected her pyjamas and headed into the bathroom.

Had Belle been lying to her? But why would she lie? Nothing was missing from her room, and what would be the point in denying she'd knocked the things off the coffee table? They both knew she was the only one home alone, and why lie about something as unimportant as making a mess? Unless she hadn't done it. Lucy decided to forego the bath and instead took a very quick shower. Unease hung heavily over her for the remainder of the night.

Hugh walked out the back of the pub with an armful of rubbish and spotted the police officer circling his parked bike. He calmly dumped the rubbish into the skip bin then wiped the sweat from his forehead with his arm. 'Can I help ya there, mate?'

The cop seemed to study Hugh silently for a moment before moving away from the bike. 'Just thought I'd come by and introduce myself.'

'Didn't know cops made social calls. Having a slow week or something?' Hugh didn't like the way the guy was sizing him up but, then again, he was doing the same thing so he guessed that made them even. He reached over and snagged his T-shirt from the fence where he'd tossed it earlier and tugged it over his head.

'Nate Pearce.' The cop put his hand out and Hugh hesitated only briefly before he accepted the greeting.

'Hugh Thompson.'

'Where you from, Hugh?'

'The city.' He really had nothing against this guy, but standing around chatting was not getting the dry wall up in the guest bathrooms.

'So you saw the chamber of commerce's ad then?'

'Nah, I've been looking at this old place for a while now. I didn't even know about the ad until Baxter mentioned it the other day.'

'What made you decide to move out here to the sticks?'

'Everyone needs a change now and again. Look, it was great to meet you, but I've gotta get the bathroom finished by this afternoon in time for the electricians to turn up tomorrow.'

'No worries,' Nate Pearce said but made no move to leave. 'I'm hearing a few noises about bikers coming to town.'

'Bikers?'

'This is a pretty quiet town and I really want to keep it that way. I wouldn't like to see anyone bringing any kind of trouble here, if you know what I mean.'

'I don't know what you've been hearing, but it's not about my pub and it's got nothing to do with me.'

'Well, we don't have a problem then, do we?' Nate said with a brief grin that was more a warning than a friendly gesture. 'Nice meeting you.' He went to turn away but stopped and Hugh clenched his jaw irritably. 'You know, for some reason your name rings a bell. Have we met before?'

'Doubt it, mate.'

The cop gave a small grunt. 'I'm usually pretty good with names.'

Hugh turned away, hoping he'd take the hint and leave but when he turned back the guy was still standing there.

'Never mind, it'll come to me.' He gave Hugh a brief nod as he went back out the rear gate of the pub and disappeared behind the tall tin fence into the car park.

Hugh trudged back upstairs. Having a cop digging around in his past was not something he felt particularly comfortable about. Hitting the nails in with a little more force than was actually needed, he felt his good mood evaporate.

Seven

Lucy was filling up the water in the windscreen-washing buckets when a ute pulled up next to the bowser. She straightened slowly, wiping her hands on her jeans before turning to find Hugh getting out of the driver's side.

Part of her was disappointed that he wasn't riding his bike—there was something undeniably sexy about a man in leathers and a helmet. She had no idea how long she'd had this strange fetish, but she hoped to God he was unaware of her attraction because she wasn't sure she could live with the humiliation if he knew about it.

Lucy shook off her inappropriate thoughts as she walked towards him. 'Don't tell me you traded in your bike?'

'It'd be a cold day in hell before that happened,' he said before standing back to join her as she eyed the vehicle curiously. 'It was getting a bit hard to carry building supplies on the back of a bike, so I had to make a trip down the mountain to buy a work vehicle.'

'Ahh,' Lucy nodded. 'All that's missing now is the kelpie in the back.'

'I don't think I'm ready for that kind of commitment just yet,' he said.

If ever there was a flashing warning sign that had to be it. *Not that she was thinking of having any kind of commitment in the first place*, she told herself firmly. 'How are the renovations going?'

'It's safe to say after the last two all-nighters, I never want to see another paintbrush ever again.'

'So you'll make your grand opening?'

'It was touch and go there for a while.'

'Congratulations. I didn't actually think you'd be able to do it in time.'

He gave her a mock injured look, before shaking his head mournfully. 'Nice to see that good old community spirit coming out there, Lucy.'

'I've never been able to get a tradesman to work to a schedule before.'

'Nothing to it. You've just got to know how to handle them, that's all.'

Lucy's eyes narrowed. 'You offered to pay them double to get it done, didn't you.'

'I'm not giving away my secrets. But, if you ever have any trouble with tradesmen again, let me know and I'll see what I can do,' he said with a grin. 'So you'll be coming along on Friday night to the opening?'

Lucy shook her head as she shut the draw of the till. 'I'm not much of a pub person.'

'The *Emperor* is a pub. My place is somewhere you can relax and have a drink or a meal.'

'Well, *I* heard it's going to be a bikers' pub. Complete with bar fights and everything.'

Hugh gave a gruff chuckle and shook his head. 'I hate to disappoint you, but the kind of bikers I'm aiming at prefer a latte or a fifty-dollar bottle of wine over a beer, and look forward to a luxury room to fall into after a long day of riding.'

'So you really are trying to bring bikers to town?'

'*Weekend* bikers. It's an untapped tourist market. The whole town can benefit from this if they'd just listen to reason and stop throwing up barriers because they're too afraid of change.'

Lucy saw the frustration on his face and felt a twinge of sympathy. It had to be hard to come into a town as a stranger and have to fight for every inch of change, although he hadn't exactly done himself any favours by shunning everyone upon his arrival. 'Bundah's been a small town for a long time. The thought of being overrun by strangers is a little unsettling for most people. It just takes time to get used to.'

'Well, if they don't embrace this opportunity, they'll miss out. Everyone has a chance to make a good living from this. The whole town can cash in on it, and it's not just some get-rich-quick scheme. It's a market that can continue to grow each year.'

'I'm sure they'll come around eventually,' Lucy assured Hugh.

'Once the tourists start coming here, other business-savvy people are going to see what an opportunity this place is, and the locals will miss out on getting in on the action. Change is going to come whether the town likes it or not.'

That much was true. Already there were more people driving through town, particularly on weekends. It was all anyone could talk about, but the initial excitement and curiosity that had come with Ken's newspaper promotion had slowly turned to suspicion and wariness as things had begun to change more quickly than anyone had anticipated.

Lucy battled with her own feelings on the subject. Only a few years ago the local primary school numbers had dwindled and the townspeople had been praying for a miracle to bring some young families to Bundah to help boost numbers again. Now it seemed those prayers had been answered, but it wasn't bringing with it the community harmony everyone had been expecting.

Lucy was happy to sit back and see how things settled before she got too concerned, but she knew there were certain elements in the community who weren't. She had a feeling the murmurs of discontent she had been hearing would soon become a roar, particularly if Hugh's weekend bikers didn't turn out to be quite as tame as he was making them out to be.

The phone rang as Hugh left the shop and Lucy went out into the office to answer it.

'Hello Lucy, dear,' Marg said, and Lucy couldn't help but smile at the sound of the familiar voice. She'd grown to love Ken's much older sister, who had moved to Sydney as a young woman and lived there ever since. It was after Ken bought the servo that Lucy first met Marg, when she'd call looking for Ken, even though it was rare her brother was ever here. Eventually, Lucy had realised that the woman was simply after a chat and they had started talking regularly. Lucy appreciated the older woman's warmth, wisdom and sense of humour, and by now she thought of Marg as an important person in her life.

'How are you, Marg? How are your hands today?'

'The gloves you sent are working wonderfully; that's what I was calling you for, to thank you.'

'I'm glad they're helping.' It was such a small thing to do; she'd seen a pair of heated gloves that you warmed in the microwave to help ease arthritis pain, and she'd bought them after Marg had said the cold mornings were playing havoc with her hands and she was finding it hard to do her beloved knitting and crocheting.

'You're such a good girl, Lucy.'

Lucy smiled and felt about ten years old again. They chatted for a little while longer and then Lucy had to hang up as a customer had pulled up outside. Marg played on her mind a lot that afternoon. Would that be Lucy one day? Sitting by the phone and hoping Belle called her to have a chat now and again? The way things were going at the moment, her beloved daughter would probably have her sent to a nursing home and then forget all about her.

Posters had appeared all around town, announcing the grand opening of the top pub. Hugh had renamed the place the Coach House Hotel, and Lucy had to admit it suited the stately old pub perfectly. A barbecue was planned, as well as live bands playing over the whole weekend, and rumour had it that Hugh had been advertising the pub to various social bike groups in the district and offering special discounts on accommodation packages.

She'd heard that he'd been looking for extra staff for the restaurant he'd been renovating and had hired Terry, an ex-shearer's cook with a flair for gourmet cuisine. He cooked like Colin Fassnidge in the kitchen, but dressed like a truck driver in blue singlets and shorts. She didn't know much about the man, but he seemed to spend a lot of his time watching the horse races on the TV over the bar when he wasn't working.

As Friday afternoon approached, it appeared the rumours were true, as a steady influx of bikes began arriving in town and the whole place became a hive of activity.

Lucy called in Ernie, her part-time assistant, to help out as the increase in traffic had been keeping her too busy to get to any of her paperwork. It was strange to look up the main street and see people walking around aimlessly, browsing even. People in Bundah didn't browse; they came in to get supplies and then they might stand around and chat, but they never browsed. The café also looked to be doing a roaring trade. When Lucy walked down to do the banking she could see Steven and Russell were in their element, chatting and flirting with all the new customers. It seemed that Steve also had a biker fetish. She waved as she walked past and smiled when the big man fanned himself with his hand as he turned away from a leather-clad bike rider.

Lucy had to admit, Mavis's fears about being overrun by unsavoury bikers seemed to have been put to rest. There were bikers in town all right, but they weren't the Sons of Anarchy kind. These bikers had expensive-looking riding gear, and she hadn't seen anyone under the age of fifty.

'You here to try a sausage sanga?' Hugh asked, tongs in hand, manning a large stainless steel barbecue in the courtyard of the pub. He'd caught her as she popped her head in to check out all the action.

'Sure, why not.' The truth was she had smelled the cooking sausages all the way up the main street and her mouth was watering. 'Looks like a great turnout,' she said as she looked at the crowd of people milling around, a slice of bread and sausage in one hand and a glass of beer in the other.

'Better than I had hoped, actually.'

'Yeah, well, this old place has been closed for so long, not many locals would turn down the opportunity to come and take a look at what you've done to it.'

'And you thought all that secrecy wasn't going to work,' he told her smugly.

He had a point: denying everyone access to the renovations had obviously whet the town's appetite, although she suspected his secretive behaviour had not solely been to pique public curiosity.

'Well, congratulations.'

'Thanks. Now I just need to keep the clientele coming.'

'It looks pretty positive so far. How did you get them to come up here?'

'I've been building up a partnership with a lot of social bike groups over the past year or so and I started spreading the word. And I'm working with a few guys I travelled with for a bit last year. We're putting together a list of the best rides in Australia to go in a major bike magazine next month. The ride through the hinterland and up the range is bound to spark a lot of interest. It's the kind of ride social bikers dream of.'

'Wow, you've really put a lot of thought into all this.'

'Had to. I've got everything I own tied up in this business.'

'I like the name,' she said, pointing up at the wooden sign attached to the top of the building.

'Yeah, I decided to do a bit of research into the pub,' he said almost sheepishly. 'Apparently this place was a stopover on the old coach route. Thought it was kind of fitting since it'll now be a bit of a stopover on the bike trail.'

'I'm impressed.' And she was. Who would have thought under that tough image lurked an amateur history buff.

More people arrived wanting sausages, so she took hers and left him to it.

As she bit into the hot sausage, Lucy saw Russell sitting at a table in the courtyard chatting in his usual flamboyant way with two companions Lucy hadn't seen before. She had to swallow the hot mouthful quickly as Russell caught her eye and waved her over. 'Lucy!' he called, drawing the attention of quite a few people nearby. 'Over here.'

Wiping her mouth self-consciously in case of any stray tomato sauce, Lucy approached the trio with a smile. As she drew closer and noticed the fashionably dressed, older woman seated at the table, she felt incredibly underdressed in her jeans and Baxter Fuel Depot T-shirt.

'Lucy, I'd like to introduce you to my dear friend, Twiggy. Twiggy, this is Lucy.'

'Hello, Lucy,' the woman said, holding out a perfectly manicured hand, fingers tipped down. Lucy wasn't sure whether she was supposed to shake it or kiss it. She decided on giving it a brief shake, self-conscious about the state of her own dirty fingernails and the slight whiff of petrol that hung about her uniform.

Lucy had to force herself not to stare at Twiggy, but it was hard not to. She was dressed in a pair of stylish white pants and a gauzy burnt orange top, with a set of stilettos that looked impossible to walk in.

'And this is Jerome,' Russell went on, his hand lingering on the arm of the attractive young man sitting next to Twiggy.

'Hello,' Lucy said, and was given a brief once-over by the man and a somewhat dismissive greeting.

'Twiggy and Jerome own a string of hair salons in Melbourne and Sydney; you may have heard of them?

Madam Latoy?' He didn't give Lucy time to shake her head but continued excitedly, 'Anyway, they're about to open one right here in Bundah.'

'That's great. Welcome to town.'

Jerome didn't look particularly thrilled by the idea, but Twiggy gave a serene smile and took a dainty sip from her wineglass.

'Well, it was nice to meet you both, but I'd better get back to work. See you, Russell,' she said, noticing Jerome had lost interest in the conversation already and had taken out his phone.

As she made her way across the courtyard, she caught Hugh's eye from where he still stood serving sausage sandwiches. He gave an exaggerated eye roll and looked back at the table she'd just left. It seemed an odd arrangement and she wondered how on earth Madam Latoy's would fit into a place like Bundah. Oh well, she dismissed, scrunching up her paper napkin and tossing it in the bin, it wasn't her problem. She had enough to worry about trying to keep Ken's wayward filing system in some kind of order, and she spent the remainder of her Friday buried beneath paperwork.

Her mobile rang just before knock-off time and she saw Nicole's name flashing across the screen.

'Get in the shower and find something nice to wear,' was Nicole's greeting.

'Excuse me?'

'You and I have a date tonight.'

'Why? Where are we going?'

'The Coach House. It's the grand opening.'

'I was there this afternoon so I've already made my appearance.'

'No, we're going to do the grown-up version. Come on, Luce, we haven't had a girls' night out in forever. Please? I want to get dressed up and go out somewhere.'

'Then take your husband,' Lucy said, tucking her mobile between her chin and shoulder as she packed away her desk.

'He's working, and the kids are at their grandparents for the weekend.'

Lucy gave an irritated sigh. She really didn't feel like going out; after the long working week, all she wanted to do was curl up on her lounge.

'You do that every weekend,' Nicole argued. 'Come on, you need to get out of that house. You're becoming an old spinster.'

It did Lucy no good to moan and complain about it; when Nicole set her mind to something, she never let it go. In the end it was easier just to go along with it, and that's how Lucy found herself staring at her wardrobe and wondering what on earth she was going to wear.

In the end she decided on her good jeans, knee-high boots and a long sweater top. She even went as far as putting on makeup for the occasion, only because if she didn't Nicole would drag her back inside and do it for her. At least this way Lucy could control how much she used. A little voice in the back of her mind suggested, somewhat smugly, that maybe she was making an extra effort to look nice for a certain publican she was bound to bump into tonight, but she dismissed that with a silent scoff. She was doing it to keep Nicole happy. And that was all.

Eight

'This will be good for you, you'll see,' Nicole promised Lucy as they walked into the newly refurbished pub. The warm glow of the timber floorboards freshly polished and brought back to their former glory made an excellent first impression.

'Wow. This is amazing,' Lucy whispered as she took in the soft lights and the tasteful leather lounge chairs scattered in casual groups around the bar. The background music floated through the air gently and added to the relaxed atmosphere. The bar had been restored with stone features and lots of glass shelving and mirrors. It was a sophisticated combination of modern and original fixtures and the whole thing was so un-Bundah-like that for a moment Lucy felt disorientated.

'Ladies,' Hugh greeted them, his hooded gaze holding Lucy's steadily.

'This is incredible.' Lucy saw him incline his dark head slightly at her compliment and seemed satisfied by her genuine delight.

'Now, this is what I'm talking about,' Nicole declared. '*Finally* some class,' she said, nudging Lucy lightly then ordering their drinks.

'On the house. Enjoy your evening.' Hugh handed over the wineglasses, giving Nicole a wink. Lucy rolled her eyes as Nicole turned a delicate shade of pink and giggled like a teenager.

The two of them settled into a couple of leather chairs and quietly observed the crowd for a few moments. The place was packed with a mixture of both locals and visitors.

'Who would have thought we'd ever be sitting in a boutique pub in the middle of Bundah?' Nicole said, sipping at her wine.

'You reckon Hugh's weekend biker thing has potential?' Lucy asked.

'Who knows, but I was reading an article not long ago in one of the Sunday papers and it talked about the huge popularity of these social motorbike groups. They're older people wanting more comfort and less thrill for their dollar. I think he's onto something.'

'For his sake I hope it works out. He must have spent a fortune on renovating this place.'

'If anyone can do it, I think it'll be Hugh Thompson.'

'And you'd know this from the whole twenty minutes of conversation you've had with the man since he arrived in town?' Lucy responded with a drawl.

'I know it, Ms Smartypants, because I *know* people. I reckon this guy has had to fight for everything he's ever owned. He doesn't seem the type to go into something he wasn't sure he could win.'

'You really have missed your calling, Nic,' Lucy said, taking another sip of the crisp wine. 'Your talents here as a mere mortal are wasted.' Lucy let her gaze roam the room casually, but an uneasy feeling settled around her as she noticed more than one table seemed to be deep in conversation, casting the odd glance in her direction. Was she imagining it? Maybe she was being oversensitive.

'Go on and mock me if you will. But I'm telling you, our Mr Thompson is an intriguing man . . . kinda like someone else I know.'

'Come off it.'

Nicole shrugged a slim shoulder. 'You've both been burned before. You circle each other like a pair of prize fighters trying to work out where the weakest point is in each other.'

Lucy stared at her friend as though she'd lost her mind. She *did not* stare at Hugh Thompson. She tried her best not to look at him at all.

'You know, if you'd both just let down your guards a little bit, you might discover how much you have in common.'

'Thanks, Dr Phil, but I'm having a small life crisis at the moment with my teenage daughter, so I really don't need to be taking on a man, especially one as emotionally high maintenance as Hugh Thompson.'

'Oh, please! A crisis? That child of yours has to be one of the most well-adjusted teenagers I've ever met. You want to know what a real crisis with a teenager is? Drop by my house any day of the damn week and take a look at what my daughter dishes out.'

'Christy? What's she been up to?'

'My God, the child's twelve going on twenty-one. I've had to go up to the school to deal with her rude behaviour towards the teachers. She's moody, disrespectful and dresses like she's taken up streetwalking as a career choice.'

Maybe Belle's sudden change of personality was Lucy's punishment for having it so easy for most of her parenting life. Secretly she was relieved that her daughter wasn't twelve. At least if this was some last-minute burst of rebellion, there weren't years of high school left to endure!

'I'm getting another drink, want one?'

'No thanks. I'm good.' Lucy lifted her barely touched glass and watched her friend head across the polished timber floorboards to the bar. Young Jason McAlister was behind the bar now and Lucy found herself looking about the room in search of that annoyingly familiar face.

'Lucy.'

Lucy looked up at her name and her ready smile slipped a notch. 'Hello, Stewy. I didn't know you were back.'

'Came up to Aunty Jean's funeral.' She saw him sway a little and he put his hand on the back of the seat nearby to steady himself.

Great. He'd been drinking. This was going to be interesting. Lucy eyed the man warily. The last time she'd seen him things hadn't ended well and she really didn't want a repeat performance tonight. 'I saw the announcement in the paper the other day. I'm sorry. She was a lovely lady.'

'Yeah. She was.'

The conversation petered out and Lucy's eyes darted around the room hoping Nicole was on her way back.

'You sent my money back,' he said.

Lucy felt her stomach drop. She really didn't want to get into all this now. 'Yes, I did.'

'I wanted to help.'

'I know. But I couldn't take it.'

'Why? Was my money not good enough for you or something?'

This was why she tried to avoid Stewy whenever possible. He was unpredictable when he drank. Sometimes he was melancholy, but occasionally he could get aggressive.

'Mick was my best mate. I loved him like a brother. I owed it to him to look after you and the kid.'

'It doesn't matter now.'

'It does matter!' he said, raising his voice and leaning closer. 'Why don't you just let me help?'

'I don't need help. I didn't want—'

'Didn't want *my* help. That's what you mean, isn't it.' He gave a dry scoff.

Lucy could smell the alcohol rolling off him in waves and knew there would be no reasoning with him tonight.

'Do you have any idea how much guilt I've had to live with? Taking care of you would have at least made me feel like I'd done something to fix things, but you wouldn't even let me do that, would ya.' He swayed again as he tried to straighten. 'You're selfish. Just like every other woman I've ever known,' he added morosely.

'I think you should go home, Stewy,' Lucy said quietly, realising they'd drawn the attention of a few people in the room. All the whispers earlier now made sense.

'You don't tell me what to do!' he yelled.

'No, but I do. I'd suggest you do as the lady suggested and go home, mate.'

Lucy gave a small sigh of relief as she looked over and saw Hugh standing behind her.

'It's none of your business. This is a private conversation.'

'Not from where I'm standing it's not. Now step away and get the hell outta my hotel before I throw you out,' he added pointedly.

Something obviously registered in Hugh's voice to make Stewy take a second glance at the man who now stood almost over the top of him. He took a step back, losing his balance slightly as he bumped into a chair behind him and let out a string of expletives.

Lucy slowly released a shaky sigh as she watched him walk out of the pub. She tried to ignore the hush of conversation around the room. If there was one thing Bundah loved, it was a good old-fashioned public drama.

'What was that all about?'

She shook her head and reached for her wine glass. She had to concentrate on keeping her hand steady. 'It was nothing. It happens now and again.'

'If this has happened before, then it sounds like you need to go and see that cop about taking out some kind of AVO against him.'

'It doesn't happen that often, and I'm sure Nate has better things to do.'

'It's his job. Go see him or I will.'

Lucy put her glass down and stared at the man irritably. 'Look, I'm really grateful that you were here to intervene, but you don't get to tell me what to do and you sure as hell don't get to interfere with my life.'

'Don't get too excited—I'm not interested in getting mixed up in your life. I'd have done the same for anyone being harassed in my pub.'

Lucy felt a blush creeping up her neck at his dismissive remark but she held his gaze. 'Just mind your own damn business,' she snapped, wishing she could think of something scathingly witty to cut him down to size.

'You were the one who said that was impossible in this town,' he pointed out.

They were both oblivious to Nicole, who had just returned. 'It's good to see you two kiddies playing so nicely.'

'Do what you like. I have a pub to run.' Hugh turned and left abruptly, sending a scowl at Lucy as he went.

'Well, that obviously went weil. What happened?' Nicole asked, taking a seat.

'Stewy stopped by and Hugh stepped in and sent him on his way, but then went on to tell me what I should be doing about it.'

Nicole gave a commiserating grimace. 'Yeah, I thought he might come home for the funeral.'

'Apparently, you were correct,' Lucy said taking another sip of her wine.

'I feel for the guy. It must be hard living with the fact he killed someone, but you've been putting up with his crap for too long. Enough is enough, Luce. It was years ago. He needs to get over it—he's screwed up.'

Lucy nodded in agreement. Stewy had moved away from Bundah after his release from prison, and had started sending money spasmodically over the next few years. Each time, Lucy returned it, diplomatically but firmly.

He'd come back to town to see her after his release and she really had felt for him. He was consumed with guilt over the death of his best friend. She'd tried to point out that Mick had been old enough to know what he was doing, that they had all had been drinking that night. In truth, it had been an accident waiting to happen. Mick and his mates had a reputation for wild parties and even wilder antics. It was only ever a case of when, not if someone got seriously hurt. Unfortunately, Stewy just couldn't seem to give up on the idea that if only he could take care of her, then somehow it would help make up for his part in Mick's death.

'Seriously, you shouldn't have to put up with this every time he sees you, Luce.'

Lucy held up a hand in warning. 'It's only when he's been drinking, and don't you start. I'm not going to Nate. I just want to forget about it.'

'So that's why you bit off Hugh's head? Just because he told you to go and report Stewy?'

'No, not only that,' Lucy said defensively. 'He threatened to go over my head if I didn't do it. That's why I told him off. He has no business interfering in my life. I don't even know the man.'

'He was trying to look out for you. Why do you have to be so damn defensive about everything? Why can't someone do something for you now and again? It's not a weakness to ask for help, you know.'

'*I didn't ask*. That's the point and, quite frankly, I'm sick of everyone always telling me how ungrateful I am just because I prefer to take care of myself. I'm not useless. I actually manage quite well, and yet, because I'm not pathetic and needy, I'm somehow being too strong or too well adjusted!'

'That's the problem. You are *too* strong and *too* good at taking care of yourself. So good, in fact, that you can't see how you keep pushing everyone who cares about you away. Everyone needs a hand now and again.'

Oh, but it is, thought Lucy. She knew all about being weak and depending on people. No one could ever really know someone, so how could you trust them? Nope, the only person you truly knew was yourself . . . although lately she'd been finding herself considering things she'd never have given a second thought to before, and most of them involved Hugh bloody Thompson.

As she walked out the back of the pub a little later to head for the car park, she saw Hugh. He intercepted her on the back verandah, where tables were set up for the soon to be opened pub restaurant.

'Look, I know you told me to mind my own business before, and ordinarily I would. But I've had experience with this sort of thing before. The only way you can deal with this is to get your boyfriend the cop involved.'

'Nate is not my boyfriend. Not that *that's* any of your business either.'

'No, I figured it wouldn't be. Not much about anything is any of my business apparently.'

Maybe Nicole had been closer to the truth than Lucy wanted to believe. She did tend to overreact a little when people tried to tell her what to do.

'You and the cop do seem pretty friendly.'

'In case you haven't noticed, *everyone* in Bundah is friendly.'

'*Most* people in Bundah are friendly,' he corrected, and she moved to turn away. 'Okay, my mistake but, boyfriend or not, this is a police matter and I wouldn't be very neighbourly if I didn't advise you to take it seriously.'

Lucy turned back reluctantly. 'I guess I should thank you for helping out tonight. He just kind of caught me off guard.'

'Apology accepted.'

'I wasn't apologising, I was explaining.'

'No, it sounded more like an apology,' he smirked before she walked away.

Lucy could feel him watching her as she made her way to her car and drove out of the car park. She was determined not to look at him in the rear-view mirror. 'Annoying bloody man,' she muttered to herself.

Nine

Lucy flipped through the mail on her way inside after work, passing over the few bits of junk mail and sighing at the bills. She dropped it all on the kitchen table unenthusiastically, before starting on dinner.

'How was your day?' Lucy called out when she heard Belle's bedroom door open a few minutes later.

'Fine.'

'Don't eat anything, I'm getting dinner,' Lucy told her as she watched her daughter heading for the fridge.

'I'm starving,' Belle complained.

'Well, it won't be long. By the time you set the table it'll be ready.'

Lucy finished chopping up the salad and heating up the lasagne she'd made the night before.

It had been a frustrating day. She'd spent far too long trying to balance the till, which hardly ever happened, and searching for a missing invoice. She couldn't wait to leave work and get home to a nice glass of moscato and forget about work until tomorrow. Tomorrow . . . a strange thought crossed her mind. Earlier when she'd left work, she'd been thinking about Hugh and the night at the pub and suddenly she couldn't recall if she'd locked the door behind her as she'd left.

The moment the thought entered her head, she knew she was done for. She *did* set the alarm . . . didn't she? Of course she did. It was routine. The argument went on silently for the next few minutes until she sighed irritably. There was no way she was going to be able to relax until she checked, and if she *had* left it unlocked, she couldn't let it wait as this was her responsibility. Damn, damn, damn. For the life of her, she honestly couldn't remember locking up.

'Where are you going?' Belle asked when Lucy picked up her bag and withdrew her keys.

'I forgot something at work. I'll be back in a minute. Leave the dishes, I'll do them when I get back,' she added wearily, thinking about the bottle of wine sitting in the fridge that she'd been saving to have when she could sit down and relax.

The streets were all but empty as she drove through town. The only sign of life was out the front of the new pub. There were a number of parked cars and light spilled from the building out onto the footpath. She hadn't seen

Hugh since the pub opening. She tried to ignore the leap of her pulse at the thought of him.

She pulled up out the front of the service station and opened her door to get out. A car door slammed nearby and she turned to see the outline of a dark shadow of a vehicle in the parking bay beneath the shady willow trees. The roar of an engine broke the still night and Lucy threw her hand up in front of her eyes as a row of bright spotlights along the top of the vehicle's cabin blinded her momentarily, as it pulled onto the road, heading out of town.

Lucy's heart thudded painfully against her chest. *Who the hell was that?* she wondered, frowning after the vehicle and trailer, now a tiny shape in the distance. Tourists who'd been pulled over for a break maybe? They clearly weren't desperate for fuel if they didn't even bother waiting around.

Lucy turned her attention to the shop. Inside, the security lights were on, and a quick tug on the front door proved that it was locked tight. 'Idiot,' she muttered before heading around to double-check the side door.

As she circled around the front of her vehicle, she froze as a blur of shadow disappeared around the corner. Lucy looked around but there was no sign of anyone else; the place looked deserted. She grabbed the car door handle and scrambled inside, locking it behind her. This was ridiculous. Why was she so damn jumpy all of a sudden? It was probably just the shadow of a branch from the trees. Surely if someone had been there they would have called out to her? Unless whoever it was hadn't wanted to been seen. What if she'd startled a burglar?

With shaking hands she turned the key in the ignition, but nothing happened. Lucy dropped her head against the steering wheel and forced herself to remain calm. *This is silly.* This was also the reason she never watched scary movies: she didn't handle stress terribly well. A tap at her window made her let out a scream, before it registered someone was calling her name.

'Everything all right, Luce?'

Lucy jumped at Nate's voice. She'd been so busy stressing over nothing that she hadn't even heard him pull up. She wound down the window and summoned a smile. 'The car won't start. I think I might have flooded the engine.'

'You're finishing late.'

'I just came down to double-check I locked the door when I closed up.'

'Want me to take a look under the bonnet?'

'I think it'll be okay if I just give it a few minutes. She's a temperamental old thing sometimes.'

'Maybe it's time you looked at getting a new one?'

Lucy put her finger to her lips. 'She's a bit sensitive when you start talking about newer models.'

'Seriously, Luce, I know you like your ute, but it's becoming a bit of a dinosaur. It's got no airbags, no crumple zone, no traction control. It'd be a death trap in an accident.'

'Well, I'll just keep avoiding accidents like I have been for the past seventeen years I've owned her for.'

He watched her silently for a little while, and Lucy tried not to squirm under his gaze. This was partly why she'd never been able to let their relationship stray beyond friendship.

He was always in cop mode and she just couldn't seem to shake that sense that he was trying to peel back her layers.

'You didn't happen to see anyone before you pulled up, did you?' she asked.

'No. why?'

'I thought I saw something . . .' Lucy shook her head, feeling stupid. 'Never mind, my head's all over the place tonight.'

'I'll take a look around,' he said, moving away.

There was no mistaking Nate's 'cop' tone, so she didn't bother trying to argue. As she waited in the car, she looked around at the darkened streets and scoffed at her earlier fear. There was nothing in Bundah to be scared of.

'Everything seems to be okay. No sign of anyone around the back.'

'Thanks, Nate. It was probably nothing to start with.'

'Give the car another go now. If it won't start, we'll leave it here overnight and I'll give you a lift home.'

Lucy turned the key in the ignition and the engine roared to life, giving off a strong whiff of petrol in the process. 'See? Runs like a dream,' she said with a grin.

Nate rolled his eyes but didn't say anything more on the matter. 'Sure it does. Take care, Lucy.'

Now if she could just turn her brain off for the rest of the night and get a good night's sleep, she'd be fine.

Lucy was at her desk keying in numbers on her calculator when Ken came through the front door the next day.

'Afternoon, Lucy. I'm just dropping some invoices in for you,' he said, placing the papers on her desk before turning away.

'Okay, thanks,' she said, glancing up. 'Ken, before you go, can I see you for a sec?'

He glanced at his watch before giving her a nod.

'I'm having trouble with the fuel tally.' When Lucy had done the morning fuel level readings from the underground reservoir, checking the daily takings against the figures, they had been out quite significantly. Ernie had been doing the last few dip readings and at first Lucy thought he'd somehow written down the wrong figures, but the longer she'd been trying to untangle it the worse it had been getting.

'You're the book-keeper, Lucy. No good asking me, that's why I employ you.'

Lucy mentally counted to five before speaking. Ken was a great community leader, but as a boss he was frustrating. He wasn't overly demanding; she had the freedom of working her hours around whatever she needed to do, and she was given a free rein over the office as manager, but she found it incredibly annoying when he did things without telling her. 'That's the point, Ken. I can't do my job if I don't know when you've taken money out without telling me. I need to know when you do anything with the accounts.'

'What are you talking about?'

'Did you take money out of the till and forget to write it in somewhere?'

'No, I did not.'

'Well, the takings don't match the fuel dip numbers.'

'It can't just disappear. There has to be a number written down wrong. Just leave it for now. I'll come back later and see if I can find out where you've gone wrong.'

Maybe she'd just been looking at it too long with a tired mind. It irked her to have her boss take over. She took great pride in her management role; it wasn't a large business by any means, but she'd started out here as a cashier and had worked her way up to accounts manager and eventually overall manager, before the previous owner had retired and sold the business to Ken a few years ago.

For the most part she still loved her job, and if Ken would just stop meddling in the accounts there'd be no problem. Sometimes she wondered if Ken was beginning to lose the plot. He often forgot to tell her when he'd paid a bill or made some kind of arrangement with the bank, and it frustrated her no end to have to go back and fix all his mistakes.

'Oh, and don't forget it's Marg's birthday tomorrow.'

Ken gave a long-suffering sigh as he paused at the door.

Lucy glanced up at that and frowned, before striving for a calm, non-judgemental tone she was far from feeling. 'It would make her day to hear from you. She seems a bit lonely lately.'

'If she's lonely, it's no one's fault but her own. I set her up in a fancy apartment; she's got everything she could ever want. If she decides to live like a flamin' hermit then that's her problem.'

'I think it's hard for her to go out alone and meet people. Maybe you could go down and see her, or bring her out here for a visit. I'd be happy to—'

'Babysit her? Because that's what you'd be doing, and quite frankly I'm paying you to work, not sit and talk to my sister all day. You know maybe you need to start looking after your own family before you start telling other people how to take care of theirs.'

'I wasn't trying to tell you what to do, I just thought—'

'I've heard Belle's been going off the rails lately,' Ken cut in.

Lucy blinked in surprise at his sharp tone.

'Maybe *you* need to start paying closer attention to your daughter and leave my sister to me,' he said bluntly, leaving Lucy to stare after him, her cheeks growing warm in mortification at having been chastised about how she raised her child.

He really could be an insensitive jerk when he wanted to be. Fine, she thought angrily, closing the books in front of her. Ken could go over the mess he'd made of the books. She'd already wasted far too much time today already.

Ten

Lucy closed her eyes as she listened to the meeting going on around her. She hadn't been sleeping well over the past few days. The last place she wanted to be was sitting here listening to Mavis incite a coup on new businesses in Bundah.

'It's going too far, Ken. We need to have some kind of regulation for what type of businesses are being allowed to open.'

'We have the usual council regulations in place, Mavis.'

'It's getting ridiculous. What on earth do we need another hairdresser in town for?'

'So we don't have to be stuck with hairstyles from the eighties any more?' Nicole whispered in Lucy's ear.

Madam Latoy's was certainly stirring up an ants' nest around town since it had opened almost a fortnight ago.

Lucy had been filled in on the gossip by Russell and Steven, who were more than happy to talk about their celebrity-like friends who had descended upon Bundah with all the subtlety of a tsunami. Twiggy apparently was not French; in fact, she'd grown up in a town very much like Bundah somewhere out around Longreach way, but she *had* been a burlesque dancer in Kings Cross for a few years before making a career change into hairdressing. Her much younger partner, Jerome, however, was very much a Frenchman, and his heavy seductive accent was wooing more than its fair share of Bundah's female population.

'It seems a bit of an odd location for them to be setting up a salon,' Lucy had said as she'd listened to the boys gushing about the newcomers.

'Well, about that,' Russell had said, leaning closer to Lucy and lowering his voice a fraction, even though they had been the only three in the café at the time. 'Word has it that young Jerome's wandering eye attracted attention from a certain high-profile A-lister who happened to be Twiggy's biggest rival, and Twiggy was not happy. She knew we'd made the move and decided that a little country air might do her young stud some good.'

Steven had chuckled a little. 'Of course, we don't *officially* know any of that. Twiggy's version is that she wanted to get back to her small-town roots for a while,' he'd said with a conspiratorial wink.

Whatever the reasons for coming to Bundah, the two made a scandalous couple and the gossip mill was in over-drive about the obvious age gap between them. Personally,

Lucy thought that if Twiggy could manage to look that good at sixty-something, then she *deserved* a hot young stud of twenty-five. Although she did have to wonder whether Bundah was going to be able to hold their attention for very long.

'Come on now, Mavis. A little healthy competition is good for the town,' Ken was saying.

'Healthy competition?' Mavis spluttered. 'I'll have you know my prices have always been extremely reasonable. You just wait and see how much these city people want to charge.'

'Then you'll have nothing to worry about. Look, bringing new business to Bundah is a good thing. There will be plenty of opportunity for everyone. Residents who at the moment take their money out of town will be able to spend it in Bundah. We need to give people choice,' Ken said calmly to the murmuring group of concerned business owners gathered in the hall.

'You wouldn't be so gung-ho about it if another real estate agency opened up. It's all right for you, Ken, you're the only one making any kind of profit around here,' Mavis sniffed.

Nicole hummed under her breath beside her, providing the soundtrack for the drama unfolding before them.

Lucy bit her lip to stop giggling, but she couldn't help but hold her breath nervously as she caught Ken's frown and the colour begin to rise in his face.

'I certainly hope you're not suggesting that I'm putting myself ahead of this town, Mavis?' Ken huffed. 'Nobody has fought longer or harder to get this initiative off the ground than me, and at quite a substantial cost to myself, I might add. This is for the long-term benefit of our town.'

'Well, that's all fine and dandy, but what about those of us whose takings will be affected in the short-term?'

'I appreciate that this is going to bring changes to the way we've always done things, but we cannot stay still while the world moves on around us. This is an opportunity to take a look at how you run your business and maybe make some improvements. It can be a positive, not a negative.'

'The man really should go to Canberra; he's a born politician,' Nicole whispered.

He certainly knew how to work a crowd; although, Lucy noted, there were a few people who didn't seem placated by his remarks—most notably, Mavis, who had sat back down, arms crossed and lips shut tight.

Lucy had to concede the woman had a point. Ken was probably the least affected by all the new businesses coming into town, not to mention the fact he was making money from both rentals and sales. She felt a little sorry for Mavis, but then she reminded herself that quite a few women went to hairdressers in Tenterfield, so Mavis wouldn't be losing their business seeing as she'd never had it in the first place.

It always came down to change and some people fought hard before they would accept it.

The main street was quiet by the time the meeting concluded. Lucy, running late as usual, had left her ute parked out in the street and had cut through the back of the top pub and down the small laneway which ran along the side of the premises to the hall.

It wasn't late, but the moon wasn't as bright as it had been earlier and Lucy shivered in the cold breeze. She wished she hadn't watched so many crime shows on TV, with their dark alleyways, shadows and strange noises. All she needed now was the creepy music escalating in the background, she thought with forced bravado. *Would you get a grip,* she told herself firmly. These were hardly the back streets of New York—this was Bundah, for goodness sake. At worst that rustling behind her was someone's cat out hunting for mice. As she entered the laneway beside the pub she picked up her pace. As did the rustling behind her. Her heart rate spiked at the sound of her footsteps echoing off the tall tin fence that lined both sides of the laneway, and the heavier, much louder sound of someone else's footsteps following her.

She turned to look over her shoulder, preparing to scoff at her overactive imagination, but caught the movement of a dark shape before it slipped into the shadows. The clouds moved overhead and the laneway grew darker. Any remaining calm she'd strived to hold on to disappeared as she made for the gate that led to the side of the old pub. She slipped her hand through the small gap cut into the tin panel, releasing the latch and pushed the gate open, which gave a loud creak of protest. As teens, they had often used the laneway to cut across town when they'd wanted to sneak away from school at lunch time to buy hot chips.

She couldn't hear anything over the pounding of blood in her veins as she ran up the dark side of the hotel, not pausing to see if whoever had been behind her was still there. Ahead she could see the light from the main street and she aimed for it, slipping out into the street and breathing heavily. She didn't stop to see if anyone appeared from the laneway behind her, she just headed for her car, fumbling with her bag as she searched for her keys. *Good thing you're not in an actual horror movie,* she thought, *or you'd be dead by now.* She almost laughed out loud but then a shadow fell across her and she screamed, swinging her handbag wildly.

'Woah. Hey, calm down. It's me.'

Lucy opened her eyes and found herself staring up at Hugh.

'What's happened?' He was already looking around, searching the dark street for any sign of what might have set off the hysterical woman before him.

Lucy wished she could sink through the footpath and disappear.

'Are you okay?' he asked again, his expression worried.

'I'm fine. You just scared me.'

'No kidding.'

'You don't sneak up behind someone at night like that—what's *wrong* with you?' she demanded, terror melting into anger now that she realised how silly she'd been . . . and had a witness to it.

'I heard someone running up the side and thought I had a burglar.'

'I was using a short cut.'

'You use that short cut often?' he asked, folding his arms across his chest as he watched her.

'No. Not any more.'

'You sure you're okay? You look a little pale.'

'I'm positive. Sorry to disturb you,' she said briskly, before turning away to rummage in her bag for her keys, muttering under her breath as she failed to find them.

'Problem?'

'I can't find my stupid keys.'

'Maybe you dropped them while you were out jogging?' he asked, keeping a straight face when she turned her narrowed eyes on him. 'I'll get a torch. Come on inside.'

She wanted to tell him she was fine to wait out here, but a quick glance around the empty streets soon changed her mind and she followed behind him with as much decorum as she could muster after having screaming like a banshee only a few moments ago.

She waited as he went behind the bar and brought out a big square torch.

'You want to stay here while I go take a look?' he asked.

'No. I'll come. Two sets of eyes will be better than one.'

She followed Hugh along the narrow side of the building, her eyes following the surprisingly bright beam of light from his torch. 'I came in through the side gate,' she said, pointing at the opening in the tin fence and standing back as Hugh pushed it open and walked through.

'You were coming from the CWA hall?' he asked, shining the torch up and down the length of the laneway before aiming it back on the road. 'Did I miss anything?'

'Just Mavis trying to recruit a lynch mob to put a stop to new businesses opening up in town.'

'What?'

'Well, to be more precise, a new *hairdresser*.'

'Ah,' Hugh nodded. 'I see. Well,' he said, 'there's no sign of your keys out here. Maybe you left them inside the hall?'

'I guess I should go and check,' she said with a sigh. She didn't need this tonight. All she wanted to do was to go home, have a nice long bath and go to bed.

Stepping out onto the street in front of the CWA rooms, Lucy gave a frustrated groan.

'They didn't waste time locking up tonight,' Hugh commented, taking in the small hall sitting in absolute darkness before them.

'Damn it.'

'Come on, I'll give you a lift home, and tomorrow morning I'll take another look for your keys in daylight.'

What else could she do? Stumbling around out here in the dark wasn't getting them anywhere. No sooner had she thought this than her toe caught a pothole and she tripped forward, slamming into Hugh's solid back.

He let out a surprised grunt but turned to catch her instinctively, his hands resting on her hips, holding her tightly against his body. It happened so fast, Lucy was too surprised to step back immediately. Up close his chest was broad and firm. Beneath her hands she could feel the soft fabric of his T-shirt and, through that, the warmth of his chest as it moved up and down in time with his breathing. Swallowing hard, Lucy forced herself to take a step back. 'Sorry.'

'No worries.' Hugh's voice sounded husky. 'Did you check your pockets for your keys?' he added after clearing his throat.

'Of course I checked my—' Lucy stopped, her hand moving to her front pocket automatically. She let out a small groan and closed her eyes briefly. 'How did you know?'

'Well, if it wasn't your keys digging into me, then you were really pleased to see me.'

What an idiot! Why hadn't she realised they were there before? Admittedly she'd been preoccupied, thinking she was being chased but, still, why hadn't she checked her pockets? *Moron.* 'I don't know why I put them there. I usually put them in my bag,' she muttered, wishing she could rewind the last twenty minutes and start over.

'You can admit it, you know,' he said as they turned to head back to the main street.

'Admit what?'

'That you used it as a ploy to get me alone in a dark alley.' She heard the grin in his voice even before she looked over at him.

'In your dreams,' she scoffed but was grateful to him for making light of the whole awkward mess. They came out from the side of the pub and back onto the footpath of the main street and Lucy held her keys up in a farewell wave. 'Thanks for helping me search. Sorry I wasted your time.'

'It wasn't a complete waste,' he said without elaborating. 'I'll follow you home.'

'What? No. I'm fine.'

'Humour me, okay? Look, something obviously spooked you earlier, and I wouldn't feel right letting you drive home alone.'

'It's Bundah. I just had myself worked up over nothing. You don't need to escort me home.'

'You want to be responsible for me tossing and turning all night wondering if you made it back?' he asked, lifting an eyebrow.

'Heavens above, we wouldn't want that, would we.' It seemed useless standing here arguing about it—Hugh Thompson seemed to have a stubborn streak in him. 'Okay, fine, if it makes you feel better.'

She unlocked her car and climbed inside and, by the time she'd clipped up her seat belt and started the engine, she heard the roar of his big bike start up from the car park down the other side of the pub.

Lucy pulled away from the curb and within a few moments saw a headlight in her rear-view mirror turn onto the street behind her. As silly as it seemed, she had to admit she felt safer. She wanted to brush the whole thing off as just an overactive imagination, but something continued to niggle her. Someone had been in that laneway behind her and had vanished by the time she'd made it to the main street.

Lucy parked the ute in the driveway and saw Hugh pull up out the front of her house. She'd expected him to simply wave and keep going once he saw her arrive home safe and sound, but he turned the bike off and was removing his helmet by the time she approached him. The engine ticked in the sudden silence between them.

'Thanks again.'

'No problem.'

There was a moment of awkward silence before Lucy remembered her manners. 'Do you want to come in for a cuppa or something? It's the least I can do for dragging you out like this.'

'Sure. A coffee would be great.'

'Okay.' Holy crap. What was she doing? She did a quick mental check of the condition of the house and hoped it wasn't too much of a mess. Before she'd left this evening she'd barely had time to scoff down an early dinner and have an argument with Belle about yet another party she wanted to go to; there'd certainly been no time for cleaning up.

She unlocked the door and scanned the kitchen and lounge room as she walked inside, breathing a sigh of relief that Belle had at least done the dishes.

'Belle, I'm home,' she called out as she placed her handbag on the entrance table and headed for the kitchen.

'Nice place,' Hugh commented, his gaze moving around the house as he took in the pressed-tin ceiling and original fretwork of the arches in the hallway.

'Thanks. It's pretty much all original. Old places have far more character than the new ones.'

'I agree, although the restoration can be a killer.'

'I was lucky with this, it was in pretty good condition when I bought it. I just upgraded the tiles and carpet a few years ago.'

'Have you thought about it?' Belle asked, coming out of her room and removing the earphones from her head. She stopped dead in her tracks when she saw Hugh across the room.

'Belle, you remember Hugh?'

'Hi,' she said, eyeing him suspiciously.

'I had . . . car trouble and Hugh followed me home to make sure I didn't break down again.'

Lucy saw Hugh glance at her but he didn't comment. 'Hi, Belle.'

Belle turned her frown onto her mother, ignoring the visitor. 'So have you?'

'Have I what?' Lucy asked.

'Thought about the party.'

'For goodness sake, Belle! I just walked in the door and we have company,' Lucy said pointedly, giving her daughter a don't-mess-with-me-now look which, being a teenager, Belle simply ignored.

'But Mum! Please. Just this once.'

Lucy busied herself switching on the coffee machine and getting down two cups, before telling Hugh to take a seat at the kitchen table.

'Belle. There are going to be boys out there a lot older than any of you and your friends. I don't want you in that situation.'

'But we'll stay away from them. Mum, please!'

'No. I'm not discussing this any more. You're not going out to a party on a property that far out of town.' Why did it have to be tonight of all nights that Belle wanted to wage World War III? She wasn't in the mood to be diplomatic, and she sure as hell wasn't in the mood to be placating an unreasonable, hormonal teenager.

'Sorry about that.' Lucy muttered as she let out a slow breath after the door down the hallway slammed.

'Look, I'm no expert on parenting, but I do remember how frustrating it was to be that age. Maybe a compromise could smooth things over.'

'Yeah, well, I remember all too well what it was like to be a teenager. I also know what goes on at those parties. There's no compromise on that. You don't have any kids?' Lucy asked as she inserted the coffee pod into the machine.

'Nope.'

'Have you ever been married?' There was something about his adamant answer that had piqued her curiosity.

'Nope.'

'You got something against marriage?'

He let out a soft chuckle and shrugged. 'Nope. Do you?'

Lucy realised with a small start that she'd been surveying the width and shape of his shoulders beneath the fabric of his well-worn T-shirt.

'No . . . Not really.'

'It just wasn't for you?' he asked curiously.

Lucy shrugged uncomfortably before adding milk to their cups and bringing them to the table. She might have started this little Q&A but she wasn't sure she enjoyed being on the receiving end. 'I guess I never found anyone I could see myself living with for the rest of my life.' She slid the sugar bowl over to him and took a seat.

Hugh raised an eyebrow lazily. 'So you've never had any near misses? No one ever came close to tempting you into tying the knot?

'Nope.'

'Interesting,' he nodded, as though pondering her answer thoughtfully.

'What's that supposed to mean?'

'Either Belle's dad was a real prick, or he was the perfect man no other guy could hope to compete with.'

Lucy frowned. 'He was young. We were *both* young.'

'What does that mean?'

Lucy gave him an irritated look. 'It means that I was seventeen when I got pregnant and neither of us were ready for marriage, let alone the responsibility of raising a child together.'

'You seemed to step up and handle it okay.'

'*I* didn't have much choice, did I? Anyway,' Lucy smiled softly despite herself, 'Belle was the best thing that ever happened to me. I wouldn't change any of it even if I could.'

'Where's her father now?'

The smile faded from her lips. 'He's dead.'

A moment of silence followed her answer. 'I'm sorry. That must be hard for Belle.'

Lucy turned her cup around in front of her. 'He died before she was born.'

'So it's just been you and Belle ever since?'

'I've got family. My parents are really great. They live in Tenterfield, so they're close by and we see them all the time. And we had Mick's dad, Fred, until he died when Belle was about three.'

'But no guy in your life?'

'It's not like there's been an abundance of opportunities to meet eligible bachelors in Bundah,' she said.

'You could have left town.'

Lucy nodded. 'I could have, I guess. But I like it here.'

'Not many opportunities for kids though.'

'No. But Ken's initiative is at least bringing a few new jobs to town. And, who knows, in time that might make a difference.' As in most small towns in rural Australia, the lack of any major industry other than farming led to all the young people either leaving town in search of work or remaining at home and facing long-term unemployment.

There was silence for a few moments.

'So car trouble, huh?' Hugh said eventually. 'I take it your daughter has a problem with you having men over?'

'I don't *have* men over,' said Lucy.

'I thought that's why you made up the car trouble excuse.'

'No, I don't need an excuse to have company.'

'So what's going on then? There's more to it.'

Lucy studied her coffee cup. 'I didn't want her to hear I overreacted.' She didn't particularly like his insightfulness. It made her feel exposed and rather vulnerable. 'There's been a few odd things happening lately. I didn't want her to start worrying.'

'What kind of odd things?'

Lucy shrugged awkwardly. 'Nothing I can put my finger on for sure. Just doors unlocked that I thought I'd locked, and little things moved around inside the house.'

'Like maybe someone's broken in? Did you call the cops?'

'No,' she said. 'And before you say it,' she added, cutting him off, 'I haven't reported it because there's nothing missing, and I can't say for absolutely certain that I didn't just forget to lock the door behind me.'

'Then tonight could have been more than just an over-active imagination?'

Hugh's words brought back the uneasiness she'd been feeling for the past few days. 'Put together with all the little things you've been dismissing, I think this adds up to something that you need to report. Does Nate know about your friend at the pub the other night?'

'No,' Lucy said, taking a sip of her coffee and striving to keep calm despite the dangerous terrain this conversation was entering.

'In light of this new turn of events, don't you think maybe he should?'

Lucy tried to imagine Stewy rummaging through her belongings and following her in the dark. Would he do something like that? They had a past, for sure, but he only got upset when he'd been drinking, and she didn't think that the footsteps she'd heard had sounded like drunken stumbling. She shook her head. 'I'm pretty sure it's got nothing to do with him.'

'How do you know?'

'Because . . .' God, she hated being interrogated! Why was everyone poking their noses into her business all of a sudden?

'Maybe he's trying to scare you into needing him.'

'I don't think he's that smart,' she said, trying to make light of it, but Hugh's stare didn't waver in the slightest.

'Something spooked you tonight. What was it?'

'I thought I heard someone walking behind me down the laneway, but it could have been an echo or something. It really doesn't take much to scare me.'

'Look, I don't want to frighten you, but you need to at least consider that this is all linked somehow until you can prove otherwise. From now on, don't walk anywhere alone. Tomorrow I'll come over and put a new lock on the front door. The one you've got's not worth a cracker.'

'Not that I don't appreciate all this, but changing locks? Don't you think that might be a little extreme?'

'Better to be safe than sorry.'

Lucy was suddenly very tired. She didn't want to be scared of her own shadow. She wanted her nice, quiet, predictable life back but she knew he was right. It wouldn't hurt to take a few precautions.

'I'll come over after work tomorrow and fix that lock.'

'Thanks for . . . everything. I appreciate it. Really,' she added sincerely.

'You're welcome. I'll see you tomorrow. Lock up behind me.'

She turned the lock and sighed, pushing away from the front door and flicking off lights as she went. She couldn't be bothered with that bath she'd been dreaming of earlier, she was too tired. All she wanted was bed and oblivion.

But lying in bed later, she found that sleep didn't claim her as quickly as she would have liked. Instead she found herself thinking about a certain leather-clad male in ways that were far from platonic, or even appropriate for that matter. It proved to be a very restless night's sleep.

Hugh sat at his computer late into the night, the coffee cups stacked up on each other beside him as he stared at the screen. He'd lain in bed, unable to shake the conversation he'd had with Lucy earlier that evening. He wanted to know why a woman like Lucy had remained unattached for so long. He wasn't dismissing the cop, the guy was making it pretty obvious he thought Hugh was already encroaching on his territory as it was, but Lucy didn't seem to be concerned.

The guy at the pub was a concern, and after the weird stalker episode, his gut was telling him not to brush things off as merely coincidence. He needed to dig deeper into Lucy's past to try to find out what was going on.

He googled newspaper search sites, using Belle's age as a guide to how far back to start the search, and it didn't take him long to find what he was looking for.

A local man was killed late last night after the vehicle he was riding in the back of rolled at high speed. The man, twenty-two-year-old Michael Monroe, died at the scene. The driver, also a Bundah local, Stewart Gibbons, had a blood alcohol level three times the legal limit and was uninjured in the accident. He is due to face court tomorrow. Two other underage passengers sustained non-life threatening injuries. The group of men were on their way to a party when the accident occurred.

Unable to find anything further about the accident, Hugh closed the computer and went back to bed. The newspaper hadn't told him much, but he got the general idea. While Lucy had been at home pregnant with his child, her boyfriend had been out partying. And good old Stewy from the pub had been the driver who'd killed him. There was definitely history there, but was this Gibbons guy stalking her? And, if so, why now after all this time?

First thing tomorrow he was going to go out into that laneway and take a look around. He'd be willing to bet that not everything that had happened tonight had been in Lucy's imagination.

Hugh stifled a sigh as he looked up from restocking the fridge to see Nate Pearce walking in the front door of the pub. He'd been half expecting a visit, given the guy seemed to thrive on making himself a pain in Hugh's arse.

'Can I have a word?' he asked when Hugh slowly straightened up but didn't offer a welcome.

'Sure.'

'Maybe out the back?' the cop said, looking across at two men dressed in leather riding gear, reading the paper as they leisurely finished a latte.

Hugh stared at the man for a long moment, before calling out to Jason to watch the bar for him.

He led the way out to an empty lounge area and gestured for the cop to take a seat.

'I've got a bit of a problem.'

'Oh?' Hugh lifted an eyebrow curiously.

'Seems there's a bit of an epidemic happening around town. Somehow kids are getting hold of drugs, and I want to stop it.'

'And you're telling me . . . why?'

'Call it a friendly warning. I noticed the other day you have an interesting tattoo on your back.'

Hugh kept his face expressionless, but he already knew where this was headed. 'Lots of people have tattoos, far as I know it's not a crime.'

'It's not. But the interesting thing about tattoos is that sometimes, for a certain element of the community, they're used as a way to show loyalty to a particular group . . . like an outlaw motorcycle gang, for instance.'

'Just because I ride a bike doesn't mean I'm in a gang.'

'No, but given that tat on your back, the odds are that if you're not still in a gang, then you were once connected to one.'

Hugh felt his gut clench at the cop's words, but years of experience had conditioned him to keep his face blank. 'I've got work to do.'

'I haven't finished yet.'

Hugh remained standing and glared at the cop, his mind turning over a hundred different things at once.

'It seems a strange coincidence that as soon as you got here, drugs started turning up in my town.'

'Me and at least a dozen other newcomers.'

'Yeah, but as far as I can see, none of them have possible connections to the underworld.'

'I'm just minding my own business, trying to make a go of this pub. Besides, even if there was any merit to your half-arsed theory, seems to me a bloke would have the right to leave his past behind him and start over.'

'As long as that bloke wasn't bringing drugs and trouble into my town,' the cop agreed with stony resolve. 'I've got my eye on you, Thompson.'

'Knock yourself out, mate.'

Hugh didn't go straight back into the bar; instead he pushed open the door that led out to his quarters and slammed it shut behind him. He crossed to his kitchen, bracing his hands on the benchtop, and closed his eyes. *Shit, shit, shit!*

He should have gotten the stupid tat removed, but it covered a large portion of his back and wasn't that easy to get rid of. He should have done it anyway. Once it'd been a symbol of something important. It had given him an identity, a sense of belonging and acceptance. Now it was a stark reminder of a life he'd left behind. He was usually careful to keep it covered, considering it was a fairly easily recognisable club insignia.

The last thing he needed now was some wannabe detective piecing together his past and holding it over his head.

Eleven

Hugh rolled the bike to a stop behind the pub and cut the engine. He'd been out of town for the past three days, making new business contacts he hoped would pay off in the coming weeks. It had been a flying visit to the city, and he'd thought he'd find it hard to drag himself away from civilisation once he got there, but he was surprised to discover he'd been wrong. A few hours of dealing with traffic and crowds and the fast pace of people hurrying from one place to another and he'd found himself craving the peace and quiet of Bundah.

He pulled off his helmet and swung his leg over the bike. Heaving his gear sack up onto his shoulder, he turned to walk up the back path to his private quarters at the rear of the pub. A noise caught his attention as he was about to slide the key into the lock, and he paused to listen. It was coming from the alleyway between the pub and the bakery next door. Quietly he lowered his bag to the ground and crept his way towards the alleyway.

Easing his head around the corner, he found a small group of kids sitting on the ground, their backs against the wall of the pub, talking quietly. That's not all they were doing, he noticed as he spied an empty bottle of alcohol and syringes lying discarded nearby. He'd left the city to get away from this shit, he thought angrily as he stepped out into the alley, his heavy boots grinding the loose rocks and cement of the worn path as he stormed towards the group of strung-out kids.

They swivelled their heads towards him as he approached and scrambled to their feet, some more unsteadily than others, before scattering in all directions. All except one young girl, who stumbled and tripped, falling at his feet in a heap as she tried to force unsteady legs to run away.

Hugh gave an irritated sigh and reached down to lift her to her feet. He blinked as she tossed her head back and brushed her long hair from her face and a wave of disappointment and dread washed through him.

'Let me go,' she snarled, trying to pull her arm free of his hold.

'Take it easy, you'll fall over if I let go. Calm down.'

'I'm perfectly fine,' she said with a slur.

Hugh peered closer and noticed that her pupils weren't dilated, which was a good sign, but he caught a strong whiff of spirits, Bourbon if he had to hazard a guess, and his initial dread eased a little.

'Your mother is going to have a fit when she finds out you've been hanging around with deadbeats like that lot,' he said.

'She already knows and there's nothing she can do about it,' the girl snapped, stumbling as she tried to pull away once more.

'Nice. That's really mature of you. Come on, let's get you inside and sobered up before we call her.'

'I'm not going anywhere with you,' Belle said, dragging her feet as he turned to head back into the pub.

'You're not staying out here by yourself in this condition. Now move it,' he snapped, fighting hard to hold on to his patience. He wasn't used to dealing with drunk teenage girls; his expertise was more along the line of hardened criminals and drug pushers. But he knew enough to know his usual form of communication wouldn't be useful when dealing with a teenage girl from Bundah.

Once inside he pulled out a chair at the kitchen table and sat her in it. 'Stay,' he ordered as he turned away to put on the jug.

'I'm not a dog, you know,' she said indignantly.

He ignored the comment, but kept half an eye on her as he moved around the kitchen to make some coffee. Maybe it was the shock of being dragged inside, or maybe she hadn't been as drunk as he'd first thought, but sitting there at the table she seemed to be coming to her senses faster than he'd expected.

'I think I'm feeling better now. I'd like to leave.'

'You better have something to eat first.' He took out the frying pan and dropped two strips of bacon into it. 'Trust me, you'll thank me later. You better give your mum a call and let her know where you are.'

'I'd rather not call my mother,' she said stiffly as she watched him warily from the table.

'I can't imagine why not,' he said sarcastically. 'You're going to have to face the music sometime. I'm pretty sure she's going to know you've been drinking the minute she sees you.'

'She's not home.'

Not home? That was unusual. 'Where is she?'

'Maybe she's out on a date.'

Hugh was surprised by the flare of reaction the thought caused him, but he managed to hide it from the smug teen sitting across from him. 'Good for her.'

'Don't you want to know who with?'

'None of my business,' he shrugged, taking a sip from his mug. 'So what exactly *were* you doing hanging out with that bunch of idiots anyway?' Time to change the direction of this conversation.

'They're my friends.'

'Nice friends. They left you behind, in case you didn't notice. What could you possibly have in common with any of them?'

'You wouldn't understand.'

'Try me.'

'They understand about my mother being overprotective. They know that I need to escape from all that every once and a while.'

'By giving you drugs?' he asked, hitching up an eyebrow doubtfully.

'I don't *do* drugs.'

'You just drink?'

'Sometimes.'

'You think that's a smart way of dealing with things?'

Belle shrugged and scowled at him. 'It works.'

'From what I hear, you're a smart kid . . . It'd be a shame to throw all that away on a bunch of losers who seem hellbent on pulling you down with them.'

'They don't judge me,' she snarled.

'They're not your friends, Belle. They're addicts and they'll eventually push those drugs on you too. I've seen it happen a million times before, and one day you'll be left lying in that alleyway with a needle sticking outta your arm and your life will be over. Is that what you want?'

'Of course not! There's no way I'd ever do drugs. But you have no idea what it's like being me.'

'Excuse me if I don't shed a tear for how hard your life is. Where I come from, kids are dying in the gutters because they have no one to give a shit about them. They don't have a mother who loves them. They don't have someone who works their arse off to provide them with a decent future. They're sleeping on the streets and forced to prostitute themselves just to eat. You think you've got it tough? Sweetheart, you have no idea what hard is.'

'Stop it! You don't know anything about me.'

'True. I do know, though, that you have countless possibilities ahead of you and if you keep doing what you've been doing, you're going to throw them all away.'

'If you're so smart, how come you're in Bundah?'

'There's worse places to be.'

'There's nothing here,' she said with a dismissive glare. 'No action, no adventure, nothing but rules and gossip and cows.'

'Well, if it's adventure you're after, hanging around those losers is a sure way never to find any. They're the kind who'll still be sitting around here getting stoned when they're forty.'

'I'm not staying here a minute longer than I have to.'

'Good for you.'

'If my mother had any say in it, though, I'd never be leaving.'

'You're lucky she wants you hanging around.'

'Did your mother kick you out when you were a kid?'

'That would imply she actually knew I was there in the first place,' he said drolly. 'No, my mum was hardly ever home. She wasn't exactly the maternal kind.' *Understatement,* he thought. He only remembered seeing her a handful of times before they found her in some dive of a motel, dead from an overdose. His old man had been drunk more than sober while Hugh was growing up. It was a good thing he'd been a resourceful kid—he'd practically had to raise himself.

'Come on,' he said, pushing his memories back into the box way back in the dark where they belonged. 'I better get you home.'

'I bet you can't wait to tell Mum all about how you saved the day,' she muttered.

'Not my circus, not my monkey, kid.'

'What?'

'It's none of my business.'

'Funny, you say that a lot for someone who seems to be always in the middle of everything.'

'What's that supposed to mean?'

'You're always hanging around Mum, following her home the other night like some big hero. I heard you stepped in at the pub the other day when that creep Stewart Gibbons was hassling her. You like her, don't you?'

'I respect anyone who's worked hard and made a good life for themselves.'

'You won't get anywhere with her, you know.'

'Yeah, well, life's full of disappointments.'

'You give up pretty easy,' she scoffed.

'I didn't say *I* was the one going to be disappointed,' he said before standing to place his cup in the sink.

As they headed through the darkened streets, his irritation at the teenager beside him softened a little when he saw she'd fallen asleep, her head resting against the window. In sleep she lost the bored, obnoxious attitude and looked much younger than her seventeen years. He woke her up when they reached the house and Hugh took her keys to unlock the door. Belle headed straight for her bedroom, with no more than a grunt of farewell. He checked the windows and doors were secured before letting himself out the front door, making sure it locked behind him.

Twelve

Lucy walked into the office the next morning and switched on the lights, dropping her handbag on the desk. She hadn't even switched the computer on when the phone rang.

'Baxter's Fuel Depot,' she answered, trying not to sound as weary as she felt.

'Luce, it's me,' Nicole announced briskly.

Something about her friend's tone warned her this wasn't going to be a friendly catch-up chat. 'I just found out Rick Toovey died last night.'

Lucy froze for a moment as the news sunk in. 'What? How?' Rick Toovey had started school with Belle. He was just a kid. Lucy had spent years helping out at the primary school, listening to kids read, and Rick had always been such a well-mannered, nice kid.

'He apparently overdosed on drugs. His parents found him in his room and called the ambulance, but it was too late.'

'Oh my God,' Lucy whispered. 'Drugs? But he was such a good kid.'

'I know,' Nicole said sadly. 'Jackson's really worried. The hospital's had half-a-dozen kids over the weekend, from two separate parties.'

'Here?' Even as she said it, Lucy knew she sounded naive, but it just didn't seem possible. Drugs had never been a problem in their little town before. Sure, there'd always been marijuana, but never *hard* drugs . . .

'Thought you'd want to know. I'm guessing there's going to be a lot of kids in shock today.'

Lucy realised the school would probably be holding some kind of special assembly to inform the kids, but her heart ached for Belle and the rest of Rick's classmates who'd be grieving for their friend today. Hot tears rolled down her face as the implications continued to sink in. Yesterday the Tooveys had a son, and today they didn't. She couldn't imagine the pain they would be going through.

The bell jingled, announcing someone coming into the shop, and she quickly wiped her hands across her face before hurrying out of the office. She came to an abrupt halt when she discovered Hugh waiting at the counter. Her gaze darted to the window to search for his bike; she was positive she hadn't heard it pull up. The driveway was empty.

'I'm on foot today,' he explained, following the direction of her gaze.

Lucy lowered her eyes; her lashes still felt wet from her tears and she felt self-conscious standing in front of this man in her present state.

'Are you okay?'

Her hope that he wasn't paying too much attention was dashed. 'I'm fine. What can I do for you?'

'You don't look fine. What's happened? Is it that guy from the pub? Has he been back?'

'No, it's nothing to do with that,' she said. 'I just had some sad news. What do you need?' She didn't want to talk about it, she just wanted to serve him and get him out of the shop.

'I was hoping you had some electrical tape,' he said slowly, clearly still not convinced she was fine.

Lucy moved from behind the counter and walked to the far row of shelves and held up two different types for him to inspect.

He took a step closer and reached for the thicker one, but closed his hand around hers and waited until her gaze flew to his in surprise. 'Tell me what happened.'

She wanted to tell him to mind his own business, she planned on telling him to mind his own business . . . but somehow that gentle look in his usually hard eyes was her undoing and she found herself telling him about Rick Toovey. 'It's just so . . .' She shook her head helplessly. 'Those poor parents. I don't know what I'd do if I lost Belle,' she whispered and fresh tears filled her eyes once more.

Hugh didn't speak, he didn't try and soothe her with platitudes, he just tugged her closer and held her head against his chest while she sobbed. Beneath her cheek, his black T-shirt soaked up her tears, smelling of freshly cut timber and sandalwood. After a few moments she gathered back what remained of her composure and pulled away, wiping her eyes and going in search of a tissue from behind the counter. He followed and she took in the damp patch on the front of his shirt with a silent groan. Great, cover the guy in snot and tears—way to keep things professional.

'I'm sorry about messing up your shirt,' she said as she threw the tissue in the bin and reached for the tape he'd placed on the counter.

She saw him glance down briefly before shrugging. 'I've had worse spilled on me.'

Somehow, despite the lightness of his tone, she detected a certain truthfulness to the statement and wasn't comforted. Lucy dropped her gaze, feeling out of her depth and unsettled by the support he'd just shown her. 'Is that all you need today?' she asked, nodding at the tape.

'That's it.' He handed over the money and as Lucy rang up the purchase she tried to act as though nothing had happened.

'Well, there you go . . . and thanks,' she said quietly.

'Anytime. Will you be okay?' he asked as he moved to turn away.

'I'll be fine,' she waved off his concern.

He paused as though he wanted to say something, but then seemed to think better of it, turning away and heading through the door without looking back.

It took Lucy a minute to realise that the bleeping in her sleep wasn't her alarm clock going off but the phone ringing. She sat up in bed, reaching for the phone, her heart skipping a beat at the late-night call.

'Mum . . . it's me.'

'Belle?' Lucy blinked and rubbed a hand over her face, trying to wake up. It didn't make any sense that Belle was calling her when she was supposed to be in bed, asleep.

'I have to hand over the phone,' her daughter said, then a male voice took over the conversation.

'Lucy, this is Mitch Goodard. Apparently my son decided to have a party and announced it to the world on Facebook . . . It was supposed to be a small bonfire with only a handful of his mates, but when I came over to check on them I found a heap of underage kids in amongst them. I can't be responsible for underage drinking on my property. Lucy, I'm sorry, but you need to come and get Belle.'

'Belle's out there? *Drinking?*' She felt the colour draining from her face. 'I'm so sorry, Mitch . . . I had no idea she'd left the house.' She was mortified. Mitch was a regular customer at work. What must he be thinking of a mother who allowed her child to roam the countryside at all hours of the night? 'I'm coming straight out there now. I'm so sorry about this.'

'No worries, Lucy. I just thought it would be better coming from me, rather than the cops delivering her home in the back of a paddy wagon.'

Lucy didn't remember getting dressed or grabbing her keys, all she was aware of was sitting behind the wheel of the ute and watching the road unfold before her, the surrounding darkness cocooning her. Arriving at the house, she saw Belle sitting on the front steps of the large farmhouse next to three other teenagers wearing matching expressions of surly indignation.

As she walked towards them Lucy fought to control her temper. Belle stood up and walked past without a word, heading for the car.

'Belle.'

The teen stopped and turned to face her mother with a scowl.

'Apologise to Mr Goodard,' Lucy said, somehow remaining calm.

'Sorry,' Belle growled out before turning and continuing towards the car.

The door slammed and Lucy clenched her teeth. 'I'm so sorry about this, Mitch.'

'Kids, hey,' he answered with a tired chuckle. 'Don't be too hard on her, we've all been there before.'

Lucy stiffened at Mitch's words and the memories of her own misspent youth. She wasn't the same generation as Mitch, he was older by a good ten years, so she didn't think he was aiming his comment directly at her . . . Still, it stung a little.

'But after all this business with young Toovey, kids messin' around with drugs and all, I wasn't too keen on taking responsibility for a mob of underage teenagers out here. It's not just a bit of innocent fun and a few drinks nowadays.'

Lucy bit back a sarcastic scoff at that. *Innocent fun?* Maybe that's how they'd all seen it as kids, but looking back as a parent, there was nothing innocent about losing your virginity in a smelly old swag next to a shearing shed that smelled of sheep poo. There was nothing innocent about getting so drunk you passed out. *Oh yeah, good times,* she thought.

'Thank you for calling me, Mitch. Do you need me to drive any of the other kids home?'

'Nah,' Mitch said with a slight grin, 'their parents are on the way. I reckon it'll do 'em good to sit here and stew a bit.'

Lucy waved as she turned towards the ute and took a long, deep breath before sliding in behind the wheel. *Just keep calm,* she told herself repeatedly as the ute bounced across the dirt driveway.

From the corner of her eye, Lucy saw her daughter staring moodily out the front window, arms crossed and a definite don't-even-say-it attitude radiating from her.

'Well? Aren't you going to start the lecture?'

Lucy clenched her teeth and forced back her seething anger. 'I'm too furious to talk to you at the moment. And it definitely wouldn't be in your best interests to say anything right now.'

She hated being angry, hated feeling disappointed and betrayed. She hated even more that she knew deep down her daughter felt just as bad.

'I knew I should have got him to call Hugh instead of you,' she muttered.

'Hugh?' Lucy said, frowning. 'Why on earth would you have called him?'

'Because at least he remembers being young and making mistakes and he's cool about it.'

Lucy pulled the ute to a stop on the side of the road and turned to face her daughter. 'And exactly how would you know all this?'

Hugh sat up in bed, immediately alert, but unsure what had woken him from a sound sleep. Then he heard it again: someone was beating on his back door.

He grabbed his jeans and pulled them on, not bothering to do them up, before heading out to answer the insistent banging.

He pulled the door open with a growled, 'What?', but stared when he saw who it was. 'Lucy? What's happened?'

'Why didn't you tell me?'

His first thoughts were that something terrible had happened to Belle, but her furious expression suggested he was somehow to blame. 'Tell you what?'

'That when I was away the other night you found my daughter with those kids and that she'd been drinking,' she said in a low, dangerous tone.

Oh. That. Hugh let out a long sigh and rubbed a hand across his chest as he eyed her warily. 'I promised her I wouldn't say anything.'

'You *promised*?'

He held her angry gaze, but inside he was surprised to discover he was feeling a little nervous. *Seriously?* A five-foot four-inch woman had him quaking in his shoes? 'Well, yeah.'

He saw her eyes narrow as she continued to glare at him. 'You thought it was perfectly fine to promise a seventeen-year-old kid not to tell her parent that she was out drinking?'

Well, put like *that*, it didn't sound so great. 'No. I agreed not to mention it to you if she stayed away from those kids. We made a deal.'

'Oh,' she nodded as she crossed her arms, and he knew he was in for it. 'That's why I just had to go and pick her up from a party, fourteen kilometres out of town at two-thirty in the morning! Because you know, *making a deal* with a teenager couldn't possibly backfire on you.'

He was smart enough not to make any comment. She was kind of intimidating when she was angry, and he found it just a tiny bit of a turn on.

'You're *supposed to be* an adult,' she said dropping her folded arms to poke him in the chest. 'From now on, you tell me *anything* that relates to my daughter, do you understand me? If you see her so much as sneeze, I want to know about it.'

Hugh leaned against the doorjamb and studied the irate woman in front of him. 'You do get why she's sneaking around, don't you?'

'Because she's a teenager; it's what they do.'

'That, and because she knows she can't compromise with you. You're smothering that kid.'

'And you're such an authority on parenting?'

'Not at all, but I remember the harder adults tried to control me, the more determined I was to break the rules.'

'Yeah, well, I remember being a teenager too, and I don't plan on letting my daughter make any of the mistakes I made.'

'I'm not trying to tell you how to raise your kid—'

'Really? Could have fooled me.'

'But I've seen this before, all too often. Kids will fight you all the way if you try and bend them. In the long-run you'll lose her.'

'I'll raise my child the way I see fit,' she snapped, her hands clenched tightly at her sides. 'And next time you think about making a deal with my daughter. *Don't.*' Her eyes flashed before she turned away and moments later he heard the slam of her car door and the rev of the engine as she drove off.

He watched the red glow of her tail lights fade into the night before closing the door. *Well, bugger me,* he thought with a slight shake of his head. He'd really believed Belle had been shaken up enough to snap out of it. Just goes to show how far nice got you in this world.

Thirteen

When Lucy arrived at work she found Ken sitting at her desk. She bit back her annoyance at his making himself at home in her office, even though it was technically his office and his business and he could sit wherever he darn well pleased. However, it was unusual for him to be here this early and something warned her that this wasn't a social call.

'Morning,' she said, hanging her bag on the back of the office door.

'Lucy,' Ken said without taking his gaze from the screen before him.

'Can I help you with something?' she finally asked when it became clear he wasn't going to fill her in on the reason for his visit.

'I'm just checking something.'

'Okay. Can I help you find whatever it is you're checking?' If he messed up her files she was going to be extremely annoyed, she thought, watching his one-finger typing.

'I'm just looking through the security footage.'

'Why? What's happened?' said Lucy, instantly alarmed. What on earth would he need to do that for? Had they been robbed overnight?

'I'm surveying security footage to see how many customers haven't been paying for their fuel,' he told her with a few more hard bangs of his finger on the keyboard.

'What are you talking about?'

Ken looked up, piercing her with a severe glare. 'Lucy, it has been brought to my attention that you've given away my fuel on at least one occasion recently. I'm going through security footage to see if I can find any further incidences before I decide if I'm going to take any further action.'

'Are you *serious*?' said Lucy.

'I take my businesses and my money very seriously, Lucy. You should know that by now.'

'Well, I have no idea what you're talking about.'

'You were overheard yesterday telling Ted Brownhouse, and I quote,' he said sitting back in his chair, '"Don't worry about it. Ken won't miss a few litres of diesel."'

'Your informant forgot to mention the bit where I said fix it up next time you're in town.'

'And that makes it better how?'

'Ted forgot his wallet. He lives like an hour up in the hills. You expect me to make him drive all the way home for fifty bucks of diesel?'

'Yes, I do. I don't run a charity.'

'It's hardly charity. It's just common decency. Ted's a regular customer—has been for the past forty years.'

'I don't care if he was the founding father of Bundah, no one gets free diesel. Next thing you know, everyone will be "forgetting their wallet".'

'I can't believe you're making an issue of this.'

'And then there's the other matter.'

'What other matter?'

Ken nodded at the money drawer sitting on the desk; clearly he'd taken it out of the safe. 'I've counted that till and it's short.'

Lucy frowned. 'No, it's not. I balanced it last night before I left.'

'Feel free to double-check it,' he said graciously, waving his hand over the desk. 'In fact, I'd prefer you to.'

This was utter bullcrap, Lucy thought angrily. She didn't have time for this today, it was the end of the month and she had a heap of paperwork to do. Unlocking the lid, she quickly began counting notes, jotting down the amounts on the pad before her. A few minutes later she frowned down at the total.

'Well?' Ken prompted.

'It's out by five hundred dollars.'

'I'm disappointed, Lucy.'

'It balanced last night.'

'So you say.'

Was he seriously implying she had something to do with this discrepancy? 'I'm telling you, Ken. This balanced last night when I locked it into the safe.'

'And yet this morning it doesn't. How do you explain that?'

'I'm not the only one with a key to the safe,' she pointed out tightly.

'If I'd taken it, it wouldn't be an issue now, would it?'

'I cannot believe you're accusing me of stealing your money.'

'I'm not accusing you of anything, I'm simply asking why the till doesn't balance.'

'I don't know, Ken. All I can say is it did last time *I* locked it away.'

There was a deathly quiet moment as they eyed each other across the desk.

'Giving away fuel is one thing, but when I'm no longer able to trust staff with unlimited access to my money, I'm afraid there's no other way around it. I have to let you go, Lucy. As of today.'

Lucy stared at Ken, dumbstruck. This couldn't be happening.

'I'm sorry, Lucy. I just don't see how I can keep you on under the circumstances.'

'Ken, this is ridiculous,' Lucy finally managed. The last thing she'd expected when she'd come into work this morning was to be fired.

'I was hoping we could do this quietly,' he said calmly. 'I'm sure you don't want the rest of the town hearing about this.'

'You can't go round spreading rumours about people without any evidence. I didn't *do* anything wrong,' she said, throwing her arms in the air. 'For goodness sake, Ken, I've worked here for seventeen years.'

'The numbers don't lie, Lucy. There's clearly a discrepancy here, and you're responsible for the book-keeping. Look, I admit it's not a great deal of money in the grand scheme of things and I'm not an unreasonable man. I understand being a single mother in this day and age is a tough job, but you could have *asked* for money, there was no need to steal it. I'm very disappointed, Lucy.'

'Ken, I did *not* steal any money!'

'I'm sorry, Lucy. I really am. But if you leave quietly, I won't bring the police into it. We'll just leave it at this,' Ken said, getting to his feet slowly.

Lucy felt ill. She stared at Ken, standing at the office doorway waiting for her to leave.

In a daze, Lucy gathered her few possessions from her desk—the photos of Belle she'd tacked up on the wall above her work station, the rather sad-looking peace lily she had a love-hate relationship with. She couldn't leave it behind. She'd rather take it home and kill it there than leave it here. This couldn't be happening.

Outside in her car, she stared out the windscreen numbly. She'd just been fired. She'd never been fired before in her entire life. What was she going to do now?

She would have appreciated a bit of Fred's candour right now. One of his blunt pep talks might have stopped her feeling so bruised and fragile. Lucy closed her eyes briefly, and blinked back her tears. 'I don't know what to do, Fred,' she said quietly.

'Don't let the bastard win.' The words were as real as though they'd been spoken in the small confines of the car. *Don't let him win.*

She let out a breath and took another one. She'd done nothing wrong. She had nothing to be afraid of; she should call Ken out and demand to see some kind of evidence to prove she'd done anything wrong. But the thought of Nate becoming involved, the humiliation of him charging her with something, was too much to bear. Ken had said he wouldn't take it further if she left quietly. It was risking employment suicide to have a mark like embezzlement against your name in a small country town. No one else would ever hire her if they so much as suspected there was any truth to Ken's rumours.

She had no job.

She turned the ignition and drove away from the service station. She hadn't been without a job in the past seventeen years. She was one of the lucky ones, she knew that, but the thought sent a wave of panic through her. How was she going to send Belle to university if she didn't have a job?

Reaching the town limits she told herself to concentrate on the road. Her gaze travelled along the main street and she mentally checked off her chances of employment. Most of the shops were family owned and run and, until they managed to entice visitors to town, that was not going to change. Her eyes fell on the old post office and for a moment her hopes rose. The café was one business that was actually doing very well. She pulled into a parking spot and, after a brief hesitation, pushed open her door.

As she went in she smiled at a few people she knew, not stopping to talk. She wasn't in the mood for social chitchat today. She stood at the front counter and waited for Russell as he put the finishing touches on the cappuccino he was making.

'Lucy, how are you, chicken?' he asked when he came back after delivering the order to the table. 'Oh my goodness, you look terrible.'

'Thanks, Russell. I needed to hear that today,' she muttered.

'What's going on with you?'

Lucy looked around the café before lowering her voice a little. 'Do you think I could talk to you and Steve for a minute . . . in private?'

'Of course you can, sweetie. Come on back,' he said, lifting the counter for her to slip through.

'Hey Lucy! Wow, you need some under-eye concealer. Late night?'

This visit could have been a huge mistake, she thought as she touched her face gingerly. 'Guys, I was just wondering is there any chance you might need some extra staff? Even part-time?'

'Is this for your daughter? I was only thinking the other day she'd be a great little waitress. I can just see her in an adorable little French maid's apron,' Russell gushed.

'Russell. Remember what we talked about?' Steve warned.

'Oh. Yeah. I forgot,' Russell sighed. 'Apparently Mr Purse Strings over there has decided we have to tighten our belts. The renos cost a bit more than we were expecting.'

'Oh.'

'Sorry, sweet cheeks.'

'That's all right, It was just a thought. No worries,' she smiled and tried not to feel deflated.

'Is she eighteen yet? Because there's always the top pub. Your Mr Thompson seems to be going great guns up there. I heard he was expecting a big group this weekend,' Steve said helpfully.

'It's not actually for Belle, it's for me,' she admitted reluctantly. Work for Hugh? Flashes of their last conversation went through her mind and she cringed. Considering she'd pretty much told him to grow up, he'd probably enjoy watching her ask for a job.

'For you?' Russell repeated, surprised. 'Why?'

'Ken and I had a slight . . . disagreement this morning,' she hedged, conscious of the café owners' inability to resist a piece of juicy gossip. They were perfectly suited to small-town living.

'So you walked out on him? Good for you, girlfriend!' Russell clapped gleefully.

'Something like that,' she agreed. 'Well, I'd better get up to the pub and see if Hugh needs some help. Could you let me know if you happen to hear of any work? I'll take anything at this stage.'

'Of course we will, cupcake. We're on the case!'

'Good luck, Luce,' Steve called as she waved goodbye.

She left the car where it was and walked up the street to the top of the hill where the Coach House sat. She had to admit Hugh had done a fantastic job on the old hotel. It held pride of place in the main street now, with its freshly painted exterior. It brightened up the entire street.

Inside it was fairly quiet, with only a few men seated at the bar and two women at a table on the far side of the room.

Hugh came out from behind the bar, carrying a tray of drinks for the women. She caught the women's bright smiles and had to bite her lip to stop the amused snort that threatened. It seemed that Hugh was fast becoming a local celebrity. Her smile died as he looked up and caught her watching him.

'Do I need a stiff drink before you launch into round two of tearing strips off me?' he asked, stacking the dirty glasses he'd just collected onto the bar.

This was going to be awkward. 'No. I'm not here about that.'

She didn't want to ask him, she *really* didn't want to . . . but now was not the time to think about pride. She needed a job.

'You got a day off work or something?'

'Or something,' she said wearily. 'Listen, word is you're about to get pretty busy. You don't by any chance happen to need any extra staff, do you?'

'Staff? What? You?'

'Yeah,' Lucy said, letting out a long breath. 'I understand if you're not hiring at the moment, but if you get busy and you need a hand, I'm available.'

Hugh searched her face intently. 'What happened?'

'Nothing. I'm not working at the servo any more. I just need some work if it comes up,' she said, brushing off his concern.

'I can offer you a bit of casual work—some cleaning, filling in out in the kitchen, bit of paperwork here and there. Is that okay?'

'That would be more than okay,' Lucy assured him, feeling as though she were in a bit of a daze. She hadn't expected him to give her a job on the spot. 'I just need something to tide me over until I find something permanent.'

'Okay, so how soon can you start?'

'Now.'

He gave her a crooked smile. 'You don't waste time.'

'Nope. I'm here, you may as well use me,' she shrugged.

Hugh dropped his gaze from Lucy's bright smile. 'You may as well use me,' she'd said. If she only knew what kind of thoughts that innocent sentence had evoked, she'd probably slap him across the face.

His mind briefly went to the spreadsheet he'd been slaving over the night before. He knew hiring another staff member wasn't the smartest financial move right now, but he pushed the thought away. He saw behind Lucy's blasé expression. He knew enough about her to realise losing her income would be causing quite a bit of stress.

Always the hero, a self-deprecating voice mimicked inside his head. *When will you ever learn?*

'All right then,' he said, forcing his thoughts back to more appropriate business matters. 'I'll show you around and get you sorted.'

As they were going through the paperwork in the office, Hugh sat back in his chair, watching her as she filled in her details. 'So what happened?'

She looked up at him and he could see she was troubled. 'I honestly have no idea. I walked into work this morning and Ken was sitting at the desk waiting for me.'

'Surely he gave a reason?'

Her gaze skittered away from his and his internal alert system kicked into gear. 'Lucy?'

'He accused me of embezzling funds.'

'What?'

'The till was out five hundred dollars this morning. It balanced last night. He said unless I left quietly he'd take it to the police.'

'He has to have proof before he can fire you.'

'Apparently not.'

'Fight him on it. If nothing else, you can sue him for defamation.'

'Maybe where you came from you could get away with that, but out here once a rumour starts floating around town, the truth doesn't matter. Ken has enough sway to put doubt in people's minds. You think I'd ever get another job in town if people believed I'd embezzled money from someone?'

'Ken Baxter has his finger in every pie in town. He's a real estate agent, stock agent, owns how many businesses? He can't be sparkly clean, surely people wouldn't automatically believe his word over yours?'

'I'm not willing to risk it.'

Hugh watched her go back to writing, feeling outraged on her behalf. 'Are there cameras in the office? Anything to prove you balanced the till last night?'

'Yes. I don't know how they'd prove it balanced though.'

'As long as it shows you didn't pocket any cash, then he can't prove you took it. And you said he was there before you arrived this morning?'

Lucy nodded.

'Then maybe it'll show him removing the money.'

'He was checking the security footage when I walked in. I have a funny feeling there won't be anything incriminating left behind.'

'Only one way to find out.'

'What? Where are you going?'

'To take a look at that footage.'

'But . . .'

Hugh came around the desk and took her hand, pulling her along behind him as they headed out the back of the pub and down the laneway.

'This is crazy. Ken's not going to let you look at the footage.'

'Probably not. But if he's not there he won't know, will he?'

There was no sign of Ken's car when they arrived at the servo, but Ernie, who worked part-time, was sitting behind the counter watching something on his phone.

'Just follow my lead,' Hugh said, releasing her hand as they walked into the shop and around the counter.

'Hey! You can't go back there,' said Ernie, jumping to his feet before noticing Lucy behind Hugh. 'Oh. Hi, Luce. Um, you aren't supposed to be here. Ken was pretty clear on that. I don't know what you did, but he's not happy.'

'Lucy left in a hurry earlier and we've come back to collect a few of her belongings. It won't take a minute.'

'I don't know, If Ken finds out . . .'

'Ken doesn't have to know. We'll be two seconds,' Hugh said, ushering Lucy into the office ahead of him. A car pulled up at the bowser and Ernie stood looking anxiously back and forth between Hugh and the car.

'You go on; we'll be straight out,' Hugh urged with a friendly smile, before following Lucy into the office. 'The computer,' he said, nodding towards the desk.

Lucy quickly keyed in her password but it was instantly denied. 'He locked me out,' she said, sounding surprised and offended at the same time. She quickly tried again. 'Jerk,' she muttered under her breath as the computer granted her access.

'You have hacking skills I don't know about?' Hugh asked, looking over her shoulder.

'Hardly. It's just lucky Ken is terrified of forgetting his password and never changes it. He uses the same one on everything.'

She logged into the security footage and brought up the history. Hugh gave an irritated sigh when he saw that there was no saved data or recordings for the past forty-eight hours.

'He's wiped it,' sighed Lucy, disappointment heavy in her tone.

'If we could get the hard drive to a professional, they could find the deleted files,' Hugh said.

'Maybe I can get Nate to seize it and have it looked at?'

Hugh shook his head. 'Not without some kind of warrant. Not legally, anyway.'

Lucy hung her head, dejected. 'Forget it. It's not worth it. I refuse to resort to stealing property. Come on, let's go before he accuses me of anything else.'

'So, why would good ol' Ken resort to fabricating a lie just to get rid of you?' Hugh asked as they headed back to the pub.

'I have no idea. I honestly don't know what's going on around here any more. The whole place is going crazy. Ever since—' Lucy stopped, suddenly remembering who she was talking to.

'The newcomers all started arriving,' he finished drolly.

'Well, yeah.'

'You're a suspicious lot, you Bundah locals,' he said with a shake of his head.

'It's just a coincidence, I guess.'

'Yeah, well, it wears kind of thin after a while, getting the finger pointed at you all the time.'

'What do you mean? Who's accused you of anything?'

'Your mate the cop thinks I'm behind the drugs arriving in town.'

Lucy swivelled around in suprise. 'He *said* that?'

'He said it seemed suspicious that my arrival coincided with the sudden spike in drug-related activities in town.'

Hugh didn't like the flash of uncertainty he saw cross Lucy's face. 'You're not seriously thinking he's right?' he asked with a frown.

'No, of course not,' she said, and he was relieved when she seemed to shake the notion off. 'Nate's a good man. I'm sure he was just doing his job. He obviously realises you've got nothing to do with it or you'd be locked up by now.'

'Yeah, well, let's just say I can relate to the whole false accusation thing,' Hugh grunted. 'So, what are you going to do about Ken?' he asked after a moment of silence.

Lucy sighed. 'Nothing. He was a pain in the neck to work for anyway.'

Hugh admired the brave face she was putting on. She had to be feeling gutted by the whole thing.

'Thank you for helping me out with some work. I really appreciate it.'

'No worries. You'll be doing me a favour.'

She smiled grimly and he gathered that he hadn't fooled her with his sudden need to employ extra staff.

'I appreciate what you're doing. I'll keep looking for a more permanent job and be off your hands as soon as possible.'

'In Bundah?'

'Yes, in Bundah. Something will come up. I'll put the word out that I'm looking for a change, and sooner or later something will come up.'

He wanted to argue that she wasn't being realistic, but he noticed the drawn, worried look around her eyes, so he kept his mouth shut. She'd had enough to deal with today.

Nicole sat at the bar the next day, her beautifully manicured nails tapping irritably against the side of her wineglass as she fumed not so silently. 'That snake! How dare he pull a stunt like that!'

Lucy had managed to brush away most of the curious and surprised expressions over her sudden appearance at the Coach House. For the most part she had been able to get away with the explanation that it was time for a change, but not with Nicole. There was no getting anything past her.

'He probably did me a favour really. He's been doing my head in lately with the books. He liked the idea of a manager when he bought the business, but he can't give up the reins and that just doesn't work. Plus we've always clashed, personality-wise.'

'Only because you're the one person he can't push around. You're a threat to him because you call him out on his crap. Not to mention he's been trying his best to get his hands on Stringybark. That's been a bone of contention between the two of you for years.'

Lucy gave a grunt of acknowledgment.

'It's still no reason to fire you, for goodness sake! No one can do that job as well as you. He's crazy!'

'Maybe it's a good thing. Maybe this is the universe's way of setting me on a new path.'

'And at least there are advantages to this job,' said Nicole, lowering her voice as her gaze followed Hugh across the room.

Lucy shook her head at her friend and went back to unpacking the dishwasher beneath the counter. Like she needed to add any more drama to her life at the moment. No thank you.

Lucy looked up as Hugh walked into the office, closing the file she was working on and putting away the receipts.

'So how was your first full day?' he asked.

'It was fine. Although, hopefully by the end of the week everyone in town will have been informed of my career change and things will settle back down,' she said wearily, thinking of how many times she'd had to repeat the 'needing a change' monologue throughout the day. 'Thank you, Hugh,' she added, filing the envelope of receipts in the cabinet beneath the desk. 'I know you're probably not really in a position to be hiring more staff at the moment,' she said a little awkwardly, waving at the computer. 'I couldn't help noticing . . . I am doing the books, after all.'

Hugh gave a brief smile before shrugging. 'I figure you're probably a good investment. Jason's pretty useless at anything other than bar work, and I hate dealing with the office stuff, so you're a godsend really.'

'I just wanted you to know that I appreciate it. Especially after the grief I gave you over Belle the other day.'

'She's your daughter. You had every right to be pissed off at me.'

'No. I can see that you were trying to help.'

There was a moment of awkward silence, as they looked at each other.

'Well,' Lucy said, breaking eye contact as she picked up her bag and stood up from the desk. 'Guess I'll see you tomorrow.'

'See you then,' he said as she came level with him in the doorway.

Lucy felt her pulse rate pick up as she eased past him, her arm brushing against his T-shirt. She ignored the heady scent of man, which seemed to be mixed with some kind of libido-inducing fragrance created to trap unsuspecting females.

Well, that wasn't so bad, she told herself as she walked to her car. Inside, she glanced at her flushed cheeks and bright eyes in the rear-view mirror. Oh God, who was she kidding? She was going to have to find a way of protecting herself against Hugh Thompson if she was to be working this close to him. The man was dangerous.

Later that week Hugh heard Lucy come in through the back door of the pub and looked up as she poked her head into the office.

'Would it be all right if I start at eight tomorrow so I can leave a half-hour earlier in the afternoon?' she asked.

'Sure.'

'Thanks.' Her face beamed, lighting up her eyes which gave him a warm sensation inside his chest.

He shouldn't be feeling this pleased at putting a smile on her face. 'You got another date or something?'

'A date?'

'Leaving early . . .'

Lucy gave him an odd look and he instantly felt like an idiot. *Why the hell had he said that?*

'I'm going to visit my parents over the weekend. I didn't want to be driving down the range in the dark.'

He didn't like the frown she was wearing. He was in trouble . . . again.

'And what do you mean, *another* date?'

'I just figured . . . Belle said last time . . . when you were gone overnight . . . that you were out on a date . . .' *Just shut up now, idiot, while you're ahead.*

'She *said* that?'

Hugh turned back to the screen and pretended to be interested in the spreadsheet, wishing he'd never opened his big mouth in the first place. 'None of my business,' he muttered and realised too late that it came out sounding a lot harsher than he'd intended.

'I *wasn't* on a date. Mum had day surgery and I went to stay with my parents overnight to help out. And you're right, it was none of your business.'

She had every right to sound pissed off—he couldn't for the life of him work out why he'd brought it up. Still, the relief he felt that she *hadn't* spent the night with Nate, as Belle had led him to believe, almost made him grin before he remembered it wasn't supposed to matter one way or the other to him. 'Why don't you just finish up at lunchtime and leave then. That way you'll be there long before dark.'

'Are you being extra nice to me now because you feel guilty?' she asked, looking at the computer.

'No. I'm thinking of my employee's welfare. I want you back in one piece.'

'Well, thanks for the offer, but I have to wait for school to finish before I can go anyway.'

He raised his eyebrow at her and she continued, 'Belle's lost her stay-at-home-alone privileges for a while, so she's coming with me this time.'

'I see.'

Her heavy sigh drew his attention back to her face.

'You don't approve?'

'I didn't say anything,' he said.

'You didn't have to. She thinks the sun shines out of your butt, you know,' she said wearily. 'And who could blame her? You're the cool adult who *treats me like a grown up, not like a kid,*' she mimicked her daughter to a tee.

'Sorry.'

'No, you're not,' she said, shaking her head.

'I am. I didn't mean to undermine your authority. I was just doing what I thought was right at the time. I tried to stay out of it.'

'You took her side.'

'I didn't take anyone's side.'

'Oh, for goodness sake,' she huffed. 'It doesn't matter. Forget it,' she said, standing up abruptly.

Hugh did the same, stepping in front of her to block her exit from the office. 'I can't forget it. It's not a matter of taking sides. I thought we'd cleared the air about that, but obviously we haven't. I did what I did to help a kid in trouble. And I'm sorry, but I'd do it again. I may not have read her the riot act, but I told her a few home truths about where life could take her if she threw away what she had.'

Hugh saw Lucy's eyes lose some of their anger and continued on quickly. 'I'm not a parent, okay? I have no idea what it must be like to draw the hard line every single day, but I do know about kids getting mixed up in trouble and, I have to tell you, I don't see Belle being one of those kids. Yeah, she's rebelling a bit now, but she's got her head screwed on straight and she's going to be fine. You've done a great job with her—she cares about what you think and she really doesn't want to disappoint you.'

'Then why is she continuing to do stupid things?'

'She went to a party and had a few drinks,' he said lightly. 'In the grand scheme of things, it's not the worst she could do. And these kids she's been hanging around? She's not into them. She had her little taste of the wild side and I'm willing to bet she's done with it. She'll blame you, of course, and say you're making her stay away from them, but deep down I'm willing to bet she's relieved.'

'It gets lonely being the bad guy all the time,' said Lucy, blinking a little too fast.

Seeing her eyes glisten sparked an emotion Hugh hadn't felt for a very long time. Without thinking, he reached out and pulled her to him.

There was a brief moment of surprise before she yielded to his embrace, her lips soft and supple beneath his. He'd wanted to do this so many times in the past few months, it was hard to believe it was finally happening and that it was even better than he'd imagined.

A knock at the door startled them, and Lucy pulled out of his arms, taking a hasty step away.

Hugh growled out a 'What?' and the door opened to reveal a wary-looking Jason announcing there was a problem with a beer delivery at the counter. Rubbing his hand over the top of his head irritably, Hugh told him he'd be right out and Jason backed out and shut the door, leaving them looking at each other in awkward silence.

'Lucy—'

'I'd better get back to work,' she said, cutting him off and turning her back.

He wanted to say something to put her mind at ease, but he wasn't entirely sure he knew the right words. He wasn't even really sure what the hell had just happened. *You acted on the urge you've had ever since that first day you arrived in town, dickhead.*

He hadn't meant to, but he'd be lying if he said he hadn't hoped it would happen some day. Their timing just never seemed to be right. He watched her hit the keyboard with sharper than normal strokes as she typed something into the computer. She was pissed off at him . . . again.

'Lucy.'

'I have to get to work.'

'Why are you angry?'

'I'm not angry. I'm busy.'

'It's because of the kiss?'

Lucy closed her eyes briefly but still refused to look at him. 'I work for you. What just happened,' she paused, nervously pressing her lips together, 'can't happen again. It's unprofessional.'

'What just *happened* was between you and me, not between a boss and an employee.'

'We shouldn't have gone there.'

'Well, we did. And we'll talk about it later, okay?'

She didn't answer; just bent her head over the paperwork and ignored him. He was torn between wanting to stay and make her acknowledge the kiss, and taking the life raft thrown to him by the knock at the door. The coward in him won out for now: he needed to get his head straight and come up with a logical argument to counter the negative one he was sure Lucy was busy preparing.

Lucy groaned and dropped her head onto the desk. What was happening to her well-ordered life? Everything was going wrong. What was she thinking? She couldn't have a . . . a . . . whatever the hell one had with a man like Hugh Thompson. She'd just lost her long-term, safe, *full-time* job. She couldn't afford to lose this one too, even if it was supposed to be temporary. What happened when he got sick of her? He wasn't going to want to work day in and day out with an ex fling!

She had savings she could live off for a while if she had to, but they were reserved for helping set Belle up at uni next year. How could everything be falling apart on her? She'd always been so careful.

Her mind slipped back to the kiss and her shoulders drooped in defeat. It was no point trying to lie to herself that she was some kind of victim in all this—she'd wanted that kiss just as much as he had. Maybe even more. Hugh had snuck into her dreams at night more times than she could count. She'd known it was only a matter of time before whatever it was between them ignited.

He was the most annoying, sometimes arrogant, frustrating man she'd ever met. But he was also kind. That more than anything else had broken her resolve. He hadn't needed to give her this job. Yes, his business was picking up and was busy, but he hadn't been as desperate for help to the extent he'd made out. He'd given her a job out of kindness. And as angry as she'd been over his little deal with Belle, after the initial shock had worn off she'd realised he'd stepped in and taken care of her daughter, made sure she was safe. He could have turned his back on her, left her and those kids to their own devices, but he'd stepped in and put a stop to it.

Maybe part of her anger had been sparked by jealousy that her daughter thought he was so damn cool while she was the fun police. It wasn't his job to be the bad guy, it was hers, and she knew she owed him an apology for that.

Below the surface she felt the simmering awareness between them. The smart thing would be to walk away before it went any further. She could pretend the kiss meant nothing and continue working for him. It was only a kiss after all. But something told her there was no going back to friends after this, no matter how hard she tried to forget. The mature thing to do would be to wait for Hugh to come back and talk this through rationally like two adults.

She wasn't feeling very mature all of a sudden, though, and before she could talk herself out of it she scribbled a quick note, promising to make up her hours next week and telling him she'd left early for her weekend away. She could be an adult on Monday. Right now she was going with the bury-her-head-in-the-sand option. A weekend with her parents was just what she needed—some place out of town and away from temptation.

'So let me get this straight . . . he kissed you, and you ran away to Tenterfield for the weekend?' Nicole said, staring at her dumbfounded.

'I didn't *run* away,' Lucy hedged. 'I'd already told him I was going.'

It was late Sunday night and Lucy had decided she needed an objective opinion, having spent the weekend agonising over her dilemma.

'I can't believe you!'

'What was I supposed to do?'

'Umm, I don't know, maybe jump his bones?'

'Nicole!'

'I'm serious. Jesus, Luce, you're a grown woman. You're allowed to do those kind of things, you know.'

'I knew I shouldn't have told you,' Lucy muttered, slumping in her chair.

'Rubbish, you wanted to tell me so I could tell you what you're too chicken to tell yourself.'

She hated her best friend sometimes—like now when Nicole knew how her mind worked better than Lucy did herself. She felt like a schoolgirl with a crush. Only worse.

'Luce, trust me, you need to take this bull by the horns and ride the sucker for all he's worth.'

'I seriously worry about you,' Lucy said, shaking her head, stunned sometimes by what came out of her friend's mouth. She looked like such a lady.

'Not half as much as I worry about *you*. I'm not kidding, it's not healthy to live like a nun all the time. When was the last time a hunk like Hugh Thompson walked into town? This doesn't happen every day—it's taken almost twenty years to happen the first time! You may never get a chance like this again.'

'Well, if you're so damn eager, why don't you go ride him yourself,' Lucy snapped.

'Let me tell you, if I was in your shoes, not married to a sex god and blissfully content to be so, I would.' Taking pity on Lucy's discomfort, her friend gave a long sigh and reached across the table to take her hand. 'I love you like the sister I never had, but I swear to God, Luce, you are an idiot if you pass up this opportunity.'

'It's not that simple, Nic. May I remind you I'm dependent on him for a job at the moment? It kind of complicates things a little.'

'Why?'

'What do I do when he gets tired of me? I still have to turn up to work. Awkward much?'

'Who says he'll get tired of you? What's with the Little Miss Pessimistic routine?'

'He has a plan. A three-year plan to be precise. He's selling the pub and moving on after three years.'

'Well, a lot can happen in three years. And, anyway, it's three years away! We're talking about right here and now! You can't plan everything in life. You don't have control over every single little detail, Luce. I've been trying to tell you this for years. You've been holding on to everything so tightly, but it's time to start letting go a bit.'

'You're worried I'm suffocating Belle too?' She couldn't keep the betrayal out of her voice.

Nicole shook her head and smiled gently. 'No, honey, that's not what I'm worried about. I'm worried about what happens when you can't hold on to her any more and you're *forced* to let go. What are you going to do when she leaves next year?'

'I'll worry about next year when it happens. Maybe then there'll be time for all . . . this,' she waved her hand in the air, not even able to say Hugh's name at the moment.

'Look, Christy and I are going to Sydney for the weekend, how about I take Belle with us? It'll do you both good to have some time apart, and you'll be able to think things through without having to worry about anyone else.'

Lucy's initial reaction to this suggestion was panic. She knew what Nicole really meant was without Belle here Lucy would have one less excuse to use against taking things further with Hugh.

'You can't put living off until the perfect time. Life is about taking chances and grabbing whatever opportunity comes your way *now*. You deserve to be happy and to have some fun for a change, and I'm willing to bet Hugh Thompson knows *all* about having fun.'

Lucy thought about Nicole's words as she drove home in the dark. She wasn't a nun, she argued silently, sending a brief glance into the rear-view mirror and catching sight of herself momentarily. Well, maybe her hair could use a bit of a revamp. She couldn't recall the last time she'd been to the hairdressers; it was maybe six . . . seven months ago? She'd resorted to trimming her fringe herself when it got to the point of driving her crazy a few months ago. She looked at her reflection and frowned. Maybe it wouldn't hurt to lash out on a new colour and style. Everyone had been raving about Madam Latoy's, maybe she should see what all the fuss was about. She gave small snort as she dropped her gaze from the mirror. 'A nun,' she muttered. Well, she'd show Miss Nicole Smarty Pants. By the time Madam Latoy had finished with her, there would be nothing remotely resembling a nun.

Fourteen

Monday morning was every bit as awkward as Lucy had been expecting. She did her best not to be alone with Hugh and for the most part it worked. The phone rang constantly, and she was busy taking bookings for an upcoming group of bikers wanting to base themselves at Bundah for the long weekend. For a while Lucy thought she'd managed to avoid any mention of Friday morning and that kiss, but her relief was short-lived when Hugh came into the office at the end of the day and shut the door.

For the longest time neither of them spoke, until Hugh finally moved into the room and sat on the edge of her desk. 'How was the weekend?'

'Fine. It was good. Yours?' she asked casually.

'Long. I spent it going over in my head everything I wanted to say when I saw you today.'

'You don't have to say anything. Really. We'll just move on.'

Hugh gave a dry laugh, looking down at the floor before lifting his gaze to meet hers. 'I have to tell you, this is a first for me.'

'What is?' Lucy asked cautiously.

'Caring.'

Lucy felt her breath catch at his frank response, but remained silent.

'I don't do this,' he said. 'I have no idea what's happening. I don't know when it started, or why the hell I can't get you out of my head, and you sure aren't making things any easier when you keep running away.'

'Yeah, well, I don't do *this* either,' she said, pointedly.

'So what are we going to do about it?'

Lucy opened her mouth then shut it abruptly. What *were* they going to do about it? Her mind was flashing up all kinds of good ideas, but she pushed them away quickly. 'It's too . . . It's complicated. I don't need any more disruption in Belle's life right now. We're barely getting through this whole curfew thing as it is. Adding *this* into the equation is just asking for trouble.'

'How? I'm not talking about moving in with you.'

'Oh, so I'm just supposed to be on call for whenever you feel a need to—' She stopped and swallowed awkwardly before continuing, 'You're after a friend with benefits?'

'No, that's not what I meant,' he said with a frown. 'I just meant it wouldn't have to interfere with your time with Belle.'

'I don't know how that would work . . .'

'Why don't we just play it by ear and see where it takes us?'

Nicole's pep talk the night before played over in her mind and held back the automatic dismissal of the idea she would have given only a few days ago. Maybe she really had painted herself into a bit of a corner over the years, holding on too tight in her determination to control the rest of her life the way she hadn't been able to control her early adulthood. She didn't want to become some jaded old spinster, too set in her ways to enjoy life. She just hadn't realised everyone else had been able to see the path she was heading down and she couldn't.

Lucy found herself nodding slowly.

'Do you want—?'

'Would you like—?'

They both spoke at once, before smiling ruefully.

'You go,' Hugh said graciously.

'I was just going to say, if you didn't have any plans, would you like to come over and have dinner with me and Belle this evening?'

He seemed surprised by her invitation, but covered it quickly, shoving his hands into his front pockets and giving her a nod. 'Sure. Yeah, that'd be great.'

'Okay,' said Lucy, rubbing her palms along the sides of her jeans, feeling an attack of nerves as she mentally searched her memory for a pantry list, wondering what in the hell she was going to cook. 'Well, I'd better go home and get started. Just come over whenever you're ready.'

'I'll just get Jason sorted and wait till Cassie arrives for her shift, then I'll be over,' he said, easing aside so she could walk through the doorway.

Lucy straightened her shoulders as she headed to her car. This was a good thing, she told herself firmly. She wasn't committing to anything; they were just playing it by ear . . . Somehow, though, she had a funny feeling that by agreeing to this she'd opened up a huge can of worms she had no hope of closing.

The chicken was on and the rice was cooking. Lucy counted out three sets of cutlery and handed them across to Belle as she glanced at the time.

'So, is this going to get awkward?' Belle asked, snapping Lucy's attention back to her abruptly.

'What?'

'Come on, Mum. Everyone thinks he's hot. He's single. You're single.'

'He's my boss,' said Lucy, hoping she sounded a lot more composed than she was feeling.

'So?'

'So, he gave me a job when he didn't have to and I'd like to do something nice to thank him,' said Lucy, concentrating on stirring the pot of honey mustard chicken on the stovetop. 'It's just dinner, Belle,' she said.

'Well, if you did like him, I guess there'd be worse guys you could invite over. Maybe it's time for you to start thinking about finding someone . . . I mean, next year it's going to be pretty different around here,' Belle said. 'I don't want you to be lonely, Mum,' she added quietly.

Lucy swallowed over the lump of emotion her daughter's words provoked. 'I'll miss you, Belle, so much. But I don't want you to worry about me, okay? I'll be fine,' she said, feeling a fierce surge of love for this child she'd had the privilege of spending the last seventeen years with. 'I love you, kiddo.'

'I love you too, Mum. I'm sorry we've been fighting so much lately,' she said, dropping her gaze to the table.

'I just want you to be happy. Safe and happy. I'm not trying to hurt you when I say no to these parties. I'm just trying to protect you.'

'I know, Mum, but I'm not you . . . or Aunty Claire. I haven't even had a chance to prove to you that I can be responsible. Don't you see how unfair it is?'

Lucy closed her eyes briefly. Hugh had basically been saying the same thing all along. Maybe she did need to loosen the apron strings a little. 'Maybe you're right. But,' she added firmly as her daughter's eyes lit up with excitement, 'school still comes first and these parties are not going to be a regular occurrence. If one comes up and I know who's going, I'll think about it.'

'Awesome! Thanks, Mum,' Belle squealed, crossing the kitchen to throw her arms around Lucy's neck. 'I've gotta go call Amy and tell her.'

There was a knock on the door and Belle made a detour, throwing the door open and welcoming Hugh inside with a wide grin, before disappearing into her room.

'What was all that about?' Hugh asked a little uncertainly, staring after Belle.

'That was what a happy teenage girl looks like,' said Lucy with a wry grin. 'I know, something we haven't seen around here for a while. 'Dinner won't be too long,' she added.

'Looks like you two are getting on better than last time I was here.'

'Thank goodness.'

She led him back towards the kitchen, handing him a beer from the fridge as he took a seat at the bench.

His hand covered her own on the bottle and Lucy looked up at him warily.

'Just relax,' he said. 'We're taking this slowly, remember?'

Lucy managed a weak smile, but his touch set off a riot of butterflies inside her and she wondered if maybe she was in fact closer to being a nun than she'd realised. If a brush of his hand could do this to her, what on earth could the rest of him to do?

Over dinner Belle was unusually chatty and for a moment Lucy caught a glimpse of the daughter she'd thought she'd lost. For the most part, Lucy was content to sit back and listen to the conversation going on about the overseas travel Belle was intending to do. 'Have you been to many places?' she heard Belle ask Hugh after she'd finished relaying her bucket list of places to go.

'I've been to Bali,' he said.

'That's all?'

'Belle,' Lucy admonished from across the table.

'Well, I just thought you must have been to more,' she said with a touch of defensiveness in her tone. 'You seem to know a lot of stuff.'

'I read a lot.'

'I wouldn't have picked you for a reader,' Belle said.

'Why?'

'I don't know. You've got tats . . .'

In her daughter's defence, Belle did seem slightly embarrassed by her quick assumption, but Hugh just chuckled at her candour.

'Sometimes we make choices when we're young that we have to live with for the rest of our lives,' he said quietly. 'But you should never let them define you.'

Lucy stared at him thoughtfully, mulling over his words.

'Getting your tats was a bad choice?' Belle asked curiously, undeterred by politeness to leave the topic alone.

'One of many, I'm afraid. If you're lucky, you can hide most of your mistakes, but some of us can't do that,' he said with a lopsided grin as he glanced down at his forearms. 'But just because you make some bad choices doesn't mean you have to keep paying for them for the rest of your life. Sometimes people see past the mistakes, sometimes they don't. It doesn't really matter, as long as *you* know you've changed. You are the only person you should be trying to please. You've got to be able to live with yourself.'

The conversation changed after that to lighter topics, but Lucy couldn't help but be a tiny bit impressed by Hugh's theory on life. He was a bit of an enigma, this stranger who'd arrived in town and stirred up her nice quiet life. Little did he know he was weakening her defences at an alarming rate.

'I'm going to my room. To watch a movie,' Belle announced once she'd finished washing up after their meal. 'I'll be wearing headphones,' she added pointedly, before disappearing, leaving Lucy, mortified, in the kitchen.

'Does that mean she gives her approval to move this along?'

'It means she's going to get a few extra nights on kitchen duty after that,' Lucy said.

'She's a good kid.'

Lucy hung up the tea towel and searched for something else to keep her hands busy. 'Coffee?' she asked hopefully.

'I'm still full from dinner. Can we sit for a while?'

Sitting seemed harmless enough, except if she was within close proximity to him, then she had no idea what might happen. She felt like a powder keg with a match hovering over her fuse.

Lucy led the way across to the lounge and sat down nervously. Hugh sat beside her and leaned back, seemingly completely at ease, one arm stretched along the back of the lounge chair.

The TV was playing to itself but Lucy found herself grateful that there was something to fill in the awkward silence that had fallen between them now that Belle had left the conversation.

A rerun of an old *Baywatch* episode was playing, and Lucy rolled her eyes as Pamela Anderson's cleavage bounced its way across the screen in slow motion.

Hugh caught her expression and gave a sly smile as she caught him watching the screen with interest.

'Really?'

'What? I'm a guy; it's hardwired into us.'

'Makes it a little hard for the average woman to live up to that kind of male fantasy,' Lucy said.

'Luckily we have many fantasies, so there's pretty much one for every kind of woman,' he shrugged.

'Oh?'

'Wanna know one of mine?'

Lucy couldn't help but smile at his playful mood. A few weeks ago, if anyone had said she'd be sitting on her lounge discussing fantasies with Hugh Thompson, she'd never have believed it, and yet here she was. 'Sure,' she finally said with a droll look.

'Lately I've been thinking a lot about you, and a pair of high heels.'

'Ahh, a heel fetish, huh?' she nodded reflectively. 'I do think a man having a love of shoes is a good quality. We could go shoe shopping together.'

'And you just went and ruined a perfectly good fantasy,' he shook his head mournfully.

'Well, if you're looking for that,' she said nodding her head towards the TV screen,' I'm about to really ruin your day because, firstly, I'm thirty-four, I have stretch marks and these,' she said, cupping her breasts, which made his eyes widen, 'are not fake. They were working boobs. They *fed* a baby . . . you know, the job they were actually designed for? And, as a result, they are no longer perky and round.'

'Lucy, if you expect me to uphold my end of the bargain, then don't . . . do that,' he said, his gaze determinedly fixed on her face.

Lucy froze, removing her hands and placing them in her lap and silence followed once again.

'Would you relax,' he finally said after she wriggled yet again, trying to find a position that wasn't either screaming, *Get the hell away from me!* or *Here I am, take me now!*

'I'm relaxed,' she said.

'I can see that,' he told her, eyeing her as she perched on the edge of the seat, her back ramrod straight.

This was ridiculous, she chided herself irritably. She was a grown woman, for goodness sake. Her gaze fell on his arm along the back of the lounge and followed the tribal design that poked out from the sleeve of his T-shirt and wrapped around his bicep.

'How many do you have?' she asked, looking up at his face to find him watching her.

'A few,' he said, and his tone held an odd note of vulnerability.

'You regret having tattoos?'

'Not the tattoos in general,' he said, glancing down at his arm. 'More like the time in my life they represent, I guess. You got any?' he asked, looking up at her.

'Tattoos?' she asked, surprised enough to laugh. 'Nope. I almost got one once though.'

'What happened? Changed your mind?'

'My parents found out I was planning it. They grounded me and I missed my trip to the big smoke to get it.' She'd been so excited. She'd planned on surprising Mick with a big love heart and *Mick Forever* written inside it, on her shoulder . . . Thank God for small mercies, but at the time she'd been devastated.

'Your parents were strict?'

'They weren't that bad. I was a bit of a rebel. After my sister died, I became a real handful for a while.'

Hugh didn't say anything and she was glad; it was a long time ago, but the emptiness never went away. She should have a big sister to call and complain about teenagers to when times got tough. She should have a big sister to visit and nieces and nephews to spoil rotten. She should have someone to recall childhood stories and mischief with, but she didn't. Drugs took her sister away and Lucy missed Claire every single day. 'That's why I know that if you've got a kid who's determined to do something, they'll eventually find a way to do it, because I did.'

'Belle doesn't strike me as overly rebellious. Not compared to her mother, it seems,' he said lifting an eyebrow, a smile hovering on his lips.

'Thank goodness,' Lucy said with heartfelt conviction, 'but it's a hell of a lot harder to keep one step ahead of kids nowadays. They have mobiles and Facebook and Instagram . . . technology in general . . . It's scary. And you hear people saying things like, "Well, you're the parent, don't let them have a phone", or "Don't let them use the computer".

Which of course in theory is fine, except you want your kids to have a phone because you worry about where they are and what they're doing. And keeping them off computers? Easier said than done when the school introduces them to it in kindergarten these days . . . Technology is something they actually need and you can't keep them away from it.'

'Yeah, I hear you. It's no picnic parenting in a technical world.'

'So what were you like as a kid?'

'I was in trouble a lot.'

'Spent a lot of time grounded too, huh?' she said, tilting her head to the side.

'No. My parents didn't do grounding.' When he looked into her eyes and saw her question, he gave a long sigh. 'They preferred to beat the lesson into me; seemed a lot more effective.'

Lucy knew a lot of people who had grown up in an era when smacking or getting the belt or wooden spoon was an acceptable punishment, but the shadows lurking in Hugh's eyes weren't put there by a whack with a spoon now and again. Instinctively she reached out and placed her hand on his knee, her heart saddened. She saw him look down at her hand and cover it with his own larger one, before looking up at her. 'I had my grandad. He couldn't do much, but he lived with us for a while.'

'Do you still have your grandad?'

'No. He passed away a few years ago. I used to visit him in the nursing home though, later . . . after I'd left home. We stayed close,' he said, playing with her fingers, idly. 'He was a funny old bugger,' he said with an affectionate chuckle.

'Tell me about him,' Lucy said.

'He'd suffered a stroke when I was only a kid, and it affected his speech, the only word he could say was *boy*. But he'd write stuff down.'

'That's sad,' Lucy said, wondering at his fond smile.

'Yeah, I guess, but you know it's weird because even with that one word, it was like he could say anything. I mean, you knew exactly how he was feeling just by the tone. We used to spend a lot of time together, watching old movies and the footy and cricket. He'd ask how my day was at school, and help me with homework. He was a really smart old bloke. Switched on, you know? Despite not being able to speak, he was still all there up top. But then he had another stroke when I was about thirteen and Dad wasn't sober enough to take care of him after that.'

Lucy saw his smile slip.

'Anyway, I used to visit him after school as often as I could, and then the visits became more sporadic the older I got. I feel bad about that.'

'You were only a kid. I'm sure he understood.'

'When he died I got a letter from his lawyer to say I'd been left everything in his will. I wasn't expecting anything, just his personal effects, you know?' he said, glancing down at her. 'But then I get this cheque.' He paused, shaking his head as though he still couldn't believe it. 'He'd been investing and managing his money right up until the end.

He'd made a small fortune. He was the only person I've ever really missed.'

Lucy smiled sadly. 'He sounds like a wonderful man and he must have really thought a lot of you.'

Hugh smiled a little at her statement. 'Yeah, I was lucky to have him. But I envied kids who had parents who cared. I'd never have admitted it out loud back then, but I did. I admire the mother you are to Belle, Lucy. Never doubt the job you've done. She may push you now, but that kid has been given the best gift a kid could ever hope for. Someone to protect and love her.'

Her heart felt as though it had ripped clean in two. She ached for the little boy who hadn't known the love of his parents. Without thinking, she leaned towards him, placing her hands on his face, and kissed him. It was a slow, gentle kiss, meant to take away pain and give comfort and he allowed her to set the pace, until comfort turned into something different and he took control. He threaded his own hands into her hair, and need, hot and raw, exploded between them. She felt the rub of stubble against her face and didn't flinch; the burn felt good, his warm lips claiming and drugging her.

Hugh broke away first, dropping his forehead against hers, his breathing uneven. His groaned expletive had her releasing a shaky breath in agreement.

Lucy finally pulled away, and realised her hands were shaking as she smoothed her hair behind her ears in an attempt to restore order to her wayward emotions.

'I'd better go now or I won't be able to keep my promise of taking this slow,' he said, rubbing his hands over his face briskly.

'You don't have to treat me like I'm some kind of virginal sacrifice, you know,' she said feeling strangely put out.

'You want me to stay the night?' he asked, raising his eyebrows in an annoyingly sexy way.

'Belle's here,' she admitted grudgingly.

'Exactly my point. I'm trying to be the hero,' he added, tipping her chin back gently. 'Besides, when this finally happens between us, I want it to be perfect. I want it planned and to be everything you hope. I don't want to have to sneak around. You're not some one-night stand, Luce.'

'I'm just saying, I'm an adult and I have done this before, you know.'

'Not with me you haven't,' he said, holding her gaze with a look that sizzled like a hotplate. 'Night, Luce,' he said, dropping a kiss on her nose before pushing himself up off the chair and heading for the door.

Holy moly, she thought, blowing out a long, slow breath after the door had closed behind him. Her gaze was drawn back to the TV screen once more, playing quietly across the room and frowned. Pam wouldn't be a quivering mess right now, and why would she be as she was every man's fantasy. Maybe the hair appointment she'd booked the other day would help give her back a bit of confidence. It had been a long time since she'd felt this off balance because of a man and she spent a long night lying in bed thinking about it.

Fifteen

Lucy looked at the time as she climbed into her car. How could it possibly be almost five o'clock already? She'd gone into the salon at midday, for goodness sake! Mind you, after all the bleaching and stripping and reapplying of colour and God only knows what else they'd done, it wasn't hard to see where the time had gone. It was certainly quite a process, this reinventing yourself thing. One that she couldn't afford to do very often, in terms of either time or money.

Walking into Madam Latoy's was like walking into a French parlour room. Everything about the salon was elegant and sophisticated, decorated in tones of gold and aqua. She'd spent a great deal of time going through hair magazines with Twiggy, and was grateful for the older woman's keen eye for style. She knew exactly what would suit Lucy's face shape, dismissing with a wave of her beautifully manicured hand the few Lucy had found, instead searching through the pages until she discovered what she was after. From that Jerome had created almost exactly the same look. He was truly a magician. Lucy had felt a small ping of guilt when she thought about Mavis, but it was like comparing a frozen box of no-name fish fingers with salmon fillets prepared by a master chef in a five-star restaurant . . . *in Paris*.

Her previous, rather one-dimensional ash blonde colour had been replaced by delicious-sounding colours like espresso, hot toffee and caramel, with sharply razored edges that framed her face and jawline. The darker base shade highlighted her eyes, and Twiggy had talked her into getting her brows and lashes tinted, so that she was almost unrecognisable even to herself.

All afternoon the strangest thing had been happening. It was almost as if, with each inch of cut and coloured hair, a weight had been lifted and her self-confidence had begun to grow. Her confidence had taken a big hit since Ken had fired her, but by the time she waked out of the salon she felt buoyant, strong and ready to face anything.

Who would have thought something as simple as a haircut could transform a person? Well, okay, maybe not transform, she amended, sneaking another peek at herself in the mirror. She still had the lines around her eyes that told her she was thirty-four years old, but she was definitely feeling better about things.

When she got home she had a sudden attack of nerves as she wondered what Belle would make of the changes, but then she remembered that Belle wouldn't see it until she returned from Sydney, and she couldn't even show Nicole. Disappointment deflated her nervous excitement. Here she was all done up with nowhere to go. It was somewhat depressing to be sitting all alone in an empty house after her journey of self-discovery.

She tapped her fingers on the kitchen bench as she looked around listlessly. *Hugh would appreciate your new look.* Lucy straightened in alarm at the direction her thoughts were taking and immediately dismissed the idea. She wasn't just going to show up on his doorstep unannounced and . . . She pulled back on the reins of that particular idea. She was not the kind of girl to show up in nothing but a pair of heels and a smile. No . . . she couldn't. She realised her heart was actually beating a little faster at the thought. Could she? Nicole had told her to go out and live a little. Everything in the universe seemed to be pointing her in that direction, and truth be told it was getting harder to keep fighting it.

Before she could change her mind, Lucy headed for her bedroom. She could be brave if she had to and it was time to prove it.

Who the hell was she kidding? There was no way she could go through with this! Lucy made it to the back door of Hugh's private quarters before her bravado gave out and she almost crumpled into a blubbering mess. This was so stupid! Real people didn't dress up in a Driza-Bone and red high heels, for God's sake, and then invite themselves over to their boss's house to seduce him. Holy crap, it sounded worse than a B-grade movie plot. *Just knock on the door, damn it!* said Nicole's voice in her head. She knew she was quite possibly losing her mind, but somehow her fist was banging on the door and she was left there gulping in lungfuls of air and feeling as though she might actually hyperventilate.

As the sounds of boots approaching the doorway grew louder, Lucy found herself preparing to flee, but then the door was opened and she was trapped in the bright glow of light from inside, like the proverbial deer caught in the headlights.

'Lucy?'

It was now or never, she thought, taking a breath. She stepped around him and headed inside. There was no turning back now. If she looked at him or even listened to him calling her, she'd lose what little nerve remained.

She fumbled slightly with the knot she'd tied before leaving the house, but she hadn't counted on nerves making her fingers turn into thumbs and ruin her graceful seduction. *I'm not going to cry,* she thought firmly, even though she felt like throwing her hands in the air and stomping her feet. Just breathe. She'd finally gotten the knot undone when she came to an abrupt halt in the centre of the lounge room and looked up to see the three stunned faces of Jason, Terry the cook and the beer delivery guy gaping at her.

This could not be happening. She vaguely heard Hugh arrive behind her and his low groan that followed. She couldn't move, she was frozen in mortified shock. This wasn't supposed to be happening. She'd managed to pick an after-work wind down to make her grand debut as a stripper? The delivery guy was leaning so far forward he was barely still sitting on the couch. Terry was so stunned that he dropped his beer can and the sound of tin rolling across the timber floorboards snapped everyone out of the stupefied trance they'd somehow fallen into. Lucy opened her mouth to scream, but all that came out was a pathetic mortified gasp of horror as she frantically pulled the coat closed and turned to hurry from the room.

'Lucy, wait!' Hugh called from behind her, catching her at the front door.

'Kill me now,' she whispered, refusing to look him in the eye.

'I can't believe you did this.'

She was too mortified to register the impressed pride in his tone right away. '*You* can't believe I did it? You were the one who put the stupid idea in my head in the first place,' she said in a low whisper.

'Yeah, well, I was telling you about a fantasy I had . . . I didn't actually think you'd ever do it.'

WTF? Lucy gaped at him before returning to wrestle desperately with the front door.

'Just stop,' he said, taking her shoulders in his hands and ducking his head to look into her furious eyes. 'Let me get rid of these guys and we'll talk, okay?'

Talk? He wanted to talk? She never wanted to *think* about this ever again, let alone *talk* about it.

He opened the door beside them and Lucy caught a brief glimpse of a large bed. 'You can wait in here if you want.'

She eyed him cautiously before stepping into the bedroom. Closing her eyes tightly in humiliation, she heard him re-enter the lounge room and the sound of low, male voices, no doubt making fun of their surprise interruption to the evening. The moment was gone—whatever fleeting moment of insanity it had been. There was no way she was waiting here like a lamb to the slaughter, dressed in high heels and sexy underwear. What the hell had she been thinking? Maybe she *was* destined to be a nun! And quite frankly, if this was the alternative, she was *happy* to be! Taking a calming breath, she slipped out into the hallway and tried the cast-iron doorknob again, and thankfully it turned this time, allowing her to make a hasty exit.

It took a minute for Lucy to identify the funny noise she was hearing over the furious amount of name calling she was doing inside her head but, when she realised what it was, she pulled the car to the side of the road and dropped her head to the steering wheel. This. Could. Not. Be. Happening.

With a weary sigh, she opened the door and stepped out, turning to eye the flat tyre with a resentful glare. She was almost home. She'd almost made it without passing another single person, and she could have contained the amount of humiliation experienced for one night but, no, karma hadn't finished with her just yet.

'How much worse could tonight get?' she muttered, slamming the door shut and circling to the rear of the vehicle as she reached underneath to remove the spare tyre from its cradle beneath the tray. The rain started slowly but within minutes had become heavy fat drops, before the heavens opened up and Lucy found herself caught in a torrential downpour. 'It wasn't a bloody challenge!' she yelled as she put her weight behind the wheel brace and tried to loosen the wheel nut. 'Undo, you bast—'

'Need a hand?'

Lucy gasped as she looked over her shoulder and found Hugh standing there, hands on hips and a grin on his damn face. 'No thanks.'

'You sure?'

'Positive,' she managed to get out through tightly clenched teeth. 'Goddamn it!' she snapped as she fell back on her butt when her hand slipped.

Hugh held out a hand and Lucy listlessly reached out and took it, allowing him to pull her to her feet wordlessly. Drops of rain clung to the ends of her brand-new razored hair, dripping down her face. She could only imagine the picture she made: drowned rat was the most obvious image that came to mind. He took her place without comment and hit the wheel brace hard, forcing the nuts undone. She was somewhat relieved that he seemed to be struggling as well; it made her feel slightly less like a damsel in distress.

When he'd finished changing the tyre, he simply opened the door for her and closed it once she was inside. Behind her, she saw the headlights of his ute, waiting for her to pull back out onto the road. It seemed they were going to have that *talk* after all. He wasn't about to let her off the hook so easily.

Unlocking the front door, she left it open for him and headed for the bathroom to grab two towels.

Hugh accepted the dry towel she offered and wiped the rain from his face, watching her quietly as she mopped at her dripping hair.

'Are you going to take your coat off?' he asked quietly.

Lucy stopped drying her hair at the husky sound of his voice and lowered the towel. 'I don't think so. It was a silly idea.'

'It wasn't a silly idea,' he said reaching out to hold her wrist. 'It was a great idea. Just the timing was off.'

Embarrassment flooded her face at the memory of those stunned expressions and she closed her eyes.

'No,' Hugh's strong voice brought her eyes open quickly. 'You have nothing to be embarrassed about. Do you have any idea how lucky those guys think I am?'

'Lucky! To have a half-naked, clearly unhinged woman barge into your house uninvited? Oh yeah, I bet they're all kinds of jealous over that.' How the hell was she going to look any of them in the eye after this?

'They were. You have no idea how sexy that is,' he said, tugging her wrist to bring her closer. 'A woman turning up on your doorstep, wearing high heels and nothing underneath that coat.'

'Well, you're wrong; I'm wearing something.'

'Show me,' he said, his eyes losing the touch of amusement of a few moments before.

When she continued to stare at him reluctant and nervous, he reached for the ties at her waist, holding her gaze steadily as he allowed the coat to fall open. For a long while his gaze didn't leave her eyes and Lucy found the anticipation tantalising. When his gaze did lower she could almost feel the heat as it moved down the length of her body.

She'd felt like such an idiot when she'd found herself looking for sexy underwear online a few weeks earlier. It was all Nicole's fault! She was the one who had kept harping on about Lucy ignoring her inner woman and that she should be embracing her sexuality. Lucy hadn't intended to buy anything, she'd just gone online to have a look . . . and she'd ended up clicking on an insanely expensive set of lingerie. It was madness and completely out of character. Now though, seeing the avid appreciation in Hugh's eyes as he practically devoured the red plunging push-up bra and the matching scrap of lace below with his hungry gaze, she was very glad for the momentary insanity that had led to her purchase.

His whispered curse came out on a low, uneven breath and sent a shot of longing through her body.

Encouraged by his obvious approval, Lucy shrugged out of the coat, letting it pool at her feet.

Slowly he moved his hands to either side of her ribcage, his thumbs moving in gentle circles against her soft skin just below the edge of the lacy bra. Her harsh breathing made her chest rise and fall, drawing his gaze to the flesh on display there.

Hugh moved his hands up the sides of her breasts and pushed them close together, before dropping his head to trail warm kisses down the side of her neck and across her chest. Finally he pushed aside the fabric to gently nuzzle at her now hardened nipples pushing from behind the lace, demanding freedom.

She reached behind and unhooked the bra. Dropping it to the floor, she couldn't stop the moan of desire as his mouth captured and lavished undivided attention upon both breasts in turn.

Lucy clutched at his arms tightly, holding on as wave after wave of sensation flooded through her body. She had to admit it had been a while since she'd been intimate with a man, but she'd never experienced this level of desire before. Ever. At seventeen sex had been an exciting, dangerous, hormone-fuelled kind of desire, but it was nothing like this. This was primal and desperate. It was a hunger that couldn't be sated. Without warning, Hugh dropped his hands and slid them down her sides until they settled just under her buttocks, before he bent and lifted her, carrying her down the hallway. 'Which door?' His voice was a low groan of longing and it sent her already pounding pulse into an even greater frenzy of anticipation.

'Last door on the right,' she gasped, wrapping her legs tighter around his hips.

He kicked the door shut behind them before crossing to the bed and lowering her onto the mattress gently. For a moment he just stared down at her with an unreadable expression. Lucy lifted her hand and placed it against his cheek as her gaze caressed his face. His jawline was angled into a wide yet defined chin. It screamed extreme maleness in any language, but it wasn't the chiselled face of a male model; it had too many imperfections for that. Under his stubble she could see pale lines of old scars, unnoticeable at a distance, but visible up this close. His lip also had a small scar on one corner, and his nose looked as though it had been broken more than once; it was reasonably straight but bore a few bumps along the top. There was no denying he was attractive, but in a very rugged way; there was nothing suave or debonair about him.

'What are you waiting for?' she asked, moving her hand along his jawline and caressing his lips with her thumb.

'Nothing, I'm just enjoying the view.'

She smiled at that, but slipped both hands around his neck and pulled him down. 'You can look all you like later. Right now, you've got work to do.'

'Yes, ma'am,' he chuckled, but their laughter was soon replaced by muffled gasps of satisfaction and low groans of longing.

There was a certain kind of poetry to lying in bed listening to rain falling on a tin roof. It was pretty near perfect when you added to the picture being wrapped in the arms of your lover after having had mind-blowing sex. Lucy stared at their linked hands resting on Hugh's chest. He hadn't said much, but then again, neither had she. There'd been no need for conversation earlier, and even now she hated the thought of intruding upon this safe, warm cocoon.

Following the length of his arm, her gaze lingered on the tattoo of a weeping angle on his bicep. It was as beautiful as it was sad. She'd seen glimpses of it before, peeking out from beneath the edge of his T-shirt, but never the full image.

'Is there a story behind your tattoos?' she asked after a while.

'There's always a story behind a tat,' he said and she felt him smile against the top of her head.

'What's the story behind this one?' she asked, nodding at the angel.

'I got that when I was eighteen. I guess at the time it summed up my life. It was pretty hopeless.'

'What about the other one?' she asked. He shifted a little and she lifted her head to follow his gaze to the other arm. This one also had an angel but it was a male version, and he looked like some kind of warrior holding a sword high above his head.

'That one I got once I'd stopped feeling sorry for myself and decided that I was going to be a fighter.'

'A fighter?'

'Not literally. More like a survivor. I worked out people who had a crap start in life went one of two ways: they either used their past to hold them down—as an excuse—or they used it to grow stronger.'

'There's a lot of deep stuff going on behind that tough exterior,' she said, tracing the slow smile on his lips with her finger.

'Don't tell anyone, you'll ruin my image.'

'Wouldn't dream of it,' she assured him. 'And what about the one on your back?' She'd never seen any hint of that, since tonight was the first time she'd seen him shirtless. The briefest of reactions flittered across his face, so quickly she wondered whether she'd imagined it. 'It's just a tat.'

'Really?' she tilted her head slightly as she studied him thoughtfully. 'Seems strange that you put so much thought into the others but not this one.'

'That's a part of my past I'd rather forget.'

His comment shut down any further discussion about the subject and it took a moment for Lucy to digest.

'I feel like a bacon and egg sandwich, you want one?' she asked brightly and was relieved when she saw the little crinkle in the corner of his eye reappear as he grinned.

'Sure. I need to regain my strength.'

'So you can make it home?' she asked, arching an eyebrow.

'Eventually. But I was thinking more along the lines of an encore.'

'Well, I don't know. I'm still undecided about whether or not I approved of the first performance.'

She shrieked when he lunged for her across the bed and dragged her back across his chest. 'From what I could hear, I'm pretty sure you liked it.'

'Big-noting yourself, hey?' she teased.

'Nope. Just stating a fact.'

'If you help me cook dinner, I'll think about it,' she grinned, but it soon faded when he cupped the back of her head and pulled her down for a long, slow, toe-curling kiss that left her breathing heavily.

'Deal. But you'd better be a fast eater.'

Lucy had mixed emotions about facing work after their weekend together; not only would she have to face her work colleagues after flashing them on Saturday, but she'd be seeing Hugh and hoping he couldn't read her confused thoughts. There was a brief moment of distraction while she listened to Belle recap the highlights of her Sydney trip, but she could only drag that out for so long.

She told herself she wasn't delaying the inevitable as she parked in front of the takeaway shop, across from the café. It was definitely a two-coffee morning. As she locked her car, Lucy did a double-take at the closed sign hanging on the takeaway door and frowned as she crossed the road to the post office café.

'Ooh la la! I told you Twiggy was a miracle worker. I love it,' Steven gushed, clasping his hands together below his double chin as he studied her new do.

She gave Steven a pleased grin. 'She is that.'

'You look gorgeous!' he said with a satisfied nod, before turning away to make her a coffee.

'It's unusual for the takeaway to be closed in the morning,' she said, looking back over her shoulder at the other side of the main street.

'You haven't heard?'

'Heard what?'

'They've left town. The whole family. Two days ago. Just packed up the car and left.'

'What? For good?'

Steven shrugged. 'That's the general consensus. Kids were pulled from school and they handed in the key to the shop.'

'But why? What happened?'

'His shop was one of the ones that were graffitied the other week, and apparently they've been receiving anonymous phone calls and threatening notes. Then Monday night as Lucas was locking up, a car full of hoons drove past and threw rocks at him. It smashed up his front window and hit one of his kids.'

'Oh my goodness, were they okay?'

'He needed to go to hospital to get stitches. Told their neighbours this wasn't what they thought country life was going to be like.'

'Personally, I think it was just too hard for them to stay, with no family support and such,' Steven shrugged. 'It's a real worry though. A lot of the new business owners are nervous. No one knows who's going to be targeted next.'

Lucy struggled to comprehend what she'd just heard. 'How have I not heard any of this?'

'I guess some people are having way too much fun doing other more pleasurable things with their time,' he wiggled his eyebrows dramatically and Lucy would have laughed had she not still been in shock at the news of Lucas and his family.

'So how are things going with that handsome man of yours?'

She should have known everyone would already have heard about the newest couple in town, but it never ceased to amaze her at the speed of which gossip could travel in this town.

'Oh, fine. It's still kind of new,' she said, avoiding Steven's inquisitive gaze. 'How are you guys doing?'

'It's been a bit quiet lately,' he shrugged, but didn't seem overly concerned. 'But I'm asking about you, don't change the subject. You don't seem yourself. Surely not trouble in paradise already?'

'Paradise?'

'Oh, honey. If that man looked at me the way he looks at you, I would think I'd died and gone to heaven. Tell me what's going on.'

Lucy bit back an impatient sigh when Steven pulled out the chair across from her and sat down, clearly prepared to settle in for the long haul. 'It's just that, well, there's still a lot I don't know about him.' She reached for the sugar and stirred it into her coffee, while Steven looked on quietly.

'Do you know the important things?'

'Like what?'

'Do you trust him?'

'Yes,' she said slowly, realising it was true.

'Do you believe that he's being honest in things he's already told you?'

Lucy thought on it before nodding slowly. She had no reason to doubt anything he'd told her so far.

'Then you already know the most important thing. Trust, my sweet, is one of the hardest things to earn and the easiest thing to break. If you have trust, you're already ahead of the game. The rest will come in time. I wouldn't worry about it too much. You know what men are like, they prefer to keep their feelings and emotions inside. Which is silly because we all know a good woman can bring it all right out when she sets her mind to it, don't we,' he said with a wink.

Lucy smiled in spite of herself. When all was said and done, she knew that she did trust Hugh. There was something in his past that he wasn't yet ready to reveal to her, but she had to believe that whatever it was, it wasn't going to hurt them now.

'Morning Jase,' she said, deciding the best way to handle the awkwardness was to act as though the whole horrible episode hadn't bothered her at all. The young bartender looked at her briefly before his face turned red and he quickly looked away with a murmured, 'Hi.'

Just hold your head up, she repeated firmly as she pushed through the kitchen doors and saw Terry busily whisking eggs in a bowl. 'How was your weekend, Terry?' she asked cheerfully.

Terry glanced up and immediately dropped the whisk, swearing as he slopped the bowl of eggs across the bench in the process.

Lucy gave a small wince and hurried from the kitchen amid the flurry of swear words hanging in the air behind her. *Well that went well,* she thought. She eased into the office, poking her head around the door to make sure it was empty, and breathed a sigh of relief when it was. At least she could have a few minutes' privacy to gather her composure before she had to face Hugh.

'What have you done to my staff?'

Or not. Lucy looked up as Hugh wandered into the office, closing the door behind him.

'Apart from traumatising them for life, absolutely nothing,' she said despondently.

Hugh chuckled, but his smile sobered a little as he reached out for her hand to pull her from the chair. 'You okay?'

'I'm fine. I've just had Belle talking my ear off since she got home about how fantastic Sydney was and how she can't wait to get down there to live. I'm beginning to think Nicole actually hates me.'

'Nah, it's a good thing. You'll see. She'll spread her wings for a while, but she'll miss her mum and come home to visit, I can guarantee it.'

'I don't know, compared to the bright city lights, Mum's pretty boring.'

'I'd have to disagree with that statement,' he said with a provocative smile.

The Coach House was busier than ever with the new verandah restaurant opening. Working together wasn't as awkward as she'd been anticipating. They'd managed to keep their hands off each other for the majority of the time, except for that one brief moment in the cold room when Hugh had steered her inside and they'd made out like a pair of randy teenagers. But other than that, they'd been completely professional.

Although there were still moments when she heard that little voice inside cautioning her against rushing into things.

There was still so much she didn't know about Hugh's past. He never volunteered anything, and she sometimes picked up on a slight hesitation before he answered questions about his life before Bundah. She couldn't quite put her finger on what it was that concerned her. He was obviously a private person, and she could appreciate that. Yet she couldn't ignore the little niggle of doubt that hovered on the edge of her happiness.

Late one afternoon as Lucy perused the display of milk in the supermarket, she heard Nate call her name.

'Hi there,' she said, looking up, but when he didn't return her smile, her own slipped a little. 'Is everything all right?'

'Yeah. No. Everything's fine,' he said, picking up an apple from the nearby display and testing its weight in his palm distractedly. 'It's been a hectic day.'

'More broken windows, I see,' she said, having passed the taped-up shopfronts on the way here. 'What's going on around here? Any idea who did it?'

'I have a fair idea, but so far haven't been able to prove it.'

'Well, I hope you get them soon. It's disgraceful.' She reached for a carton of milk and a small silence fell between them.

'Actually, Luce, there was something I wanted to speak to you about.'

The note of concern in his voice immediately caught her attention.

'How well do you know this Thompson bloke?' Nate asked.

'Hugh?' Lucy shrugged vaguely. 'Well enough, I guess. Why?'

'I saw him leaving your house,' Nate said and then paused, shaking his head when he saw her expression change to a frown. 'Before you tell me to mind my own business, just hear me out. I'm not spying on you, I was driving past and saw him,' he said quickly. 'Look, I just think you need to be careful around him. He's not . . . let's just say, I'm not so sure I trust the bloke.'

'Why?'

'I've heard a few rumours about him.'

'Rumours? Come on, Nate. You should know better than anyone that rumours rarely tell the full story.'

He shrugged his shoulders, but she saw a flicker of doubt cross his face. 'Normally I'd agree with you, but let's just say that when you keep hearing the same kinda things about someone, you start to believe there's an element of truth in there somewhere. Just be careful, all right? I don't want to see you get hurt over a fella like Hugh Thompson. You deserve better.' Nate turned and left the shop before she could think of a reply.

What was going on? Was Nate just puffing out his chest, warning her off a rival male? Or was there something more to his concerns?

Back inside the pub she found Hugh leaning against the bar. 'Should I be concerned that Nate's worried about you?' she said bluntly.

Hugh glanced up from the paperwork he was reading through, cocking an eyebrow lazily. 'Should *I* be concerned that Nate's worried about me?'

Lucy ignored his attempt at humour and placed the plastic grocery bag onto the bar. 'What does he know that I should be aware of?'

'That I'm an awesome lover and once women have had me, all other men, especially small-town cops, are ruined for them,' he said with a slow grin.

'I'm serious, Hugh,' she said folding her arms across her chest and trying to look formidable, which was difficult when she was distracted by that goddamn sexy smile of his.

'So am I, Lucy,' he mimicked, dropping the paperwork and leaning his arms along the top of the bar to give her his full attention. 'There's nothing to tell,' he said. 'The guy's obviously getting a little edgy about you seeing me.'

'That's not it. Nate's just a friend and he was worried enough to come and warn me off you. I know him, Hugh, he wouldn't be doing that unless he had some kind of reason, and it makes me a little uneasy that you won't tell me why you think he'd do that.'

'I just told you why—the guy's jealous as hell.'

'Why do you keep saying that?' It was really getting on her nerves.

'Because if it were me, I'd be doing exactly the same thing,' Hugh said, his smile disappearing as he moved around the end of the bar and came to a stop in front of her. 'He's right to be wary.' He took another step closer to trace a finger along the side of her face and Lucy somehow forgot how to breathe. 'Unlike Nate, I don't intend to leave a shadow of a doubt about what my intentions are where you're concerned.'

Lucy couldn't have formed a coherent sentence if she'd tried, but there was no need, he leaned forward and seared her with a kiss that burned like a trail of fire straight through her body. *Holy crap, the man can kiss,* the thought registered somewhere in the back of her mind; everything else was obliterated. All that mattered was that he didn't stop doing what he was doing . . . possibly ever.

'Ahh, boss? There's, umm . . . a phone call.'

She felt Hugh hesitate and she grabbed his shirt tighter in her fists as a little voice somewhere inside screamed out, *Noooooooo!*

His chuckle reverberated against her chest as he gave her one more kiss before pulling away. 'This isn't over,' he promised, uncurling her fingers from his shirt.

If it were at all possible, Lucy went even weaker at the knees at the look he gave her. *Did he even know he did that?* she wondered absently. Until now, she'd never believed those romance novels her nan had given her to read, about men whose gazes smouldered. She used to snort at the description—until she'd been on the receiving end of one of Hugh's looks. It didn't just smoulder, it scorched.

Lucy took a hasty step back and felt her face flame as she remembered where they were—standing in the pub, in broad daylight . . . for anyone to see. Not that there was anyone around, but she could hear voices murmuring outside and now that her senses weren't being invaded by

Hugh, she could also detect the clink of cutlery out on the restaurant verandah.

The man was lethal, she thought, running a hand through her hair as she straightened herself and stepped further away from Hugh as he spoke into the phone Jason had handed him.

Lucy tried not to squirm as Hugh held her gaze as he listened to the person on the other end, but when she waved and mouthed a goodbye, he shook his head, holding up a finger to indicate he'd only be one more minute.

Lucy dragged her gaze away from his, needing to gather her composure. What was she doing? What had happened to the Lucy who was happy with her own company? Over the past few days she had found herself missing every minute she was away from Hugh. It was ridiculous. She wasn't a teenager, for goodness sake.

'I'd like nothing better than to pick up where we let off, but I need to go sort out a few things,' he said after ending the phone call.

'Do you need me to stay back?' she asked.

'Nah, I've got it covered. You go on home, but wait up for me tonight?' he asked, linking his fingers through hers and tugging her forward until she felt every delicious, very-bad-for-her inch of him through her clothing.

'Sure,' she heard herself answer in a breathless tone she was positive could not be her own, and was rewarded with another of those seductively wicked grins of his before he kissed her once more and then waved her goodbye.

Feeling effectively dismissed, she tried to muster up some indignation to try to slap a bit of sense into her delusional libido, without much success. It wasn't until she pulled up at her house that she realised she hadn't gotten any answers to her questions.

Not for a minute did she believe Nate's warning was a result of misguided jealousy. She knew Nate; he wouldn't have risked opening himself up to that kind of speculation if he wasn't concerned about something. She couldn't shake the kurnel of doubt that Hugh had deliberately sidetracked her in order to end the conversation. Well, she thought, mentally pulling up her britches, she'd be ready for him next time. Tonight there'd be no distracting her with that sexy mouth of his . . . or any other part of him for that matter, she added when her wayward thoughts threw up an image of his very distracting naked body lying in her bed last night.

Hugh watched Lucy walk away from the bar and let out a long, slow sigh before he turned away and headed to his private quarters.

'Okay, I can talk now,' he said when he got through to the person who'd just called him. 'What's wrong?'

'I don't know who the hell you're pissin' off up there, buddy, but you better knock it off pretty damn quick.'

'What are you talking about?'

'I'm hearin' your name down here, and not in good circles either. You've got lots of people suddenly very interested in your whereabouts.'

Hugh swore savagely under his breath, closing his eyes and pinching the bridge of his nose. This was what he'd been afraid of once he'd realised Pearce was nosing around. The one guy he had to piss off in this place and it had to be the town cop. Fan-bloody-tastic.

Sixteen

Friday nights had always been movie and popcorn night for Lucy and Belle, but they'd become rarer over the past year, with Belle cramming in as many babysitting jobs as she could to earn extra money for another trip to Sydney in a few weeks. Tonight she was babysitting Nicole's kids and Lucy was alone, undecided about what movie to watch and not at all in the mood for popcorn.

She'd been glancing at her phone every few minutes, checking to make sure it wasn't accidentally switched to silent as she waited to hear from Hugh. When she heard his bike pull up out the front she silently groaned at the giddy feeling that followed. *How old are you again?* she asked herself.

She opened the door and smiled as she watched him amble up the path in denim jeans, leather jacket and big black riding boots. Her first impression that day so many months ago now had been pretty spot on. *Sex on legs*. Everything about him screamed virile male and stirred something primal deep inside her. The bad boy appeal was understandable in a rebellious teenager, but to find herself still attracted to bad boys, despite learning her lesson the hard way, was a bit unsettling. Why couldn't she find business suits and polished shoes, appealing?

'What a day,' he said into her hair as they held each other after a long kiss.

Lucy leaned back to get a good look at his face. 'You look tired,' she said.

'I am. You should take me to bed,' he said with a slow grin.

'I would if I thought you'd actually sleep,' she said. 'Actually, I'd rather finish our earlier conversation.'

'That's what I was trying to do.'

'*Conversation*,' she repeated slowly.

Hugh pulled her back against him and nuzzled at her neck.

'Oh no,' Lucy said, pulling away, albeit with enormous reluctance. The kisses against her neck almost made her lose her train of thought, but she backed away from his embrace and held her hand out in warning. 'You're not going to use that trick again.'

'What trick?' Hugh reached out and made a grab for her playfully.

'The old kiss-her-until-she-forgets-what-she-asked-you trick,' she said, slapping away his hands.

'I'm simply picking up where we left off this afternoon.'

'So am I. We were discussing the real reason Nate thinks you're trouble, and this time you're staying right there until you answer.' She ignored his sigh and tapped her foot impatiently. 'Do I have to make Nate tell me?'

'*Nate* doesn't know what the hell he's talking about,' Hugh said. '*Nate* should just mind his own damn business.'

'If you were in his position, would you warn me off you?' she asked.

'I wouldn't ever be in Nate's position,' he scoffed, making Lucy frown.

'Why do you dislike him so much?'

He didn't answer straight away but, when he did, he'd lost a little of his animosity. 'I don't . . .' he started to explain, before stopping. 'I've had a really long day. I think I'm just gonna head off.'

Lucy bit back her disappointment as he turned away. He did look tired, she thought, noticing the faint lines of strain around his eyes, and she felt torn between wanting to take care of him and guilty for making him want to leave. In the end frustration won. 'You're doing it again.'

'Lucy, can we not do this now?'

'When are we going to do it?'

'Why don't you just go ask good ol' Nate? He reckons he has all the facts.'

'Because I want to hear it—whatever it is—from you.'

'You want to hear it? Fine. That tat on my back? It's the insignia of a gang I belonged to. For two years I was part of a biker gang. I've done some shitty things and I've done time in prison, *happy*?' he practically growled at her, before snatching up his keys and wallet from the table and leaving.

Lucy couldn't do anything. She wanted to tell him to wait, but his words had stunned her and all she could do was watch him as he walked out of the room. She heard the front door close behind him softly, and the controlled calm of the action somehow seemed worse than if he'd slammed it.

Seventeen

Lucy frowned down at the paper the next morning as she read the headline.

Missing teenager, Ben Hudson.

Anyone knowing the whereabouts of Bundah teen, Ben Hudson, should contact police immediately.

'Belle,' she called and waited till her daughter stuck her head around the corner. 'Do you know a boy named Ben Hudson?'

'The guy who's missing? Yeah. He was in the year below me. He left school last year.'

'You knew he was missing?'

'Yeah. Nate was at school interviewing kids who knew him yesterday.'

'How come you didn't tell me any of this?'

Belle shrugged. 'You didn't ask.'

'You didn't think to mention it when we did the whole, "Hi Belle, how was your day?" yesterday afternoon?'

'Well, if you'd said, "Hi Belle, how was your day? Do you know Ben Hudson?" I would have told you.'

Of course, how silly of me. 'I hope they find him. His parents must be beside themselves.'

'I heard he was having an affair with an older woman and her husband found out,' Belle said, walking past her mother to grab an apple from the bowl on the bench.

'An affair? Who with?'

'Dunno,' she said around a large bite. 'But maybe that's why he's missing. The husband killed him.'

Lucy stared at her daughter in mute horror.

'Of course someone else swears he's knocked up his girlfriend and done a runner to the city. Half his luck,' she muttered wistfully as she headed back into her room, leaving Lucy to ponder the article silently.

Lucy felt marginally relieved that the first rumour was more than likely unfounded. From previous experience, it was usually the least exciting rumour that proved to be the truth.

Her thoughts soon turned to Hugh. She still felt miserable about the way Hugh had left last night.

She wasn't sure what she'd expected Nate's warning about him to be, but it hadn't been that he was once in a bikie gang. Was she uneasy about it? Yes. From her limited amount of knowledge about bikie gangs, they seemed to be made up of pretty scary individuals who ended up in the headlines from time to time.

But Hugh didn't seem to be the kind of guy she'd associate with an outlaw motorcycle gang. Sure he had tattoos, but so did a lot of the population these days. It was clearly a very painful subject and one he'd been warning her he didn't want to talk about yet. The prison thing *did* bother her, though. She wished he'd stayed and answered her questions. The optimistic part of her said that going to prison may not have necessarily been as bad as it sounded. Maybe he'd been young and stupid, and the experience had been enough to wake him up and shock him into making changes to his life.

She just wished he'd stayed and explained it, instead of letting her stew about it and have doubts creep into her mind. Surely the truth wasn't as bad as she was imagining?

The police station was an old timber structure with a narrow verandah. It had a picket fence and looked pretty much the same now as it had in old photos from a hundred years ago. Lucy climbed the two steps and knocked loudly on the screen door. It was early for a Saturday morning, but she'd already been around the back to the separate police residence and Nate wasn't there, but his patrol car was, so she tried the station. She needed some answers and something told her Nate knew more about Hugh than he was letting on.

Movement sounded from somewhere inside, before the front door was opened and Nate's stern expression changed to wariness as he pushed open the flyscreen and ushered her inside. 'Everything all right, Luce?'

'I don't know, Nate. I'm hoping you can tell me. What was yesterday's warning really about? And what's really going on between you and Hugh?'

'There's nothing going on. I was concerned about you rushing into anything with a stranger.'

'Aren't you a little bit too young to be acting like my father?' Lucy said, folding her arms across her chest.

'I was being a friend and looking out for your best interests.'

'I appreciate that. But I'm a grown woman and I think I'm able to make my own decisions.'

'Fair enough.' Nate shifted his gaze and beckoned her to follow him out the back of the office to the small kitchen. He began spooning coffee granules into two mugs.

'He told me,' Lucy said, deciding to come out with it.

'Told you about *what*?' Nate asked slowly and Lucy noticed an instant change in his demeanour.

'That he was once in a motorbike gang and that he'd been in jail.'

'I see.' He took his time spooning in sugar before retrieving the milk from the fridge. 'And you still think this guy is trustworthy?'

'I think he made mistakes when he was young, just like everyone else.'

Nate finished stirring the coffee and handed her a mug. 'Do you know why he went to jail?'

By the way he leaned back against the bench and crossed his arms, Lucy got the impression that whatever Nate knew was not going to be good. 'No. I didn't ask.' Well, technically she'd been too surprised by his revelation to ask and then he'd left.

'The club he belonged to made their money dealing drugs.'

She stared at Nate, stricken by the information, shaking her head in denial. *Drugs?* It couldn't be true. He couldn't be the kind of person who made money from ruining other people's lives. It wasn't possible.

'I'm sorry, Luce, I really am, but I thought you should know.'

Her mind was reeling. 'It was a long time ago,' she blurted, desperate to try and justify it.

'It wasn't as long ago as you're thinking,' he told her softly.

A trickle of dread ran through her. 'How long?'

'A little over two years ago.'

It shouldn't change things, but somehow it did. She'd thought when he'd talked about mistakes in his past that he'd meant a lot longer than two years. It took a while to digest the news. 'Well, he's making a new life now. That counts for something,' she managed to get out between stiff lips.

Nate shrugged lightly, 'Maybe,' he said as he continued to face her across the kitchen. 'Actually, I'm surprised he told you.'

This was all so confusing. She was angry at Nate for going behind Hugh's back and uncovering all this stuff and then using it to drive a wedge between them; but, then again, if he hadn't told her about it, when would Hugh have brought it up?

'I appreciate your concern,' she said quietly, 'but you need to stay out of Hugh's business. This is between me and him.'

Nate didn't reply straight away but, after a long silence and holding her serious gaze, he gave a slight nod of his head and took a sip of his coffee.

Drugs had killed her sister, and someone had *sold* her those drugs and continued to supply her with them until she'd overdosed. Drug dealers had no conscience. They didn't care what happened after they got their money, how many lives they wrecked, how many people got hurt . . . and Hugh had been part of that world once. She wasn't sure how she felt about that.

Everyone had things in their past they weren't proud of; she didn't have to look too far to think of more than one thing she'd like to go back and change, but this wasn't just a few stupid mistakes. This was being involved in a world of drugs and money and violence. Could she really trust that someone could just walk away from that?

Eighteen

Hugh tossed the pen down on the desk and rubbed his hands over his face. He hadn't been able to sleep much and had been up since before sunrise, hoping he could distract himself by doing the book work all morning, but he kept seeing that look on Lucy's face after he'd told her about doing time. He hadn't meant to say it, but he was tired, stressed and, yes, he could admit it to himself, he was jealous. Every time Lucy mentioned Nate, it grated on his nerves. It wasn't helping that it was *Nate* causing all this trouble in the first place. If he'd just kept his nose out of it, everything would have been fine.

He tipped his head back in his chair and closed his eyes. Lucy had every right to demand an explanation after Dudley Do-Right had raised his concerns but, damn it, he'd wanted more time before he told her. Deep down he knew he wouldn't have told her at all if he thought he could possibly get away with it, but that wasn't likely. Eventually he knew he'd have to come clean with her about at least some of his past.

He'd read each expression as it crossed her face: confusion, shock and then disgust. That was the one which had hurt the most. It stung like hell coming from her. He'd blown it big time. Whatever they'd had was over now. There was no way she'd be coming back from that.

This was why you should never have got involved with her in the first place, a little voice reminded him. Which was all well and good, if he thought for one minute his brain had any say in the matter. What he knew he *should* do and what he *wanted* to do were two completely different things. Common sense told him that getting involved with Lucy was not smart. But she'd gotten under his skin, and that small part of him that had always craved a normal life had somehow managed to stage a coup, gagging his common sense and taking control. And, Christ, how he'd wanted a shot at a normal life.

He eyed the phone and considered calling her. She deserved an apology for his leaving the way he had, but when he reached for the phone he saw that look on her face again and picked up his pen instead. He needed to concentrate on his business before he lost that as well. The only thing sadder than a man losing his woman was a man losing his woman *and* his pub.

Sunday night was turning out to be even less exciting than Friday night had been. Belle was raking in a small fortune with her babysitting jobs, and Lucy felt guilty for wishing she were at home so she had someone to watch a movie with. Curled up on her lounge and trying to read a book in order to distract herself from thinking about Hugh, Lucy looked up at a soft knock on the front door. Her pulse leapt as she saw the familiar outline, and she forced a steady breath before opening the door.

'Hey,' Hugh said quietly. He was standing on the verandah, his thumbs hooked in the front pockets of his jeans, as he watched her warily.

'Hi.'

'Look,' he said with a long sigh, rubbing the back of his neck with one hand, 'I'm sorry about the other night. I shouldn't have dumped everything on you like that.'

'I guess I asked for it.'

'No, you didn't. At least, not like that. Can I come in? I'd like a chance to explain.'

Lucy stepped aside, allowing Hugh to walk past. Her breath caught as his hand brushed her fingers, clasping them gently, before letting go to walk ahead while she shut the door behind them.

He waited until she took a seat on the lounge, before sitting across from her, their knees almost touching as he leaned forward. 'I gotta be honest, I wasn't planning on telling you about all that, at least not anytime soon.'

'I can see why you'd not want to tell anyone about being in jail—you'd be worried about people thinking differently about you.'

He shrugged. 'Other people, not so much, but I was worried about you . . . and what you'd think.'

Lucy looked down at her hands, fisted on her lap, and made a conscious effort to relax them.

'And I was right, wasn't I?' he said wearily. 'It has changed the way you feel.'

She could only wish it changed the way she felt about him—unfortunately, no matter how confused her thoughts were, her body didn't seem to care. That's what worried her the most. No matter what he'd done, she was still attracted to him. She looked up and saw genuine regret in his eyes. 'I went to see Nate.'

His gaze hardened, but there was a shadow of uncertainty in his expression.

'He told me why you went to prison.'

He managed to hold her gaze steadily, but she could see that his jaw was tightly clenched, as though he was holding himself in check.

'My sister died of an overdose when she was eighteen. Did you know that?'

Hugh shook his head. 'No. I didn't know. I'm sorry.'

'Really? Because drug dealers weren't too sorry when they sold her the stuff that killed her. All they cared about was taking her money.'

'Luce—'

'I know Claire's death had nothing to do with you, and I'm not saying Claire wasn't responsible for her addiction, but I lost my sister to drugs, and I cannot wrap my head around the fact that there are people out there making a living off other people's suffering. Drugs *ended* my sister's life. It almost killed my parents to lose their daughter, and it tore our family apart, and now I find out that the man I—' She stopped short of totally humiliating herself, but she didn't miss his sharp glance—'Someone I trusted was sent to prison for the very thing that took my sister's life.'

'I can't excuse what I did in the past,' he said, taking her hands in his. 'But I can tell you I've left that part of my life behind. There were things going on . . . stuff I can't explain right now,' he said, finally looking at her, and she saw a shadow of something very much like vulnerability lurking in his eyes.

'What do you mean, stuff you can't explain?'

'It's complicated.'

Lucy bit back a sarcastic snort. He'd been to prison and there was *more?* Complicated didn't even begin to explain what this was turning into.

'I guess what I'm asking is whether you can give me some time . . . You have every right to wash your hands of me now, considering everything you went through with your sister, but there's some stuff I can't deal with right now. I will in time, but I just can't bring it all up just yet.'

Part of her felt slightly offended that he couldn't confide in her, but the rational side understood that, given Nate had forced Hugh's hand, he had a right to some privacy. Their relationship, whatever it may be, *was* only new. Not many couples delved into the darkest places of their past in the first few heady weeks together. 'Will whatever it is affect us in some way?'

Hugh shook his head. 'I swear, it has nothing to do with us. Look, I never meant to get involved with anyone because I knew all this would get in the way,' he admitted, 'but you snuck up on me, Luce. If I've stuffed this thing up between us, I'm really sorry.'

What could she say to that? She hated being apart from him—despite discovering what he'd done in the past. The feelings she had for him were still there, albeit mixed with a hefty dose of confusion and a little bit of trepidation.

'It's just been a bit of a shock,' she hedged, weakening at the understanding look on his face. 'I don't want this to ruin what we have either . . . but I also don't want secrets between us.' She saw the hopeful glint in his eye return before adding, 'I can give you time, if you don't think this thing will affect *us*, but I want to know *everything* one day.'

Hugh searched her gaze for a few moments and she saw his shoulders lose some of their tension. He leaned towards her slowly and touched her lips in a gentle, probing kiss that told her without words that he was grateful she hadn't pushed him tonight.

Much later, after Hugh had gone back to the pub, needing to lock up for the night, she pondered their conversation. She wasn't some kind of saint for not pushing him about his past; she was a coward. Deep down she feared that what he'd tell her might force her to end it with him—despite the fact he'd said it wouldn't affect them. She wasn't ready to walk away from Hugh, and she was ashamed that she might be willing to live with something that she wasn't brave enough to face just so she could have him.

It had been a strained few days at the start of the week. Hugh had seemed to be giving her space but, after the first day or so she hadn't needed space, she'd needed him. So she'd walked into the office one afternoon, locked the door and given him a pretty clear sign that she wanted things to get back to the way they had been.

He'd got the message.

Lucy woke up after a much needed afternoon nap, finding herself all alone in Hugh's bed. Outside it was a grey and drizzly Sunday. She'd come into the pub to spend the day with Hugh so he could still be on hand if needed. Thankfully, things had been relatively quiet and Hugh had snuck her out the back to his living quarters for a private lunch—not that there had been much eating going on. She hadn't realised just how exhausting having a love life could be. She stretched and smiled as she turned her head on the pillow that smelled like Hugh.

She lay awake listening to the rain for a while before acknowledging that she should get home. With a reluctant sigh, she got out of bed and pulled on her clothes before pulling up the sheets and making the bed. It went against the grain to leave the bed unmade, even though she had to admit part of her was a little bit impressed by the rumpled sheets. There was something just a little bit naughty about toe-curling sex in the middle of the day. As she tucked the turned-back sheet under the mattress, her hand brushed something cold and she bent down lower to see what it was.

For a moment her hand tingled and she felt a little light-headed as she stared at the gun. A wave of fear washed over her as she looked down at the cold, black steel and felt its weight in her hand.

The creak of the floorboard sent her alarmed gaze to the doorway just as Hugh entered the room. She saw him freeze, his gaze immediately fixed on the weapon. For a moment neither of them moved, but slowly Hugh's gaze moved from the gun to her face, his expression almost blank as he waited for her to speak.

'I . . . was making the bed,' she managed to push through numb lips. He didn't move, or speak, he just continued to watch her silently. Lucy took a big breath and grabbed blindly for her senses. 'Why do you have a gun under your mattress?'

'Habit,' he said far too calmly for her liking.

'It's a habit to keep a weapon under your bed? Where the hell were you living? Guatemala?'

He shrugged. 'Different time, different life,' he said, crossing the room and gently taking the firearm from her, then placing it on the bedside table before walking across to stare out the bedroom window.

For a long moment Lucy stared at his back, unsure what to say. Normal people didn't sleep with a gun under their mattress. 'Is this another one of those things we don't talk about?'

'You don't have anything to worry about,' he said, turning back to face her. 'It's not what you're thinking.'

'I'm glad you know what I'm thinking, because I seriously have no idea where to start.'

'I don't even know why I still have it. I guess I've never really known what to do with it, so it's easier to keep it.' He crossed back to her side and took her hands in his, his gaze locking on to hers intently. 'I swear you have nothing to be scared of. I guess I'm just asking you to trust me on this.'

Lucy wasn't sure how to respond. The man had a gun under his bed.

'I should get home to Belle,' she said, hoping her voice sounded more composed than she felt.

'Luce,' he said as she reached the door. 'I promise I'll tell you everything. Just . . . not yet. Okay?'

She'd already agreed to let him have time. Of course, she hadn't known then that it would involve guns under beds, but the truth was that she wasn't sure she really wanted to know any more.

Much later that night, Hugh sat alone in the dark pub, a glass of whisky in his hand. Around him the old building creaked and cracked, the tin roof groaning after a long hot day. The sounds kept him company while he fought the urge to go back to Lucy's for the night. So far they'd only spent the entire night together a few times, when Belle had

had a sleepover with a friend; they'd never slept together while Belle was home. Tonight, though, the need to go to her nagged at him. The past few weeks he'd come to realise Lucy was the missing part of his life. He wasn't stupid enough to think it was going to be like some fairy tale, with a happy-ever-after ending. There were big issues with a relationship like theirs. It wasn't just Lucy and himself who had to be taken into consideration; there was also Belle. He would become an instant dad to a teenage daughter, and that came with a whole bunch of responsibilities he wasn't sure he was ready to handle. *Would you knock it off. Why would you even be thinking that far ahead?* He frowned at the thought; he had no idea why he was thinking long-term. His life before coming here had *never* involved thinking long-term. Ever. Nothing had been permanent.

He tossed back the contents of his glass in one long swallow and let the whisky burn its way down his throat, then reached for the bottle to splash in another measure. He stopped himself. He wasn't going there tonight. He tried never to go back to those dark times, but occasionally they'd sneak in. Those days were part of some other guy's life: a stranger, someone who died in the ashes and re-emerged clean and ready for a fresh start.

Then he remembered the promise he'd made to Lucy and the expression on her face when she'd found the Glock under his bed. If he was smart he'd end it with her right now, but lately he wasn't being all that smart. Lucy offered him the possibility of a normal life. It was close enough to touch, and he couldn't bring himself to turn away from the promise she offered.

Hugh knocked on the rear door of the police station's private residence and listened to the sound of approaching footsteps.

He noticed the grim expression on the cop's face when he opened the door, and figured it probably matched the one he was wearing. It was pretty obvious to both of them that this was not a social call.

'Can I help you?' Nate asked with strained politeness.

'I doubt it, but you're doing your best to get me killed and I'd appreciate if you'd knock it off.'

'What are you talking about?' said Nate.

'I need you to stop making enquiries about me.'

'Well, that's interesting. How would me making some enquiries through some pretty quiet avenues get back to you?'

Hugh concentrated on not gritting his teeth. He'd thought long and hard about what to do but he knew he had little choice. He couldn't afford to have Nate nosing around in his affairs any longer. He resented the fact that he had no option but to reveal part of his past he'd much rather erase from his memory.

'Once upon a time I used to be on the job. Okay?'

Nate didn't react in any obvious way, but Hugh could tell the news threw him slightly.

'You're telling me you used to be a cop?' There was a hint of scepticism, but also a note of caution, as though he wasn't entirely sure whether Hugh was joking.

'I was UC working drugs and gangs.'

'Undercover?' The cop drilled him with a hard look, obviously wondering whether or not to believe him, but after a moment he slowly nodded. 'That's why I had trouble turning up anything. I knew there was something off about you.'

'Congratulations,' Hugh said. 'Now back the hell off.'

'But that doesn't clear you of any possible involvement in what's going on around here.'

'Are you shitting me?'

'Ex undercover nark involved in a biker gang . . . Drugs turning up in town around the same time you arrive here. If anything, you just made yourself a bigger suspect. You've got more ties and connections to the underworld than anyone else around here.'

'Connections that could get me killed,' Hugh snapped.

'So you left the force and you bought a pub that would have cost you an arm and a leg to renovate. It's not unreasonable to wonder if you hadn't obtained some of the cash in illegal ways.'

'Then maybe you need to give my bank manager a call and let him tell you just how much "cash" the bank invested in my pub?'

'So maybe you need money to pay the bank back?'

Hugh swore savagely. 'You have no idea what you're messing with here. Knock off this backyard detective crap and stay out of my business. Got it?'

Nate leaned against the door frame and folded his arms across his chest thoughtfully. 'I'll keep that in mind.'

Hugh clenched his jaw and remained calm even as he itched to deck the guy. 'You do that. Now if you'll excuse me, I have personal business to take care of with a certain hot brunette with a killer body.'

His lips twitched as his comment hit its mark. He pushed aside the fact he felt like a jerk scoring points against the guy at Lucy's expense, but Nate was backing him into a corner and ignoring all the warning signs Hugh was giving him.

This was bigger than anyone could possibly get their head around and it was Hugh's life the cop was gambling with.

Lucy pushed through the kitchen doors, bringing in dirty dishes from the two early morning departures who had spent the night at the pub. She was still smiling at the husband and wife duo, feeling somewhat envious of their retirement trip around Australia—by bike. She'd only had a handful of rides on Hugh's bike, but somehow she didn't think his sleek sporty motorcycle would be all that comfortable to travel far on—at least her backside didn't think so. Being a biker's moll wasn't anywhere near as glamorous as she'd imagined—helmet hair was a serious issue, for one. No, she was happy to leave the biker side of things to Hugh—he at least looked sexy in leather and a helmet.

Lucy saw that Terry was chopping herbs as she headed for the sink to set down the tray of breakfast dishes. While the men still wouldn't make small talk with her at work, they were at least able to look at her without blushing nowadays. For that small mercy she was grateful.

Terry's attention was on the radio, which was broadcasting the hourly news. 'Did you hear that?' he asked.

'Hear what?'

'They found that kid.'

'Oh good. His parents must have been beside themselves,' Lucy said, but stopped when she saw the man's expression.

'They found his *body*,' he elaborated.

'Oh no.' Lucy stared at the cook in dismay.

'They're not saying much but it looks like a drug overdose—drug related, anyhow.'

'What on earth is going on?' This didn't happen in their town. At least, not like this. Her sister had run away to the city and become hooked on drugs there, and in Lucy's mind it had always seemed to be a big city problem, not something that happened in Bundah.

For the rest of the morning, Ben Hudson's name was on everyone's lips. Small huddles of people gathered outside shops in the main street, beside cars in the supermarket car park and at tables in the pub, all asking the same question: what the hell was happening to their town?

Theories varied, but one thing was becoming very clear—the arrival of newcomers to town at the same time as drug-related incidences increased was too much of a coincidence for most locals.

As Lucy stacked the dirty dishes a loud commotion broke out from outside in the main bar, followed moments later by Hugh's voice raised loud enough to hear. 'Don't bother coming back.'

Lucy exchanged a curious glance with Terry before heading out of the kitchen to investigate. She almost collided with Hugh as he stormed past her in the hallway, and she followed him into the office.

'What's going on? What happened?'

'The whole town's going nuts,' he grumbled, opening and closing the desk draws.

'What do you mean?'

'I just had two locals turn on a couple of my guests and randomly accuse them of being drug pushers.'

'What? Why?'

'Because apparently they *didn't like the look of them*,' Hugh growled, moving papers from the desk irritably. 'They're lucky I didn't knock them on their arses like I was tempted to do.'

'What are you looking for?'

'My keys. I need to go for a ride before I do something I regret.'

'You need to calm down.'

'I am calm. Trust me, this is calm. Do you have any idea how much harm those two idiots have done to my business? They've abused paying customers—customers I've fought hard to get here, and who can turn off God knows how many potential future customers with just one bad review.'

'I think you're overreacting a bit.'

'Overreacting!'

'Okay, maybe not without good cause,' she hastened to add, 'but we can fix it. We'll just speak to the customers, offer them a free night's accommodation—or a voucher for their meals and drinks. I'm sure if we explain what's been going on around town they'll understand.'

'Right. I'm sure they'll be completely understanding about a town full of rednecks who like to abuse tourists because the towns got a drug problem and kids are being murdered. Yeah, good luck with that.'

Lucy frowned. 'Well, maybe not put quite like that,' she snapped.

'I'll be back in a while,' he said, locating his keys and snatching them up. Hugh moved to take a step, but stopped, turning to swoop down and kiss her briefly. 'Sorry.'

Lucy gave an impatient sigh as she watched him walk out the door. Clearly this was how he dealt with frustration. His kiss hadn't been gentle or passionate, but it had been a message of sorts: his problem wasn't with her, he just needed time alone. She could respect that but clearly something else was bothering Hugh for him to fly off the handle like that. Maybe a ride would help improve his mood. At the very least it would stop any more patrons being thrown out this morning.

Mavis bustled into the bar late one afternoon and handed Lucy a stack of flyers. 'We've arranged a town meeting. People are getting sick of the way things are heading. It's time someone did something. We need answers.'

Lucy took the flyers and saw that they were advertising a meeting to take place at the high school in two days' time.

'I expect you'll be attending, Lucy. You must have concerns, with a teenage daughter and all.'

Lucy looked up from the flyer and gave the older woman a tight smile. 'I'm concerned for everyone in town.'

'Good. Well, make sure you hand those out. If we want something done about the more—' she gave the patrons in the bar a quick, unimpressed glance—'undesirable aspects of the place, then we need to make our concerns heard.'

Lucy followed Mavis's gaze and saw only paying guests. 'Surely you're not referring to the clientele here as undesirable?'

Mavis gave a delicate sniff, and busied herself gathering her remaining flyers to deliver. 'I was never a fan of these . . . bike enthusiast types.'

'They're spending money in our town. If it wasn't for Hugh opening this place, they'd never have come up here,' Lucy said, lowering her voice so as not to be overheard. The last thing Hugh needed after this morning's events was for any more guests to be offended.

'Just make sure you hand out those flyers,' Mavis reminded her firmly, before turning away.

Oh, she'd make sure she handed out the flyers all right, but it wouldn't be to support this small-minded paranoia. The youth and drug issue was something that needed to be looked at, and *that* was what she would be advocating.

The high school hall was packed, bringing home just how worried the community really was.

Ken chaired the meeting up on stage and Lucy tried to put aside her personal feelings towards the man. She might not like him but she had to give him credit for pulling together this meeting so quickly. The town was like a powder keg at the moment and people needed a chance to air their concerns. Nate and the local area command were represented, as well as Nicole's husband, Jackson, who was there to speak as the local doctor, and, as he worked in the hospital at Armidale, he would also be able to give a point of view from the front lines, so to speak.

Ken started the meeting by calling upon Jackson, who stood to give a rather harrowing report of the number of drug-related cases both the surgery and the nearby hospital had attended in the past few months—the numbers had increased alarmingly in recent months.

'These are not drugs used and made in a quality controlled lab intended for medical use. These are drugs manufactured by people who may not even have any kind of laboratory experience. We're finding a cocktail of poisonous chemicals in these tablets such as acetone, found in nail polish remover and paint thinners, antifreeze, lithium from batteries, hydrochloric acid, drain cleaner, lighter fluid, sulfuric acid and ammonia.'

Undertones of fear, anger and disgust flowed through the auditorium following Jackson's departure from the microphone.

The local area commander, Inspector Wallace, also gave a report on where they were with drug-related crime in the area, stating that crime was up at least fifty per cent on the previous year's figures and steadily growing.

'Is it true the kid they found today was tied up in this whole drug business?' a voice from the rear of the hall called out.

Ken leaned forward to answer the question but the Inspector quickly reached for the microphone. 'We are unable to speculate at this point. Police are still undertaking investigations.'

'I heard he was found with drugs in the car,' a woman called out.

'Again,' the Inspector said in a calm yet authoritative voice, 'we're still investigating the matter. No comment will be made until we have all the evidence and have a chance to look at it closely.'

'What we *can* say,' Nate added, accepting the microphone, 'is that we are not taking these spikes in statistics, both criminal and health related, lightly. We've increased surveillance and we're working hard with various agencies to find and dismantle the source of this drug problem. We *will* find out where these drugs are coming from and we *will* put a stop to them. Any information anyone has, no matter how trivial it may seem, should be directed to the police. We need people to be extra vigilant and report anything suspicious or out of place immediately. What we *don't* need, though, is widespread panic or rumours being spread. At this stage we have no suspects locally and individual persons should not be targeted. The recent spate of vandalism to local businesses will not be tolerated and anyone found harassing other community members will be dealt with by the full force of the law.'

'Well, are you at least looking in to some of these newcomers?' Margery Whitmore asked from the middle of the crowd. 'None of this stuff was happening before we got flooded with city people.'

'We are looking at all avenues,' the Inspector said.

'Common sense suggests the timing's no coincidence. It has to be someone new to the area.'

A chorus of agreement sounded from various parts of the hall and Lucy frowned as she looked around at some of the more vocal protesters. Beside her, Hugh sat in stony silence. On the other side of her, Steven and Russell were whispering nervously together.

'I knew this was a bad idea,' someone else said loudly from the back of the hall. 'I knew it was only a matter of time before they tried to bring their big city ideas to our town. Have you tried to get a park in the main street recently? You can't. Some days you have to circle round the flamin' block.'

'Yeah! I almost got run over by a crazed biker the other day, crossing the street. I don't feel safe in my own town any more,' another voice called out.

'Those bikes are dangerous, and they take up perfectly good car parks.'

'I had one guy swear at me only yesterday because I asked him to move his bike so I could park my car,' Joyce Warmsley said with a cluck of irritation.

Lucy closed her eyes briefly in resignation. Why did meetings always come to this?

Hugh leaned towards her slightly. 'Is this for real?' he asked quietly.

'I think we're getting sidetracked from the issue,' the Inspector cut in eventually.

'We never had a drug problem in this town until all these new businesses opened up,' Mavis said from the front row.

'That's ridiculous,' Nicole said, standing up crossly. 'Come on, Mavis, you know as well as I do there have always been drugs in this town—admittedly not the kind that we're dealing with now, but let's not sit here on our high horses. Do I need to remind you about the time the CWA sold hash brownies at the local show?'

A few muffled chuckles erupted about the room, as well as the odd horrified gasp.

Mavis spluttered rather indignantly before protesting, 'Someone tampered with the recipe, and to this day I suspect you and Lucy Parker were behind it!'

Nicole ignored her outburst, and continued, 'Every town has its share of kids experimenting with drugs of some kind. Thankfully here, up until now, it's been relatively mild, but all this pointing fingers at the newcomers is totally ridiculous. What's happening to our town? We used to stick together. We certainly didn't go around vandalising buildings and sending threats. It's time to start working together. We all want to find out who's responsible for what's been happening, but turning on each other is not the way to do it.'

A round of applause followed as Nicole sat down and Ken stood up, waving down the murmur of conversation to bring some form of order back to the meeting.

'Well, it seems we've covered as much as we're going to be able to cover for now. We'll wait until the police have finished their investigations concerning the young Hudson lad, and possibly arrange for another meeting to get an update on any new information,' Ken suggested and looked to the Inspector for confirmation before thanking everyone for their attendance and ending the meeting.

The hall buzzed loudly with a multitude of mini conversations. Lucy and Hugh stood up and made their way towards Nicole as she waved them over.

'Hash brownies?' Hugh asked, eyeing Nicole and Lucy sceptically.

'Pure speculation that we had anything to do with it,' Nicole shrugged. 'No one can prove a thing.'

'Did you have to bring that up in front of the whole town?' Lucy muttered.

'She needed putting in her place,' Nicole said.

'She only recently stopped talking about it after *how many years*?' Lucy groaned.

'She'll get over it.'

'I worry about your wife sometimes, Jackson,' Lucy said.

'You and me both,' he said, wrapping an arm around Nicole's shoulder and pulling her close to his side.

'You both know life without me around would be incredibly boring,' Nicole told them haughtily.

'Come on, time I got you back home,' Jackson said, taking his wife's hand and waving goodbye.

'So you weren't kidding when you said you were a bit of a rebel as a teenager,' Hugh said, breaking the silence in the car on their way home.

'Being a teen mum didn't give you a clue?' she asked, looking out her window at the quiet streets. It was hard to believe this peaceful town had evil lurking in the shadows.

'Not necessarily, no.'

'It's not something I'm exactly proud of,' she said after a while.

'We've all got things in the past we're not proud of,' he said quietly.

There was no point answering; they both knew that his past still hung between them like some huge, unspoken elephant in the room.

'I wouldn't say I was a rebel,' she added. 'But for a while . . . after Claire died, I was a bit of a handful. That's when I met Mick.'

'It would have been a hard thing to deal with, especially as a teenager.'

'I guess,' Lucy shrugged, keeping her gaze fixed out the front window. 'I had too much freedom while my parents were grieving. It wasn't their fault, they were doing their best to cope with losing a child. It wasn't as though they ignored me or forgot about me, but I definitely took advantage of their preoccupation. I did a lot of sneaking out at night and lying about where I was. Which is why I keep Belle away from the things I did as a kid.'

'You can't protect her from everything. Sooner or later she's going to make mistakes.'

'I know,' Lucy said quietly. 'But while I can, I'll do whatever it takes to protect her from whatever I can. That's my job. I'm her mother.'

The house was empty after she listened to Hugh's ute drive away. There was a strain around their relationship that hadn't been there before, an uneasy feeling that hovered between them. Something seemed to be brewing, a storm was coming, and she had no idea what it was going to bring.

Hugh sat with his legs stretched out in front of him and stared at the two men across from him. Nate had introduced his colleague as Inspector Wallace, and the man was leaning back in his chair with his arms folded across his chest as he watched Hugh with a narrowed stare.

'So tell me, what have you been doing in the time between leaving the force and coming here?' Wallace asked.

'I travelled around a bit.'

'And then came here and bought a hotel?'

'That's right.'

'Sounds like quite a substantial purchase.'

'I got it for a bargain,' Hugh shrugged.

'Have you had any contact with Leon Basio?' he asked unexpectedly.

Hugh's eyes narrowed, but he kept his voice even. 'Nope.'

'Any other members of the Rabble Motorcycle Club?'

'No. Is that all? Because I have a business to run.'

'Where would a guy like you get the money to own a place like that?'

'I'm pretty sure that's none of your damn business.'

'Well, that's a matter of opinion, isn't it? I mean, if for instance any proceeds of crime had been used in the purchase, then that would very much make it my business.'

'You want to know about my finances you better make damn sure you get a warrant. Until then, you can both get stuffed.'

'I know about you, Thompson,' Wallace snarled, leaning forward. He pushed a photocopy of a newspaper article across the desk and Hugh felt his gut churn as he caught a glimpse of the headline. **Bikie Massacre During Bungled Drug Bust.**

Hugh turned his eyes away from the paper and glared at the man across the desk. 'I was acquitted of any wrongdoing, so you can take the rest of your questions and shove them up your arse. I have better things to do than sit around here. The two of you need to get out there and do some real police work instead of wasting time with this shit.'

'I don't care if you were acquitted, there's a stink around you and, if I find any connection between you and Basio, I'll be down on you like a ton of bloody bricks.'

Hugh pushed past a younger constable sitting in the main office, slamming the screen door behind him. Today Bundah station was like cop central.

Nineteen

The next morning when Lucy arrived at work she was surprised to discover Hugh was nowhere to be found. Jason couldn't shed any light on his absence, telling her that as soon as he'd arrived at work Hugh had asked him to finish opening up and then left.

It wasn't like Hugh not to let someone know where he was. The mood had been rather subdued after they'd arrived home from the meeting. Hugh hadn't stayed long, and Lucy had been secretly glad she could fall into bed and go to sleep, but she'd been looking forward to seeing him this morning. They'd fallen into a routine of spending a few minutes alone in his private quarters, having a coffee and stealing a few precious moments together before they started the working day.

It was close to ten when he finally made an appearance.

'Did you have an appointment or something I didn't remember? Where have you been?' she asked.

Hugh glanced at her as he entered the office, and she gathered from his tight expression and grim set of his mouth that he was not in a good mood.

'At the police station.'

'Why?' she asked somewhat cautiously.

'It seems Nate and his inspector buddy were serious when they said they were leaving no stone unturned last night. Apparently I made their suspect list.'

'I'm sure they were only doing it to rule you out.'

'If it hadn't been for Nate nosing around in my business, they'd never have known about it in the first place. Thanks to him, I became a suspect.'

'Well, you can't expect them *not* to interview you. If anyone found out you'd been . . . well, you know.' She faltered slightly as he held her gaze expectantly. 'They'd be asking why you weren't questioned. If you have nothing to hide, then you don't have anything to worry about, do you?'

'*If* I have nothing to hide?' he asked.

'You know what I mean,' she sighed.

'I'm not sure I do.'

'Why are you angry at me?'

'Maybe I expected you to be a little more outraged that your mate, the copper, suspected me of being a drug dealer,' he snapped.

'He's just doing his job, Hugh. You can't blame him for that.'

'I don't believe this,' he said, shaking his head in exasperation. 'The whole town has gone crazy. Everyone's paranoid over these damn drugs.'

'With good reason. Two teens dead in the space of a few weeks? That's not right.'

'Two deaths doesn't warrant a drug epidemic.'

'*One* death is too many. Maybe where you're from, you're used to it, but there's no way people here are going to stand by and just let it become normal.'

'Overreacting and turning into redneck vigilantes sure as hell isn't the way to solve it either.'

'I don't agree with the way some people are acting, but something needs to be done. It *is* an odd coincidence that drugs have suddenly become a problem here. If it's someone new in town bringing them in, then it needs to be stopped.'

'So you think it's one of us non-local types too?'

'I can't rule out the fact that we didn't have a problem to this extent before,' she said with a shrug.

'You know you're beginning to sound a lot like Mavis and Ken right now, don't you?'

'I'm simply saying that they have a point.'

'So everyone new to town is a suspect in your opinion? Even me?'

'It's just an avenue that needs looking into,' she said, dropping his unsmiling gaze.

'That didn't exactly answer my question.'

'No, I don't actually believe you are a suspect.'

Lucy saw him go very still for a moment before he leaned back in his chair and watched her closely. She'd seen Hugh in many moods—arrogant, angry, composed—the way he was now, however, sent a flicker of alarm through her. His whole demeanour had changed, turning him cold—untouchable.

'I'm not buying it. You think there's a chance I *could* be behind this, don't you?'

'Don't be ridiculous,' she snapped, ignoring the image of a gun under his bed.

'You don't want to believe it, but it's still lurking there, isn't it?'

And that was the kicker. Maybe somewhere deep down she felt bad because the thought *had* crossed her mind. But that was before. Before she'd caught a glimpse of the vulnerability that was hidden deep within him, before she'd laid her head on his chest and listened to his heartbeat against her ear, before she'd gone and fallen for him. Her face, though, must have given away some of her confusion because she immediately saw his expression switch from disbelief to something very much like resignation.

'I know that you aren't involved, Hugh,' she said, reaching for his arm. She watched as he slowly stood and her hand dropped away.

'But there was a moment when you weren't entirely sure, wasn't there?'

Lucy shook her head, frustrated, unable to form the right words to save the situation. How had things gone so wrong so quickly? 'You can't blame anyone for the thought crossing their mind.'

'I came here to start over, but instead I'm being judged for what I did in the past.'

'You made bad choices in your past, that's fine, but, you know what, you have to own those mistakes and realise that part of that is accepting the fact that occasionally people are going to remember what you did.'

'Apparently it's too much to ask for a little privacy.'

'You're part of a small community now. Privacy is a thing of the past,' she told him.

'I could ignore everyone else thinking the worst of me. It's the fact you even considered it that hurts the most.'

'That's not fair! You know I don't believe that you're involved in any way.'

Hugh just shook his head. 'We were kidding ourselves if we thought this relationship was ever going to go anywhere. I knew when you found out about my past, it would change things. Maybe Nate did us a favour.'

His words stung.

'Come on, Luce. Could you honestly see yourself settling down with a guy like me? And, more to the point, do I look like the kind of bloke who'd be able to play house with a wife and kid?'

If Lucy hadn't been so hurt by his cold tone she might have been able to see that he was hurting as much as she was and lashing out because he felt betrayed . . . But she wasn't in a calm enough state to be thinking that logically.

'I don't recall saying I was ever planning on you being a permanent fixture,' she said, impressed that her voice had come out sounding as normal as it did, considering inside she was a broken, miserable mess. She ignored the flash of emotion crossing his face. 'Now, if you're done? I've got work to do.'

Once the door shut behind Hugh, Lucy sank into her chair and covered her face with her hands, muffling the sobs which finally broke free. She was shocked at how callous he had been. Yes, he could be annoying and arrogant, but not the cold, unfeeling bastard she'd just witnessed.

Closing her eyes she said goodbye to the fading image of Hugh, Belle and herself standing arm in arm smiling in front of her little cottage. Damn him for being able to read her every emotion like a book, and damn her for not skipping ahead to see what was coming.

Hugh swore as he shoved his helmet on his head and pulled on his gloves. Where the hell had that all come from? One minute he was daydreaming about the night before, and the next he was slipping back into a persona he thought he'd buried once and for all. It scared him how easily he could become that person again. He felt the cold chill of the past creeping up his back and suppressed the urge to shiver. He was *never* going back there.

He swung his leg over his bike and left the pub and the town far behind. He needed to get away. He didn't trust himself around Lucy right now. She was the one person he'd allowed himself to care about in far too many years, and now he'd gone and hurt her very badly. He swore long and hard once more before kicking the bike up a gear and aiming towards the horizon.

Lucy forced herself to work a solid two hours before she picked up her handbag and left the office, getting into her ute to drive around aimlessly. She had no idea where she was going, she just knew she had to get away. She'd tried to concentrate on work, but it was impossible. She headed out of town, turning off after a few kilometres down a road which eventually ran out of bitumen and turned to dirt. The paddocks of cattle and sheep passed by her window unnoticed. It wasn't until she pulled up on the side of the road that she realised where she'd been heading. Stringybark. The faded old sign hung a bit lopsided on the front gate, worn by weather and rust.

How long since she'd been out here? It had to be at least five years, maybe more. There was no reason to come here any more. She leased it to an old school friend, Ross, who had been running his cattle and sheep on it for the past ten years or so. She'd always had a soft spot for Ross. He'd been a bit of a loner during school, always seeming to be on the outside looking in, and she'd tried to include him whenever possible. It went against the grain to turn her back on someone who seemed lonely. But then she'd been swept off her feet by Mick, who was a whole two years older than her, and she and Ross hadn't spent much time together any more. When Ross fell on hard times and his family lost their property, it seemed the perfect solution to let him start his own venture on Stringybark. It was the perfect arrangement, and it had gone along without a hitch for almost a decade.

She had no idea why she'd come here: maybe it was just the furthest place from town she knew; maybe because she just needed to hear the sound of birds and cattle for a few minutes to clear her jumbled head.

Lucy got out of the car and unhooked the chain on the gate, driving the ute through and closing the gate behind her. She supposed as the landlord she was obliged to give some kind of notice before she came out here, but theirs was a private deal, and she was sure, considering she pretty much left Ross to his own devices all these years, he wouldn't object to her stopping by to see the old house again. It wasn't as though she was planning on going in, she just wanted to see it.

She slowed down as she neared the house at the end of the dirt driveway, and parked. She heard the dogs before she saw them, and when she saw the two massive Dobermans that came running to the front gate snarling, she was glad she hadn't already let herself into the yard. She checked her phone to make sure she had reception on the off-chance she was mauled half to death and needed to call for help. Then she slipped her phone back into her pocket and, eyeing the animals warily, got slowly out of the car.

The house was in desperate need of some TLC. Lucy took in the peeling white curls of paint on the walls and roof and felt bad for neglecting the old place for so long. Although clearly the sad state of the house didn't bother Ross too much, or he would have contacted her. The yard had never been wonderful, but it had at least been mowed while she'd lived there. Obviously lawn care was not high on Ross's list of priorities either, judging by the length of the grass inside the front yard. Maybe leaving the place to a bachelor was a bit of a mistake; it desperately needed a woman's touch again. Not that being a bachelor's house was anything new for this place. For a long time, Mick and his father had lived here without a woman, until she arrived on the scene.

Her years here with Mick and Fred hadn't been happy; in fact, they had been some of the worst times of her life, and yet somehow she still had a soft spot for this old place.

When she'd discovered she was pregnant, Lucy had moved in with Mick, following a rebellious fight with her parents. At first his father, Fred, had treated her as though she wasn't there, ignoring her for the most part. It had been lonely for Lucy considering she was pretty much trapped there, with only her L plates and no driver's licence to head into town whenever she wanted company. She'd started making herself useful more out of boredom than any real desire to become domesticated. The Monroe men had not been big believers in housework. Mrs Monroe had cleared off years ago and was never spoken about again. Mick had shrugged it off, seemingly unaffected by his mother's abandonment. Looking back, though, Lucy realised that had she been a little older and wiser, she'd have recognised that he was simply hiding his feelings. *Fred Monroe didn't raise no girls.* It was a common phrase she often overheard during Fred and Mick's frequent rows.

After a while, Lucy realised the only way to get on with Fred was to stop cowering whenever he spoke harshly and give back as good as he gave. One day when he was cursing about her incessant cleaning and poking her nose in his business, she turned on him furiously. 'Well, if you and your son didn't live like pigs, I wouldn't have to be such a cleaning Nazi!'

Her raised voice surprised them both, and Fred stopped giving her grief when she vacuumed. After that day, while Fred didn't exactly warm to her, he at least seemed to accept her being there and they formed a strange kind of understanding. As her pregnancy progressed, they settled into a routine of having breakfast together in the mornings, and then he'd bring out a cup of tea and they'd sit on the verandah while he read one of the many magazines he ordered by mail. Reading was the only interest he seemed to have; he read about everything from science to war, and his favourite magazine was *National Geographic*.

Mick spent long days working on the property, only returning late in the afternoon to shower and then head into town to the pub or to a mate's place. The fairytale romance she'd been holding on to as a naive seventeen year old soon turned sour. A wife and kid had not been something Mick had been planning on, and he let her know about it on a regular basis.

'It wasn't something I planned on either,' she yelled back at him one night when he'd stumbled in drunk after a big night at the pub.

'Then get rid of it!'

'That's your answer for everything, isn't it, Mick? If it's too much trouble, just get rid of it. If it doesn't fit in with your plans, just get rid of it.'

'Then why the hell are you still here?'

His scathing reply sliced her already battered heart in two, but she fought to remain calm. She was not going to give him the satisfaction of seeing how much she cared for him. 'I'm trying to make this work, Mick. This is our baby. Don't you see we have to at least try?'

'No. I don't. I just want it to all go away. You too.'

Until that point, she'd honestly believed he'd calm down after a few months of blowing off steam and accept that they would be a family. The look in his eye now ended that possibility. He didn't love her, he probably never really had.

'She ain't goin' anywhere, boy. I may have raised a moron, but I didn't raise a coward. You knocked her up, you live with the consequences. Grow up and be a man. For once in your life, finish somethin',' Fred snarled from the doorway.

In his own way, Fred had been sticking up for her; at the time, though, Lucy had been mortified.

Mick had immediately turned on his father, calling him a no-good drunk and a useless father, and asking how the hell could he talk about manning up when his own wife had taken off because she couldn't stand him?

The two men had yelled and sworn at each other, then started throwing furniture and punches and bleeding all over the kitchen. Lucy had never witnessed this kind of physical violence before, and it had terrified her. It had only ended when Mick had left the house, slamming the door behind him so violently that the doorframe had shook. That had been the last time she'd seen him. He hadn't returned home, and two days later he was dead.

Lucy's parents, whom she'd slowly begun mending fences with at Fred's insistence, had begged her to leave the farm after the funeral and come home with them, but something had held her back. Maybe it had been stubbornness, teenage pride, or maybe she hadn't been able to admit to her parents, maybe even to herself, that she was wrong.

At the funeral, Fred had remained aloof. He'd accepted his neighbours' condolences with a staunch nod and handshake, but he'd remained on the fringe of the gathering. He was a sad, lonely man who'd always kept everyone, including his only son, at arm's length, and her heart ached for him. She couldn't leave him out at Stringybark all alone. He'd let her in, had tried in his own way to take care of her, and she couldn't turn her back on him now when he had nothing left.

It was a hard-fought battle. He told her more than once to go back to her family, that she didn't need to 'hover over him like some damn invalid', but Lucy just ignored him. When she went into labour he drove her to hospital and stayed in the waiting room until the nurses told him she'd had a little girl. In the end, she *did* go home with her parents after the delivery; there were some things she wasn't willing to risk, and going out to Stringybark with only a grumpy old man who knew even less about babies than she did was not a risk she was willing to take with her new baby. But she missed the farm and, after a year, she moved back to Bundah. She was lucky enough to find Jan, a kindly older neighbour who happily took care of Belle when Lucy found the job at the servo. It wasn't much but it was something, and for the first time she felt in control of her life. She went out to see Fred every day after work, taking him out groceries and cleaning once a week. He loved Belle. His eyes would light up when she smiled at him, lifting her chubby little arms when Fred came out to greet them, and for the first time in a very long time Fred started to smile.

Lucy blinked away the memory, her eyes watering a little as the dogs continued to snap and snarl at her from behind the fence.

'Lucy? What are you doing here?'

She spun around at her name and breathed a sigh of relief when she saw it was Ross. 'I'm sorry, I guess I should have called before I came out, but it was kind of a spur-of-the-moment thing.' she shrugged a little self-consciously. 'I just wanted to come and see the old place again.'

He gave an ear-splitting whistle and instantly the dogs stopped barking, letting out a few whines before they slunk off.

'No one's going to get in here without you knowing about it,' Lucy said, staring after the forbidding-looking animals.

'You can't be too careful nowadays,' he shrugged.

'I guess not.' She eyed him doubtfully. Maybe even out here the latest unease had made people jumpy about security. 'It hasn't changed much.'

'Nah, still the same. I, ah, wasn't expecting visitors. I don't have any milk for a cuppa or anything . . .'

Lucy immediately felt bad. 'Oh, no. It's okay, I won't stay. I don't want to interrupt your day . . . I was just . . .'

She gave an embarrassed grimace. 'How have you been anyway? I haven't seen you in town for a while.'

'I don't go in unless I need something. Place has changed a bit too much for my liking,' he said, his gaze sliding away from hers and resting back out on the horizon across the dry paddocks. 'I hear you're seeing someone.'

'Oh, no. I mean, not really.' Lucy felt like an idiot as she stammered her way through an explanation. After their argument she wasn't exactly sure what their official status was. 'It's complicated,' she ended up murmuring.

'Yeah, stuff like that usually is,' he said almost wearily.

Lucy wondered again at this strange man she'd once known as a boy. She still saw parts of that lonely kid who watched from a careful distance as the rest of them laughed and teased each other. She wasn't sure she could cope with as much solitude as Ross seemed to enjoy.

'It's just that . . . I wouldn't like to see you messed up by another bloke like Mick.'

'Hugh's nothing like Mick,' she said, realising she sounded defensive, but unable to stop herself.

'Just a friendly observation.'

She was just about sick of all the friendly little pieces of advice she was getting lately. 'Thanks, but I'm pretty sure I'd be able to tell if Hugh was like Mick or not.' Wouldn't she? Yes, Hugh did seem like the ultimate bad boy, with his bike and his sometimes surly attitude, but he'd proven to be nothing like Mick personality wise. He was gentle and caring and . . .

He wasn't so caring and gentle yesterday when he broke up with you, a little voice piped up unexpectedly. *No, he was cold and indifferent, just like Mick.*

'Well, I better let you get back to work,' she said abruptly, turning back towards her ute.

'Good to see you, Lucy,' he said, shoving his hands deep into the pockets of his ripped and dirty jeans.

She looked up as she closed the door and caught a glimpse of that shy boy whom she'd befriended all those years ago and her irritation quickly dissolved. 'You too, Ross. I'm working up in the top pub now. Drop in and say hi next time you're in town.'

He gave an awkward kind of nod and stepped back, watching as she reversed and gave a wave, before heading back towards the large machinery shed she presumed he'd come from earlier.

As she drove back along the dirt driveway she glanced in the mirror one last time. In the corner of her eye she could have sworn she saw a figure of an old man, his hand raised in farewell, just like Fred had done every time she and Lucy had left him to drive back into Bundah after a visit. Lucy swallowed over a hard lump in her throat and blinked back the sting of tears. There was nothing out here for her any more. The past was long gone and it was time to let it go.

Twenty

Lucy swore under her breath as she finished putting back the contents of her handbag. She'd searched everywhere for her damn phone and couldn't find it. She tried to think again where she'd last used it and the only place she could remember was in the car back at Stringybark yesterday.

She'd had a horrible night's sleep, tossing and turning till all hours of the morning, thinking about Hugh and wondering if he'd made it home after his ride yesterday. He'd taken off in a slew of gravel. Riding a bike angry was a recipe for disaster, but she was still upset by the turn their last conversation had taken, and stubbornly refused to call him.

He'd pretty much indicated they were over, so calling him would only have resulted in him saying something cold and hurtful, and she wasn't sure she could handle that right now.

Then her thoughts had turned to work. She needed the job, so any idea of walking out on him with her held head high went flying out the window. She'd have to swallow her pride and just turn up each day until she found something else. It was going to be incredibly uncomfortable, but there were worse things in life to deal with, she supposed. At least she still had a job . . . for now. Maybe he'd fire her? She hadn't considered that possibility.

She'd tried to drown out her anxiety by getting angry, but her worries had kept returning and she'd realised she wouldn't be able to rest until she knew Hugh was okay. She couldn't help that she still cared about him, it wasn't something she could turn off, so she'd finally given in and decided to send a text message to see if he'd got home safely. That was when she'd discovered she couldn't find her phone.

She couldn't lose her phone, it contained everything: photos, calendar, emails and phone numbers. She thought of calling Ross to see if he'd found it, but it was too early to phone; but by the time she drove out there, surely he'd be awake and she'd be back before Belle left for school. Anything was better than lying in bed wide awake and overthinking everything.

It was still dark outside, though the sun was just peeking its head over the horizon and soon the sky would be filled with shades of pink, gold and blue.

Lucy opened the door and got out of the ute, noticing there were no dogs today and wondering where they were.

After a nervous glance over her shoulder, she shut the car door and headed for the machinery shed where a loud generator roared, the smell of diesel strong in the air.

The large double door was shut and she doubted Ross would hear her knock anyway with the ancient generator making so much noise. *Surely noise pollution alone would make that thing illegal?* she thought. She circled around to a smaller door at the side of the shed and saw that it was propped open with an old brick. Stopping at the doorway, she paused as she saw what was inside.

Instead of the farm machinery she'd expected, long tables ran the length of the shed, covered in an array of containers, pots and laboratory paraphernalia. The place looked like a very messy science lab.

Lucy frowned. The Ross she knew from high school was definitely no science genius, so why would his machinery shed be full of this stuff?

Along the walls were drums of chemicals and then her gaze fell on a row of neatly wrapped packets stacked on the end of the table. Lucy stared at the scene before her in open-mouthed disbelief as she processed what she was looking at.

At the far end of the shed she heard raised voices. The generator was too loud to make out what was being said, but realising there were people around was enough to snap her out of her stunned stupor. Stepping out of the doorway, she flattened herself against the outside of the shed and fought the rush of panic surging through her body. She had to get out of here. This was dangerous. *But it's Ross,* a small voice protested. *You've known him most of your life!* Clearly she didn't know him as well as she'd thought if he'd been running a drug lab right here under her nose all these years!

She'd try and rationalise it later, once she was safely away from Stringybark. Right now she had to get back to her car and pray she could drive away without him knowing she'd been here.

She retraced her steps, her heart beat thumping painfully in her chest. As she reached the corner of the shed she stopped short. The two Dobermans were circling her car, noses to the ground, sniffing intently. She eased back. She wouldn't have long before the dogs found her and either gave away her presence or ripped her apart. If she hurried, she might be able to walk around the shed and approach the car from the other side. She doubted she'd be able to make her escape without them drawing attention to her, but she stood a better chance inside her car than standing out here.

As she reached the far side of the shed, she ducked below a window but stopped as the voices grew louder.

'I told you never to call me at home. What the hell do you think you're doing?' yelled a familiar voice.

What is Ken doing out here? wondered Lucy, heart thumping.

'We got a problem. A big one.'

Lucy peeked in through the side of the window as Ross handed over a phone and Ken appeared to be reading something on the screen. She saw him look up and frown. 'What the hell is this?'

'I got thinkin' about that guy who bought the top pub. I heard a few rumours that the cops were askin' around about him, so I sent a photo down to one of our associates. Turns out we were right to be worried about him. He was an undercover cop.'

'I knew there was something off about that guy,' Ken muttered. 'Just what we bloody need.'

Hugh used to be an undercover policeman? Lucy wasn't sure how many more surprises she could take today.

'Yeah, well he won't be a problem for much longer. They're sending someone up here to take care of him.'

'Oh great, just what we need,' Ken growled. 'I told you it was a bad idea bringing them in on this.'

'You were the one who wanted to expand. The club has reach into places we could never get to.'

Ken gave an unimpressed grunt. 'Why the hell are they interested in the Thompson fella anyway?'

'Personal business, they said.'

'Well, I guess that's one less problem *we'll* need to deal with.'

'This is all getting out of hand, Ken.'

'You should've thought about that before you brought the Hudson kid in.'

'How was I supposed to know he'd start selling locally.'

'You should have been keeping a better eye on him.'

'It's time to wind it down. There's too much talk around town. We need to quit while we're ahead.'

'Just calm down,' Ken said harshly. 'We've just gotta let it blow over. Now that we've taken care of Hudson, the drug problem around town will settle down and things will go back to normal.'

A low menacing growl sounded from behind Lucy and she froze. Her first instinct was to run, but if she ran they'd be on her in a heartbeat. If she stayed here, Ross and Ken would find her. Maybe she could bluff her way out of it. If she could just make it to her car, maybe they wouldn't even know she'd seen inside the shed.

She eased away from the window but at the first sign of movement the dogs went ballistic, and she plastered herself against the tin wall, trapped. The smell of their putrid breath as ferocious jaws snapped far too close to her face made her stomach heave. If she fell, they'd pull her apart like a rag doll.

A sharp whistle cut through the air and the two dogs dropped to the ground instantly. Lucy opened her eyes and found Ross staring at her, wearing a stony expression.

'What the hell—' Ken stopped abruptly as he came around the corner. 'What are you doing here?'

'I came to see if Ross found my phone yesterday.'

'I told you to get a lock for the bloody front gate,' Ken snarled.

'Oh yeah, that wouldn't be too suspicious now, would it? I thought you said we had to keep things normal,' Ross snapped back.

'Christ almighty,' Ken said in a low whisper. 'What the hell else can go wrong? Get her into the house,' he ordered.

Ross grabbed Lucy's arm and shoved her ahead of him towards the homestead. Lucy slid her hand into the jeans of her pocket and wrapped her fingers around the keys. If she was quick, she could get inside the car and lock the doors. As they drew closer to the vehicle, Lucy trod hard on Ross's foot and pushed away. Her hand grabbed the door handle and she reefed it open. She was almost inside when she was grabbed hard around the hips and pulled backwards.

The dogs barked loudly, jumping at the sudden activity and adding to the general commotion.

'Let me go!' Lucy screamed, struggling against the tight grip Ross had on her as he pulled her along behind him in through the front gate.

'How did you think that would even work. Shit, Lucy! Don't you see you're already in a crapload of trouble? Why piss him off even more?' Ross grunted in a low, urgent voice.

'Him? Why are you talking like you take your orders from Ken?'

'Because I do. Just do as you're told and you won't get hurt.'

'Tie her up,' said Ken, following them into the house.

Lucy watched as he removed his hat and ran his hand across his bald scalp in frustration. Ross disappeared through the door leading out to the laundry and returned with a length of rope.

'Are you crazy?' she demanded, backing away from him as he approached. 'Get the hell away from me.'

Ken stepped in front of her and Lucy lashed out at his face, but he was too strong and pinned her arms.

'Tie her hands!' he grunted as she managed to elbow him in the ribs.

She struggled but it wasn't enough against the two of them, and eventually they managed to bind her hands tightly in front of her. Ken pushed her backwards and she sat down heavily on a kitchen chair, glaring at the men; inside she was quivering with a mix of fear and outrage.

This was where the drugs had been coming from; it had been right here under their nose the whole time. Lucy felt sick.

As soon as one connection was made, more began to fall into place. 'You went through my house . . . and you've been following me . . . why?'

'Following you?' Ken looked at her strangely, before his gaze fixed on Ross once more. 'Jesus, seriously? I told you to search her house and make sure she didn't have any evidence about the fuel siphoning, At *no time* did I say follow her, you moron! Were you *trying* to get us caught?'

She turned her gaze onto Ross who stood across the room looking ashen, his bloodshot eyes searched hers miserably. 'I'm sorry, Lucy,' he said, his shoulders sagging. 'I didn't mean to scare you.'

Lucy thought back to the night in the laneway. She hadn't been going crazy. Someone *had* been following her. 'Why would you do that?'

'I . . .' Ross stammered then dropped his gaze to the floor, his throat working silently as he swallowed.

'Why do you think, Lucy? The fool's had a crush on you for years. Any idiot could see that. Now if we're done with the dramatics,' Ken cut in harshly.

Lucy's head was beginning to pound. That's why the books hadn't been balancing; Ken had been siphoning fuel. 'The diesel discrepancies were all from you.' Instantly, she recalled the four-wheel drive and trailer that night she went to check if she'd locked up. 'You were stealing your own diesel,' she said thinking out loud. Why hadn't she worked this out sooner? *Because while Ken was a prick of a boss, you didn't know he was an actual criminal.* He needed a way to fund his drug business without leaving any paper trail and so he'd been siphoning cash from one of his businesses . . . literally.

'How did you think you wouldn't get caught out eventually? Your books don't balance.'

'That's right,' he shook his head dolefully. 'My office manager had been embezzling funds from my business for months. She had the perfect opportunity. Unlimited access to keys, she handled the fuel deliveries and managed the levels of the tanks. I had no idea she was selling diesel after hours on the black market.'

Lucy could only stare in horror at the man she'd thought she'd known for most of her life. He was a monster. 'You were planning to set me up. And all because I wouldn't sell you this place so you could keep your drug lab quiet.'

'You should have sold when I told you to. You and your daughter would have been set for life, but you had to dig your heels in and get stubborn. And for what?' Ken demanded.

'How could you do all this, Ken? You of all people?' she said, still feeling dazed.

'I'm a businessman; it's just business.'

'Just business? Your *business* is killing the kids of people you've known all your life.'

'It was never supposed to be sold here,' he snapped, giving Ross a deadly glare. 'That was unfortunate but, regardless, it wasn't forced down their throats. They *chose* to buy it. We're simply providing a product.'

No one could be that cold, surely? Looking at Ken now, she realised that cold might not be the right word. Indifferent? Then she realised he really believed this *was* simply business. 'Let me go, Ken. This isn't necessary.'

'I wish it wasn't, but unfortunately now I have no choice.'

Lucy struggled to hold on to her anger, knowing that if she let it go fear would replace it and she couldn't afford to fall apart. She needed to get out of here somehow, and to do that she had to keep her wits about her and look for another opportunity. She couldn't sit here and just let them get away with this.

'I need to think. Get me a Scotch.'

Ross glared at the older man but moved across the room to do as he was instructed.

Lucy held Ken's angry glare, refusing to cower. As she replayed the events over in her head, she struggled to come to terms with everything that had happened. It was like a very bad dream—one she wished she could wake up from and laugh about over coffee with Hugh. Somehow, though, she didn't think she'd be waking up anytime soon.

Hugh picked up the phone and hit call again, listening to it ring out on the other end just as it had the last five times he'd tried. When the automated voice came on, instructing him to leave a message, he cancelled the call and tossed the phone down on the bed.

He knew she was angry at him, and she had a right to be . . . again. He dropped an arm over his eyes and swore silently. He'd overreacted. He shouldn't have gone straight back to the pub after the little interview with Nate's boss. Of course the guy had known all about his history and had made him sit through a play-by-play dissection of it all, and for what? Just to make sure he knew that real police work didn't involve becoming some kind of criminal in order to make an arrest.

By the time he'd left the station, he'd been ready to hit something in pure frustration. He should have, but instead he'd gone back to the pub, knowing full well Lucy would be there. Part of him had wanted to take it out on her because of her unwavering belief in good old Nate.

It frustrated the hell out of him that she could defend the guy without hesitation; not only that, but defend his actions for treating *him* like a suspect. He'd wanted her to show some indignation on his behalf, but instead he'd basically been told to suck it up. He knew she had a point, and deep down he knew Nate was only doing his job, but his Inspector, on the other hand, wanted more than anything to be able to prove Hugh had something to do with the drug situation in town. It would be a huge feather in his cap if he could pin this on a disgraced undercover cop.

He owed Lucy an apology though, and maybe now was the time to come clean with her about the rest of his past. He could hardly expect her to understand his frustration with the system if she didn't know the full story.

The phone rang and he grabbed it, relief briefly lighting up his face as Lucy's home number lit up the screen.

'Hugh, it's Belle. Do you know where Mum is?'

Nate looked up as the front door opened and banged shut. Hugh didn't waste any time with pleasantries. 'Lucy's missing.'

The police officer frowned, 'Missing? Since when?'

'Early this morning.'

'You two have a fight or something?' Nate asked.

'What's that got to do with anything?' The cop raised a lazy eyebrow at him and Hugh swore silently. 'Yeah, we may have said a few things yesterday that got a bit heated,' he admitted reluctantly.

'Then she's probably gone somewhere to cool off.'

'She hasn't. Belle called a few minutes ago thinking she was with me. She wasn't at home when she woke up to go to school.'

'Like I said, she probably just wanted some time alone.'

'It's not like Lucy to leave Belle without letting her know where she's going. My gut's tellin' me something's happened.'

'Yeah, well my gut's been tellin' me *you're* bad news ever since I first saw you.'

'Can we put the tape measure away? Use your other head for a minute and think about it. She wouldn't just go off and leave Belle to worry about where she was.'

Nate muttered something under his breath but reached for his hat and stood up. 'Okay. I'll go for a drive and see if I can find her.'

'I'm coming too,' Hugh said, following him out of the station.

'Haven't you got a pub to run or something?'

'It's under control. This is more important.'

'When was the last time you saw her?'

'Yesterday. I went for a ride. She'd left work by the time I got back.'

'You said you had an argument? What about?'

'None of your damn business.'

'If Lucy's missing, it's very much my business.'

'Things have been a little tense between us since she found out about my past,' Hugh said reluctantly.

'I see,' Nate said, jotting something down in his notebook.

'So it all worked out nicely for you,' Hugh said in a deceptively calm tone. 'I noticed you didn't bother filling her in on the fact I was also an undercover cop. Guess that bit of info wouldn't have worked in your favour. Much better that she thought I was just some drug-dealer bikie.'

'I was just following your orders. Keeping my mouth shut. As a civilian there was no reason to mention that part to Lucy, was there?'

Hugh gave an unimpressed snort, but this was getting them nowhere.

'I'll meet you over at her place. That's where we need to start the search.'

'Last time I looked, you were also a civilian. Can't have it both ways, mate. Just let the police handle this.'

'Like you've handled the drug ring you and I both know is working in your district. Trust me, you need all the help you can get,' Hugh snapped, heading towards his bike and pulling on his helmet. The police four-wheel drive pulled out behind him and he knew his last shot had hit its mark. Whatever else Nate might be, putting an end to this drug ring operating in the district was obviously something he took extremely personally and Hugh had to respect that. They were on the same side there. Hugh had put his life on the line for all those years to eradicate the scum who made and sold drugs, and he knew first-hand the frustration the cop was up against. It didn't mean he had to like him though. Not when he hung around hoping Hugh would stuff up and he could be there to pick up the pieces for Lucy.

And look who just gave him the perfect opportunity.

Gritting his teeth, he forced his thoughts back to where they were needed. Where the hell was she?

'Where's Belle?' Nate asked when they pulled up outside Lucy's cottage.

'At school. I played it down and said her mother wanted some overtime and had started work early. I didn't see any sense in worrying her until we knew more.'

He saw the cop nod briefly and took that as an agreement. 'Watch where you walk.'

Hugh bit back his irritation at the policeman's warning and concentrated on looking around.

'Her car's not here.'

'No,' said Hugh. So where would she have gone? He still didn't think she'd have left without seeing Belle off to school first. She always put her kid first. He understood her need to protect her daughter—in fact, it was refreshing to see. The kind of people he'd hung around in the past were lucky to even remember they had kids half the time. Her world wasn't ideal—she was a single mother and it was hard raising a child by yourself—but she hadn't allowed that to impact on Belle. He respected her more than she could possibly know for that fact alone.

'I'm gonna take a look inside,' he said, heading for the front steps.

'Hold up, you can't just break into her house. There's procedures we need to go through,' Nate warned as he followed him across the yard.

Hugh took the spare key from under the mat and unlocked the door. 'Who said anything about breaking in?'

Inside, the house was deathly quiet. The soft hum of the fridge was the only noise and it gave Hugh a trickle of unease. He headed for Lucy's bedroom, stepping inside to find the bed neatly made up.

'If she got a call to leave the house in a hurry, she wouldn't have wasted time making the bed before she left.'

'Or she never slept in it to begin with,' Nate surmised slowly as he looked around. 'She could have left anytime last night after Belle saw her. She could have been missing longer than we thought.'

As worried as Hugh was, he'd secretly been hoping Nate would come up with a plausible explanation for her disappearance. He really wanted to be overreacting about this, even though his instincts told him he wasn't.

Nate walked out of the room and Hugh heard him talking on his phone. His mind was already racing. Where the hell was she?

Twenty-one

The crisp morning air had started to warm up, but Lucy still felt chilled to the bone. Her arms ached from being tied together and the chair she was sitting on was hard and unforgiving.

She'd listened to the men out in the other room argue and throw around blame for the past hour while she'd frantically tried to think of a way out of her predicament. The table was the same one that had been here when Fred had lived in the house—in fact the majority of the furniture was Fred's because she hadn't had the heart to sell any of it. Not that it was worth much. Memories of happier times sitting at this table made Lucy's eyes sting, but she blinked them away hard. If she gave in to the fear and frustration she was feeling inside, she'd never find a way out of this mess.

'I want you to drive her vehicle out along Blackbutt Road where she'll have an accident,' Ken was saying in the other room.

'How am I supposed to do that?'

'Knock her out and push the car over the embankment. There're plenty of spots out there a car could roll over, and with any luck no one will even find the wreck for a couple of months,' said Ken as he walked back into the kitchen.

Lucy glared at Ken, horrified that he could stand there and discuss ways to kill her so calmly. He'd never get away with it; surely they'd be able to tell if a car was pushed deliberately over the side of a mountain. Fat lot of good that would do her when she was dead, though.

The thought hit her hard. *Dead?* She'd never get to see Belle graduate high school, or finish uni . . . or get married and have children of her own. *Damn it, no!* She wouldn't go down without fighting, she couldn't. She had too much to lose. She had to think. Stall Ross somehow. Would anyone have missed her yet? She thought back to yesterday and Hugh's furious departure. Would he worry that she hadn't shown up for work or just think it had something to do with their fight? Surely he knew her well enough by now to know she had a better work ethic than that? How long till he thought to call her? Belle would possibly assume she'd gone into work early, although Lucy would normally ring to check on her and make sure she'd gotten ready for school in time. Would she be worried? Lucy hated the thought of that.

'Why do I have to do it?' Ross was saying.

'Because I'm just the silent investor. This is more in line with your expertise. I want her out of here before someone thinks to come looking for her.'

Lucy turned to Ross as he approached her. She tried to beg him not to hurt her, but her voice was muffled behind the gag. Fear threatened to suffocate her. She couldn't get enough air into her lungs and feared she'd hyperventilate.

Ross pulled her to her feet and tugged her along behind him towards the door. Her feet caught on the carpet and she tripped, crashing into his back.

'Lucy, don't make this any harder than it already is,' he sighed.

The statement, almost a petulant whine, was all she needed to shift her terror to indignation. Oh, she was being difficult? She was supposed to follow meekly behind and help him make it easy to kill her? *Sure,* she mentally spat. *Can I help pull the trigger for you?*

Ross put her into the passenger side of her ute, locking the door before slamming it shut. With her hands tied in front of her, Lucy was unable to move quickly enough to unlock the door and open it before he was seated beside her in the driver's seat.

Panic set in as they drove down the driveway. Time was running out. Blackbutt Road was even more remote. If they made it all the way out there, she would be completely isolated. Stringybark was a long way out of town, but at least there were still neighbouring properties.

Dust trailed along behind them as Ross sped along the unsealed road. The poor old ute wasn't designed for this kind of speed; with each pothole they hit the ancient suspension crunched and groaned in protest, jostling Lucy uncomfortably in her seat.

In the distance a flash caught her eye before they rounded a bend and lost sight of the road ahead, but it was enough to lift her flailing spirits ever so briefly. Had it been a car approaching from the other direction? Her mind raced at the thought. Would she be able to get their attention? At the very least someone would be able to report what direction they'd seen her ute going, which gave her some hope. Of course, it wouldn't do her much good if she were dead at the bottom of a mountain range. She quickly blocked that train of thought, she needed to focus. Would they see that she had a gag on? At this speed, there wouldn't be much time for another driver to get a good look at her. Frantically she tried to think of some way to get the other car's attention. They rounded a sharp bend and a silver four-wheel drive was heading towards them.

She knew that vehicle! Ted Brownhouse owned a property three places up from Stringybark. She sensed Ross's irritation at being seen, but he didn't slow down; maybe he figured the faster they went, the less Ted would see. She didn't stop to think about what she was doing, there was no time. As they were about to approach Ted's vehicle, she launched herself sideways and knocked Ross hard against the window. For a moment he lost control of the steering wheel and the ute swerved madly. Without traction control, it began to slide across the loose gravel. Unfortunately, Ross was a more experienced driver than she'd given him credit for and he righted the vehicle quickly, but not quickly enough to avoid clipping the back of Ted's vehicle, sending them both into a crazy spin.

Lucy lifted her bound hands automatically, bracing herself as she was tossed around the cabin of the ute. She hit her head against the window and then the front dash as the car came to a sudden stop against the bank.

For a long while there was no sound, and then a loud ringing in her ears began. Everything swam before her eyes as she tried to lift her head.

Beside her, Ross sat slumped sideways in the seat, his head against the side window. He wasn't moving.

She turned her head slowly and saw a dark shadow outside her window. She needed to move, somehow she knew that, but she was having trouble connecting the thought with the action. Nothing wanted to move.

The door opened beside her and hands steadied her. 'Lucy? Are you hurt? *What the hell?*' Ted gaped at her as he realised she was gagged and tied up in the passenger seat.

She groaned behind the gag and he quickly reached behind her to untie it. 'Help me,' she whispered in a hoarse voice that didn't sound like her own.

'Just sit still, Luce,' Ted told her, already grabbing his phone from his pocket. 'You could have internal injuries. Wait for the ambos to get here.'

'No time. Call Nate.'

Beside her, Ross made a small groan and Lucy struggled with the rope at her wrists. 'He's coming to. We need to call Nate and get him out here urgently.'

Ted thankfully didn't bother arguing and instead began untying the rope around the wrists. Even so, the frown he wore suggested he was trying to figure out whether he'd just stumbled across some kind of kinky role-playing or something even more disturbing.

'Can I borrow your phone?'

'Lucy, what's going on here?'

'We have to tie him up,' she said, swapping the rope for the mobile Ted held out to her. She closed her eyes and concentrated on settling the nausea that seemed to be associated with moving her head. 'I'll tell you everything as soon as I call Nate.'

'Stay there. I don't want you to move until the ambulance gets here,' Ted said as she went to get out of the ute. Lucy eyed Ross as he continued to moan beside her, but he remained relatively out of it. She watched as Ted tied his hands together, and then dialled directory assistance, asking to be put through to Bundah station. The adrenalin was wearing off and pain began to register in pretty much every part of her body as she listened to the phone ringing on the other end of the line before being diverted to a mobile number.

'Sergeant Pearce speaking.'

'Nate, it's Lucy.'

'Lucy? Where are you?'

'I'm about five ks north of Stringybark on Blackbutt Road. There's been an accident.'

'Are you okay?'

'I'm all right, but we need an ambulance. Ross's hurt. Nate, he and Ken are behind the drugs in town,' she said, her voice grave.

The phone went silent. 'Are you somewhere safe now?'

'Yes, Ted Brownhouse is here.'

'I'm on my way.'

She handed the phone back to Ted and relayed the message that the ambulance was on its way. She wanted to get as far away from the man beside her as she could, but Ted was standing guard, making sure she didn't move unnecessarily, taking his recent first-aid training seriously.

She felt clammy as a cold sweat broke out across her forehead and down her back as the gravity of the situation sunk in. She could have died today. Someone had planned her murder.

And she wasn't safe yet; Ken was still on the loose.

'Was that Lucy? What did she say? Where is she?' Hugh demanded as Nate disconnected the call and began searching his phone for another number.

'She's okay,' he said, turning his back on Hugh as his call was answered. 'It's Nate Pearce. We need an ambulance fifteen ks out on Blackbutt Road.'

'An ambulance?' Hugh butted in impatiently.

'Calm down, she's okay. I'll tell you on the way.'

Hugh didn't argue; he knew precious time would be wasted asking questions. If Lucy was in trouble they needed to get to her fast.

At least she was safe. That was all that mattered. But as the dirt road stretched beyond them, he couldn't ignore the little voice that reminded him that when she was in trouble, it had been Nate she'd called and not him.

The sound of an approaching vehicle with lights flashing signalled Nate's arrival, and right behind him was a four-wheel drive ambulance. The cars pulled up, blocking the narrow road, but with so little traffic out this way, it was highly unlikely they'd be causing any problems.

Lucy saw Ted intercept Nate in the rear-view mirror, rapidly filling him in on what had happened. A blur of colour flashed across the mirror as someone else moved past the rear of the vehicle and Lucy barely had time to process it before she looked up to see Hugh. He crouched beside her, inside the open passenger door. 'Does anything hurt?'

'Everything hurts,' she said wearily, 'but I'm okay. What are you doing here?'

'Belle called me when she couldn't find you this morning, and I've been looking for you ever since.'

'I need to get out of here,' she tried to move, but Hugh restrained her by placing a hand against her shoulder.

'The ambos are here. Wait till they look you over,' he ordered, and true to his word, two men dressed in dark blue uniforms came over, taking his place in the open door. Once the officers were satisfied that she hadn't suffered any spinal injuries, checking she could move limbs and there was no tingling sensations anywhere, Lucy was finally free to get out of the car.

Ross, on the other hand, had sustained far more serious injuries. The steering wheel had hit his chest during the collision and she overheard the ambo's mentioning the likelihood of head injuries, so it took a considerable amount of time to brace and remove him from the vehicle. Other than the odd moan and unintelligible murmur now and again, he'd not regained full consciousness.

Hugh stayed by her side, hovering like an anxious parent as she sat in the back of an ambulance and allowed the ambos to clean up a few superficial wounds while she gave Nate a brief rundown of the events of the past few hours.

'So you saw their lab? They're actually manufacturing out there?' Nate asked with a frown after she'd finished.

'Yes. It filled the machinery shed. And I'm pretty sure they're responsible for Ben Hudson's disappearance. He seemed to be connected, maybe a distributor of some kind. They weren't happy about him selling the stuff locally and alerting everyone to the drug situation in town.'

'Ken must have balls the size of an elephant to establish a drug lab in a town this size,' Hugh muttered.

'He was counting on his reputation and his connections to keep it quiet,' Nate said.

'Well, it worked. Who would think to suspect the man behind the push to find out where the drugs were coming from? He was even behind the town meeting to get to the bottom of it all, for goodness sake,' Lucy said with a shake of her head.

'The ultimate bluff. Hide it in plain sight,' Hugh shrugged.

'I need to call this all in and then get out there. Hopefully Ken will still be there and we can catch him red-handed. If not, at least we'll get the lab. Ken won't get out of this now.'

'I don't know, Nate. I saw a side of him I never imagined before. He was like a whole other person. It sounded like he'd done a good job of keeping himself out of the messier aspects.' She nodded towards the other ambulance. 'Ross seems to have done all the dirty work.'

'I'll catch up with him later. I don't think he'll be going anywhere in a hurry but, just to be safe, I've organised a guard for the hospital.' He turned his attention back to Hugh. 'Can you get her home? I need to get moving on this.'

'I'm coming with you,' Lucy said.

'The man just tried to murder you.'

'That's exactly why I'm going. Besides,' she added, 'I'm the landlord. I'm responsible for allowing this whole mess to happen.'

'I'll come along and make sure she's okay,' Hugh said, coming to stand beside her.

'I don't have time to argue with either of you so get in the car,' Nate sighed. 'You take care of Lucy, because if anything happens to her, it's on your head,' he warned Hugh as the two men passed each other.

Lucy was too surprised to say anything, and the moment was gone as Nate got in the driver's side of the police vehicle and slammed the door.

She didn't look across at Hugh. She sensed something simmering between the two men, but there was too much else going on to worry about that right now. The shock that had been numbing the severity of the situation until now was slowly wearing off. She needed to focus on doing something; if she was sent home to rest she knew she'd lose what little composure she had very quickly.

She just needed to get through this and then she could lock herself away and fall apart in private.

A large booming sound echoed out across the valley, breaking the silence of the car.

'Was that thunder?' Lucy looked up through the window at the blue skies above.

'Somehow I don't think so,' Hugh said with a wariness that instantly put her on edge.

Nate continued towards Stringybark; the trip seeming to take far longer than it should have. He spent time on the radio; the backup he'd called for was already on its way and wouldn't be too long. The whole day was turning into one big headache for the poor man, Lucy thought, watching the strain etched around his mouth in the rear-view mirror. 'Smoke,' Nate said as they rounded a bend and saw a black haze hanging above the tree line in the distance.

Unease prickled along her spine as they continued to head towards Stringybark. Her fears were confirmed as they neared the turnoff and saw flashing lights and rural fire brigade trucks pulling up, blocking the driveway.

Nate pulled up beside the grim-faced fire captain. 'What've we got?'

'Fire in a machinery shed, as far as we can tell. Dunno what was in there but it's gone off like a bomb. The boys can't get anywhere near it yet.'

'This whole area is going to be a crime scene,' Nate instructed.

'If he's destroyed all the evidence, does that mean he'll get away with it?' Lucy asked, feeling devastated by the destruction she could see ahead.

'We'll get the forensic guys up here and see what they can find.'

Lucy stared at the roaring flames still engulfing the building at the end of the driveway and felt sadness drape itself over her like a cloak. The house also seemed to be alight, caught in the explosion which they'd heard on their way. It would all be gone, burned to the ground and gone forever. Not a trace of the lives that had been lived here on Stringybark would remain, only a black stain in the vastness of land surrounding it. It hurt more than she could have imagined.

She moved to stand by the splintering old fence and stared out across the pale grassy paddocks. The fire crews were already moving to make sure the fire didn't spread; with everything so dry, the whole district would go up like a bonfire if the blaze got away from them.

She wiped quickly at the first few warm tears, cursing softly when she failed to stem the growing tide and realised she had no tissues on hand.

Almost as though on cue, a neatly folded square appeared over her shoulder. She glanced over and saw Hugh patiently holding out the hanky. 'I promise it's clean,' he said.

'A hanky?' She didn't know anyone other than her father who still used the things. 'I didn't have you pegged as the hanky type,' she said after dabbing her eyes and feeling somewhat more in control of her emotions.

He gave an awkward shrug, before hooking his thumbs into the front pocket of his jeans. 'Don't tell anyone,' he said.

Despite the severity of the situation, she smiled a little at the image of Hugh, big tough biker, ironing his hankies. At the thought of bikers, though, she suddenly remembered something.

'What's wrong?' Her sudden anxiety must have shown on her face.

'I heard something else, just before they found me. I was coming to tell you when Ken found me.'

'Tell him what?' Nate asked, coming up behind them.

She glanced up at Hugh and saw a flicker of irritation in his eyes. 'They were talking about their associates. People who knew you.'

'Knew *me*?' Hugh said, his gaze fixed to hers intently.

'Ross said he sent them a photo and they identified you. Then he told Ken that they were sending up some guys . . . to take care of you.'

Hugh swore, and Nate's expression darkened.

'You need to get out of town,' Nate said.

'I'm not going anywhere.'

'They're coming for you.'

'Then I'll deal with them when they get here.'

'Like hell you will. I'm not going to stand by and let my town get caught up in your shit.'

'So it's true? You're an undercover cop?' Lucy demanded.

If Hugh was surprised she knew his secret, he didn't show it. '*Was*. Not any more,' he sighed.

'Who are these people that are coming for you?'

'I'm not sure.'

'I think we've gone past all this secret squirrel stuff, don't you?' Lucy snapped. It had been a stressful few hours and she was not in the mood for diplomacy.

'I honestly don't know . . . for sure. I have a pretty good idea though.'

'The Rabble?' Nate asked darkly.

'More than likely,' Hugh sounded resigned. 'It was only a matter of time until word got back to them that someone was asking around about me.'

Lucy saw a dark look pass between the two men.

'Would they really do something like . . . try to kill you?' Lucy asked nervously.

'Considering I was responsible for sending most of their members to prison at one time or another, I guess they could still be a little pissed off.'

'But surely . . . they wouldn't kill you?' Didn't that only happen in movies? She was so far out of her comfort zone, she couldn't even think straight.

'They aren't the kind of people you cross.'

'Can't you do something?' she asked, turning to face Nate.

'Not much I can do until there's some kind of threat made.'

'Well, that's just great. We have to wait until these guys arrive in town and actually hurt someone before they can be stopped?'

'It's not going to get that far,' Nate muttered.

'He's right. There're measures we can take to avoid trouble.'

'Like what?'

'I'll handle it,' Hugh said stubbornly.

'That's reassuring,' Lucy said.

'This has nothing to do with who I am now. This is tied up with my past. I thought it was safe to move on. I thought if I stayed out of trouble, I'd just be left alone.'

'Surely if this is all to do with your life in the police force, then the police will be able to help sort it out?' Again she turned to Nate and saw him frown.

'We need to get you home,' he said.

Hugh nodded his agreement. 'Don't worry about it, Luce. It'll be okay.'

'Don't patronise me, Hugh. I think after today I deserve a little more respect than that.'

'I wasn't trying to patronise you.'

'Well, you were. I'm not stupid. I deserve more than a pat on the head and being told not to worry!'

'It has nothing to do with you.'

His words cut her deeply but he was right: whatever they'd had briefly was over. She lowered her gaze and hid her hurt from him. 'Nate, I think I *would* like to go home now.'

'I'll get someone to take you back into town,' he nodded before walking over to a young SES worker who had just arrived.

'Lucy,' Hugh sighed when they were alone.

'You could have explained this to me the other day, but you chose to let me believe you were some criminal. This is why you went to prison, wasn't it?'

'I needed to gain credibility with the club. Easiest way to do that was to establish contact in jail, but it makes no difference—as far as everyone else was concerned I was a criminal and I lived like one. You had a right to know what kind of background I'd had. Make no mistake—I lived and worked beside these guys. I've done things I'm not proud of. I became immune to stuff.' He paused. 'Sometimes I really felt as though I was the character I was pretending to be.' He'd never admitted that to anyone before. Hearing it out loud only confirmed how screwed up his life had been. Why had he thought he had any chance of a normal relationship?

'But you were doing a job. It wasn't real.'

'It was real enough. I was locked up with scum, day and night. I spent two months behind bars in order to make contact and integrate with the club. Trust me, it was real.' Being forced to live in a cell and being stripped of every freedom you ever enjoyed still made him break out in a cold sweat. Facing near death experiences had been less terrifying than willingly surrendering your freedom.

'But you could have told me *why* you went to prison. I would have understood.'

'It's not something that I'm allowed to talk about, Luce. Even now. I can't tell you about that part of my life.'

'Why not? You're not undercover any more.' Her frown reappeared. 'Unless it was the excuse you needed to break it off and get rid of an unwanted attachment.'

'It wasn't—' he started to protest but saw in her closed expression she already believed it. Maybe she was right, who knows. Maybe he really *was* still that arsehole, deep down inside.

'Don't worry about it. I'm not sure I even *want* to know now.'

'It's probably better you don't. I should have known better than to hope I could have a normal relationship anyway,' he said and she heard the bitterness behind the words.

'You'll never have a normal relationship until you stop hiding behind your past. You can't shut people out of your life and expect them to trust you when they don't even know who you are.'

'Then I guess I better get used to it,' he said quietly.

Nate waved her over, cutting short their conversation, but Lucy was relieved. She wasn't sure there was anything for her to add. She didn't say goodbye, she just turned away and walked to the car that waited to take her from all the destruction which surrounded her.

News had already begun to filter into town by the time Hugh arrived at the pub later that morning. Gossip was spreading faster than the fire out at Stringybark. Shocked expressions and disbelief ran rife through town as the community tried to digest the fact that two of their own were behind so much pain and destruction.

The pub had been catering for the aftermath as people gathered and pieced together clues that should have tipped them off earlier.

There was no sign of Ken and no human remains had been found once the fire brigade had been able to enter the property and get the blaze under control. Ross had been taken to Armidale where he had undergone surgery and would be under guard until he was able to be released into police custody.

Hugh had spent the remainder of the day on the phone to his contact, sourcing any information on the Rabble and Basio, the president of the club. If he could keep tabs on them, he'd be able to ascertain how serious the threat might be. He grabbed his keys and headed outside. He needed to clear his head, get some perspective on things.

He'd done calling himself names—he'd pretty much exhausted his vocabulary of profanities and that was saying something; over the years he'd gained an extensive repertoire. He was losing his edge, big time. For years he'd survived on his wits and his ability to keep a level head in any situation, but maybe he was getting used to civilian life quicker than he'd anticipated. He'd dropped his guard and become careless. Somewhere along the line he'd forgotten his plan. If he were honest with himself, his plan hadn't been all that practical in hindsight. Buy a pub. Do it up. Run it for three years. Sell it. Leave town.

Unfortunately, his plan didn't allow for the fact that he'd have to interact with other people, or that he'd find a woman who would somehow manage to get under his skin and make him do something no one had managed to make him do in a very long time . . . care. He cared about her.

He cared about her daughter. Hell, he even cared about this stupid town. He wanted this place to be *home*.

He kicked back a gear and leaned into the corner. The road blurred beneath his tyres as he pushed the bike faster. The adrenaline pumped through his body as man and machine became one for the briefest of moments. His body moved with the machine and the roar of the engine was the blood pounding through his veins. This was freedom. This was living. When he was riding he was in control, and any mistake he made was his own. *If only life were like that,* he thought grimly. A flash of memory crossed his vision and he quickly blinked it away, but it was too late.

His momentary peace was gone and, with a regretful sigh, he pulled off onto the side of the road and did a U-turn, heading back to town with no real solution to any of his problems.

Slowing down as he came into the town speed limit, he sat up and rested one hand on his thigh as he followed behind Old Donny McKay's rust bucket of a ute. McKay and his mates were part of the local population who refused to come and drink at Hugh's pub. They were loyal bottom pub patrons and nothing would budge them from drinking there. A few months ago this would have bothered him. But after observing small-town politics, he'd figured out that loyalty still meant something out here. People supported businesses, and it was a bond that was not lightly broken. Old grudges could make or break a business in a small country town—he knew he was treading a very thin line himself after having got so many locals offside while he was renovating. Lucy had warned him it wasn't the way to go about things . . . If it weren't for the younger population and the new arrivals from the city, she'd have been right about the locals. He'd be surviving only on tourists. He made a mental note to work on his reputation a little more. Maybe he'd ask Lucy for some ideas on what he should try. Then he remembered she'd probably never talk to him again after their last conversation.

A movement caught his attention as he approached two men standing beside a pair of bikes. Through his helmet he felt sweat prickling his forehead as he caught a brief glimpse of an insignia on the back of the jacket of one of the men before he turned to walk into the bottom pub. Hugh's first instinct was to turn around and ride as hard and fast as he could out of town and not look back, but he had too much to lose now to do that. He couldn't risk leaving anyone behind who might get hurt because of him.

He continued down the street and then circled back behind his pub, parked his bike and was removing his helmet as he ran towards the back door. How had they gotten here so damn fast? He'd thought he might have at least a few days up his sleeve before anyone showed up. They'd have had to clear it with the club first—unless this was not club sanctioned. The thought sat like a lump of granite in his stomach. These guys were bad, but they were at least governed by rules—*club* rules, but rules nonetheless. If this was something only a few had decided, then there'd be no rules—no hope of fighting fair. It would be brutal and messy.

He assumed they were killing time at the bottom pub, having discovered his wasn't open yet, probably asking around about him to make sure they had the right place. Shit.

He grabbed his phone and asked the operator to find the police station's number and put him through. While he waited to be connected, he kept an eye on the street through the slated blinds of the front window. It was still early, and he was grateful that the pub was locked up tight for a few hours longer.

'Pearce, it's Thompson. I got a problem.'

Hugh figured his tone must have conveyed the urgency of the situation when the cop didn't hesitate before demanding what he needed.

'They're here. I got two guys poking around at the bottom pub who I know for a fact have a shitload of warrants out on them—kidnapping, armed robbery, drug possession, aggravated assault . . . take your pick. You'll need backup, they're not going to go quietly, but this will be the only chance you get to grab them. They rarely ever come out without club protection.'

'So much for you handling it.'

'Not now, mate,' Hugh snapped. He didn't have time to get into a dick-measuring contest with the guy. 'I'm not kidding, these two are bad news. You *do not* want them hangin' around town. I'll think of a way to get their attention once you're ready to move in.'

'You stay out of it. Wallace is sending up some extra men today. I'll call and get them to step on it. Stay outta sight till I deal with it.'

'You'll never make an arrest out in the open. I'm telling you, these two have managed to outsmart the city cops for two years or more.'

'What are they really after? Why would they be willing to risk so much coming up here?'

'How would I bloody know?' Hugh snapped.

'Yeah, well, I have a theory. I reckon it has to do with this UC operative who left the force in disgrace, accused of swindling about three mill of drug money. Same bloke who then mysteriously turns up in a small town on the other side of the country and buys a pub.'

'We don't have time for this,' Hugh snarled.

'Tell me again how on a cop's wage you could scrape the money together for a place like that,' Nate continued, ignoring Hugh's warning.

'Maybe I had a rich relative who left me some money,' Hugh sneered.

'That would be convenient now, wouldn't it?' Pearce agreed thoughtfully.

'Or maybe I just got a mortgage like every other person who starts a business?'

'Maybe. But then why would hardened criminals be willing to come out of hiding just to seek revenge? It doesn't wash. They're here for more than payback.'

'Let me know when your backup arrives and we'll figure out a way to draw them out of town from there,' Hugh said, refusing to be drawn into the debate any further, and hung up the phone before Pearce could continue. Why the hell wouldn't the past just stay dead and buried? *God damn it to hell.* Unfortunately, he *did* know why these guys would take such a risk. It was becoming all too clear. They wanted the money—the stash from the drug bust that had gone so wrong.

He should have known better than to think he could ever outrun his past. The memories snaked around his soul and dragged him back into their dark and murky depths.

Twenty-two

Hugh blinked a few times and tried to clear the fog inside his head. The sickly sweet smell of marijuana hung heavily inside the clubhouse. Bodies were scattered across the floor and every other conceivable surface—some in varying stages of undress, many naked.

He glanced down at the weight on his chest and discovered a half-naked blonde draped across him like a human blanket. He shook his head a few times and forced a deep breath into his lungs, hoping it would sober him up faster. Untangling himself from the woman he had no recollection of whatsoever, he carefully repositioned her on the lounge he'd been sleeping on and eased out from under her, quietly making his way across the minefield of drunken bodies in his path.

He closed the door of the bathroom in the rear of the clubhouse and splashed water on his face, bracing his arms on the sink as he looked into the mirror, studying the image before him. Long shaggy hair, a half-beard and dead eyes greeted him. Who was this person? For a moment it shocked him that he'd asked the question. In his half-stoned condition he'd momentarily forgotten who he was, and the thought did more to sober him than any cup of black coffee and cold shower ever could. A slip like that could cost him his life and, even worse, right at the very moment he realised he didn't even care. His life was shit. He was tired. His nerves were close to being shot, and he knew he couldn't keep this up for much longer.

He let himself out the back door and lit a cigarette, inhaling deeply, before releasing the smoke in a steady slow stream. He felt the nicotine hit his bloodstream and forced his head back into the correct mindset once more. He took a few more quick puffs before crushing the stub out under his foot and picking it up to toss it in an old forty-gallon drum as he walked past. The first thing he was going to do when he got out was give up smoking.

He pushed his bike across the gravel parking lot behind the clubhouse before starting it when he was far enough away not to wake anyone else. It wasn't that he was overly considerate of his fellow bikers, it was more because he wasn't in the mood to talk to anyone and he had business to take care of. Business that didn't involve anyone back at the clubhouse.

He was on his second cigarette when the car finally arrived and parked down the street and the two plainclothed detectives got out and headed inside the café.

He gave them a few minutes before heeling the butt of his smoke and tossing it in the bin as he walked towards the café briskly. He didn't want to be out on the street any longer than he had to. This was the most dangerous part of his operation. He took every possible precaution he could think of, but you never knew when chance would turn on you and catch you out unexpectedly. Chance, fate, whatever you wanted to call her, could be a real bitch like that sometimes.

'You took your bloody time,' he said by way of a greeting to the two men seated at the table in the rear of the café.

'We're here now, so what was so important you dragged us all the way across Sydney to tell us?'

'It's on.'

That caught their attention: instantly their eyes narrowed and they sat a little straighter in their chairs. 'When?'

'Tomorrow night.'

'Where?'

'Dunno yet. Basio won't tell anyone until just before the deal goes down. He's a little spooked by recent events.'

The detectives, Collins and Mulligan, didn't miss the sting in his words. 'That wasn't our fault,' denied Mulligan, scratching his pockmarked face.

'You moved on a raid that I told you to hold off on. You got a kid killed, you morons.'

'That *kid* was a drug dealer. It wasn't any great loss if you ask me,' Collins bit out, his round pug-like eyes fixed on Hugh intently.

'I was this close to being made,' Hugh said, holding his fingers up to emphasis his point.

'And thanks to us killin' the kid, you weren't.'

Hugh fought back the urge to rip off the guy's head then and there. He hated these two bastards—they treated him like scum because he worked the kind of jobs idiots like them couldn't do. They preferred to sit at their nice safe desks and keep their hands clean, but lately they'd let their egos become inflated and were making decisions that endangered not only the entire operation but also *his* life.

They'd raided a safe house where gang members were guarding a small but expensive haul of drugs awaiting delivery. Hugh had found out and tried to intercept them—he'd known it was a set-up—but one of the young probationers they called Rocco, a new recruit to the club, had overheard him arguing with the detectives and had turned to run, before being shot in the back by the two morons in front of him.

The president of their club, Leon Basio, better known as Screwdriver due to his weapon of choice, had gotten word of a possible informant in the club and had been using the safe house as bait. Thanks to some creative evidence planting, the president was now convinced Rocco had been the informant and his initial paranoia had eased a little, but Hugh's—not so much.

His gut was telling him something wasn't right. He was on edge even more so than normal, but for the life of him he couldn't figure out why . . . yet.

'Just be ready,' Hugh snapped. 'And, this time, if I say abort you better fucking abort, because if you do anything that endangers anyone else's life—including my own—I swear to God I'll kill you both.'

'I'm gonna let that go just this once, but I think you've been hanging around scum too long, mate. You're beginning to sound like them now. Better watch yourself making threats like that, though. Other people mightn't be as . . . understanding as we are.'

'Just be ready to move when I tell you,' Hugh said, before leaving the café and making the long, complicated trip back to the clubhouse. Anyone following him would never work out where he'd come from or where he was headed.

That night he was woken with a kick to the bottom of his boot and told to get ready. He had just enough time to activate his GPS and send a message that it was happening *now*.

The warehouse was on the outskirts of the city, remote and dark. He stood around with the other members of the Rabble as they waited for the delivery of methamphetamines. It was a versatile drug for dealers: in the powdered form, it could be either snorted, ingested, injected or smoked—something for everyone.

When the truck pulled into the warehouse the bikers helped unload the wrapped packages. Hugh watched Basio signal Terrier Williams, his second-in-command, to retrieve the large duffel bag of cash from the van which the club had brought along for transporting the drugs, and he felt his pulse accelerate. At any moment police were going to come through those doors, but until then he had to remain outwardly composed. This particular operation had been months in the planning and involved not only local law enforcement but also customs and outside agencies who had worked together, tracking the shipment as it made its way to Australia.

It had taken a long time to win over Basio's trust. Every undercover op required sacrifice of some kind, but this one had pushed Hugh further than anything he'd previously done. He'd had to go in deeper and for longer. Every day you spent infiltrating a crime gang put you at greater risk of either having your cover blown, or worse, developing a relationship with the criminals you were sent in to bust. It was a dangerous game. You had to be convincing enough to deceive those you were trying to infiltrate, and yet still somehow manage to remember that you were only pretending to be part of the brotherhood. The lines had become scarily blurred for him on a number of occasions.

Hugh's role in all of this had been to discover the details of the shipment, but also to get Basio to be at the drop. Basio had never been connected to any busts in the past, and there was a lot riding on this one. Not only was it a large shipment of drugs that would thankfully be stopped from hitting the streets, but there was also a lot of pressure on the federal police to make sure all the big players were caught both in Australia and overseas.

The time was ticking: he tried not to glance at his watch, even though the temptation was like a persistent itch. Then from the corner of his eye he saw Terrier get into the driver's side of the Rabble's van. Before he could wonder at what that was about, the doors had burst open and at least a dozen armed members of the rival bike club, the Jokers, opened fire on them.

Hugh instinctively took cover, his mind frantically trying to work out what the hell was happening. He was now as confused as the rest of the Rabble, those who weren't already dead or dying on the ground. Hugh searched for Basio, catching a glimpse of him slipping out into the darkness just as a wave of AFP and tactical response officers burst into the warehouse.

The scene before him was like something out of a B-grade action flick. The delivery driver in his panic had started up the truck and driven the truck over the top of the carnage, before crashing as he tried to drive through the partially open doors.

Hugh followed Basio. He couldn't let him get away; too much was riding on his arrest.

'It's over, Basio,' Hugh called, his gun aimed at the biker.

The man slowly turned and Hugh felt the ice-cold glare of the man.

'I'm taking you back inside.'

'I don't think so,' Basio snarled.

Hugh saw him move his hand slightly. 'Don't do anything stupid. The place is crawling with cops; you're not getting out of this.'

Then a shot rang out and Hugh automatically ducked, giving Basio the opportunity to run. As he turned around, a sharp pain radiated from his skull down his body and sent him sprawling to the ground.

When he woke up he was on the side of a dirt road, with no idea how he'd got there.

By the time he managed to find help and call in his location, Basio was gone. The raid had been a disaster and somehow, in all the confusion, almost three million dollars in cash had gone missing.

He was picked up and taken to the police station where he spent the rest of the night being questioned over the whereabouts of the missing money.

'This is bullshit and you know it,' Hugh said to the detective conducting the interview. He knew his boss, Rowland, would be trying to get him out of there, but he also knew these guys would be throwing as many stall tactics as they could legally get away with to keep Rowland away.

'Really?' the young detective answered, leaning back in his chair and picking at his fingernails idly. 'Then you tell me what I'm supposed to think when I have an operative who has a record of taking some pretty big risks on the job—some might even call him a bit of a loose cannon—who goes missing at the same time as three million dollars disappears and then has no recollection of what happened.'

'Clearly I've been set up by someone.'

The detective dropped his casual demeanour and zeroed in on Hugh intently. 'And why would someone do that?'

'Because they needed a fall guy.'

'You expect me to believe your crim mates set you up?'

'I didn't say it was any of them.'

'Then who would you be accusing?'

'I don't know,' Hugh bit out irritably. 'Maybe you lot in here could get off your arses and do your job to find out?'

The detective gave a dry chuckle. 'You even talk like a bloody crim. Do you see why I'm a tad hesitant to believe your story?'

'I see why you're never going to make a decent detective. You obviously lack initiative and the ability to investigate,' Hugh said, slouching back in his chair with a tired sigh.

The interview continued to go round in circles for another few hours until eventually they had to let him go for lack of evidence. Hugh pushed through the door and fresh air filled his lungs, cleansing him of the stuffy, clinical smell of the station. A few minutes later, he sat on the train staring sightlessly out at the window. The grey concrete and blur of faceless people standing on platforms as the train sped by filled him with an unexpected emptiness.

He belonged nowhere. Officially, he was one of the good guys, but he was too good at his job, which only made the police suspicious of him. And, while he had grown close to some in the club, his alliance with them was based on a lie and he had nothing but distain for how they made a living.

He was so damn tired.

Once upon a time he felt like he was making a difference—doing something worthwhile. Lately, though, he wasn't so sure.

Twenty-three

'Lucy, I can't talk now,' Nate said as she approached him.

'You told me about Hugh and the drugs to break us up, didn't you?' she said quietly.

Nate reached the police car and unlocked the door. 'It's not what you're thinking,' he said, glancing over at her and sighing when he saw she was waiting for further explanation. 'Luce, I found out something else, something just as bad. I don't want you mixed up with this guy. He may have told you he's turned a new leaf, but I'm still not sure I trust him.'

'What did you find out?'

Nate hesitated only briefly before speaking. 'There was an incident . . . a drug bust that apparently went wrong,' he said gravely. 'Afterwards, there was suspicion about a large amount of money that disappeared from the crime scene.'

'Was there some kind of inquiry?'

'Yep, and he was cleared of any wrongdoing.'

'Well, there you go. He was innocent, so why would you be believing rumours?'

'Being *cleared* and being *innocent* are two completely different things, Luce,' he pointed out.

'Oh, for goodness sake,' she snapped.

'Thompson left the force under a lot of speculation. The guys in his own department didn't even trust him—that's saying a lot.' He sighed at her deepening frown and his face softened slightly. 'Look, you're right. I don't have any hard evidence; all I have to go on is what I hear from my sources, but I'm just pointing out that this guy has made a living out of lying and pretending to be whatever he needs to be in order to gain people's trust . . . I doubt he even knows how to be *himself* any more. I don't want to see you hurt.'

The roar of a motorbike made their heads turn as a streak of black flew past them at great speed, heading out of town.

Hugh.

Lucy heard Nate swear under his breath before grabbing his radio and calling for assistance, then shouting out to the young constable inside the station. 'The stupid bastard's going to try to take them on alone. Stay here, Lucy. I gotta go,' he said after his offsider got into the passenger seat, slamming his door shut and driving off.

Hugh didn't intend to wait around for Nate to get his act together. He wanted answers and he needed time alone to get them. He wasn't sure he could trust Nate to look the other way; he was a by-the-book kind of bloke and Hugh had learned that by the book didn't get you far on the street.

He cruised past the bottom pub slowly. The two bikes were still parked out the front but there was no sign of the riders. He didn't have to wait long. The doors swung open and the two men headed outside to the footpath. The older one, Chainsaw, Hugh knew well. For a long time he'd lived and fought beside the guy. They'd considered him a brother once. Not any more. The other one was Terrier Williams, Basio's second-in-command. He'd been at Basio's side during a split in the club a decade or so before and was the first of a new breed. The old club days were long gone. Nowadays drugs and violence were often used as both business and pleasure; the old ideals of camaraderie, family, loyalty and brotherhood thrown out the window in preference for making money.

Hugh kicked his bike into gear and revved the engine as the two men swung their gaze across the street to where he sat. Hugh snapped down the visor of his helmet and pulled out onto the road, watching in the rear-view mirror with a grim smile of satisfaction as the two bikers scrambled onto their machines and pulled out after him. He flew through town, past Nate, only barely registering who he was talking to.

Lucy.

His focus wavered momentarily and he forced himself to forget everything except what he needed to do. If he had any hope of this plan succeeding he'd have to keep his head straight . . . something he couldn't do around Lucy. The woman had had his head in a spin from the first day he'd laid eyes on her.

He wouldn't have much time before Nate would be hot on his tail, but he didn't need long—just a few minutes. If this worked, of course . . . There was a good chance he'd get himself killed in the process, but he had to give it a go. There was no other way.

Twenty-four

Up ahead, the side of the road dropped away to a small gully, edged by what he hoped was soft grass. He clenched his jaw and pushed himself against every conceivable instinct a rider had, sliding his bike onto the gravel edge of the road and bracing himself for the fall. He let go of the bike as soon as he felt contact with the dirt, and rolled as far away from the carnage as he could. He couldn't bring himself to look at the damage to his bike—that would have to wait.

Hugh took out his phone and scrolled through until he found what he was after, quickly hitting record and putting the phone back in his pocket as he heard the roar of approaching bikes. He pulled out his gun and crouched behind the cover of trees nearby; then he waited.

He knew they wouldn't risk leaving him behind if he wasn't dead; he was counting on them needing to make sure. He heard the slipping of booted feet on the gravel of the gully as they made their way down the slope to where his bike lay on its side, the hot engine still ticking in the silence.

He waited until Terrier was close enough before he lunged from behind the tree and grabbed him around the throat. 'Drop the weapon, Chainsaw!' he called, holding his gun to the other biker's head.

He watched the man weighing up his options, as he tried to plan a way out of the situation. Hugh didn't trust him, not for an instant. All the guy needed was one tiny distraction—one chance and he'd be ready to take it. A man didn't last as long as Chainsaw had in a world of violence if he didn't have the instincts of a gutter rat to keep him alive. Hugh wasn't about to give him any opportunity. He gave a nod of his head and directed him to move closer before tossing him a set of handcuffs. 'Put them on.'

Slowly the man slid the cuffs around his wrist, his eyes narrowed into thin slits of glittering hate. 'Tighter,' Hugh snapped, listening as the cuffs made a click to indicate they'd locked in place. When he was satisfied Chainsaw was secure, he quickly cuffed the other man and pushed them both to the ground, his weapon trained on them steadily.

'You're a dead man,' Terrier said in his raspy smoker's voice, and spat at Hugh's feet.

'Not like I haven't heard that before.'

'Basio's been waiting for the day he catches up with you. He's never forgiven you for gettin' Rocco killed.'

The mention of the kid's name hit a raw nerve, but he forced his expression to remain blank. 'That wasn't me.'

'It was the pigs, and you were the one who called them in.'

'It wasn't me. I had nothing to do with that.'

'Doesn't matter, you're a nark and narks are lower than scum. Must be lonely—you ain't got no friends on either side, have ya.'

'Friends are overrated,' Hugh shrugged. 'But I want some answers.'

The man scoffed and sent Hugh a petulant glance. 'I just bet you do.'

'Who was behind the ambush that night?'

'Got no idea.'

Hugh stared at the men coldly. 'I don't buy it. I've been going over that night and I've come to the conclusion that you two were workin' with someone outside the club. Who tried to set me up?'

'We're not tellin' you nothin', pig.'

'Well, that's a shame. I really didn't want to have to get dirty today,' Hugh said, pulling out his knife from the holster strapped to his leg. There was a moment of regret as he felt himself slipping easily back into character: cold, calm and deadly.

A siren sounded in the distance and Hugh muttered a curse. *Damn it, it hadn't been long enough.*

Slowly he replaced the knife and waited as Nate's vehicle and a second four-wheel drive police car pulled up in a skid of gravel, doors opening and slamming shut in quick succession.

He waited as the two police offers made the tricky trek down the slippery slope of the gully, guns drawn, surveying the scene before them silently.

Hugh's hands shook as he straightened, turning towards Nate. He swallowed back the rising nausea. That had been close. A few minutes more and he knew he would have stepped over that invisible line. There would have been no going back after that. While he cursed the fact he hadn't been able to extract the information that he needed, part of him was relieved Nate had turned up now.

Hugh grabbed the phone from inside Terrier's jacket pocket and scrolled through the list of dialled numbers. 'You're going to need to keep this quiet. My guess is they came up to scout around and report back,' he told Nate, then tossed him the phone. 'And run a check on those numbers. The last call was before I saw them, so maybe they didn't get time to report in, but I wouldn't like to risk it. I need to know who they called.'

'What the hell did you think you were doing?' Nate demanded.

'Fixing the mess I made.'

'It's not your job.'

'Not any more. But it is my mess. They don't want anyone in this town—they want me. This is my problem.'

'It might be your mess, but it's in my town, so you'll leave it up to me to deal with—you got it? You ever pull a stunt like that again and I'll lock you up too.'

'I caught them, didn't I?'

Hugh heard the low curse under the cop's breath and couldn't help but grin. 'Bet you've called me worse than that a time or two.'

'You have no idea,' Nate muttered, hauling the largest of the bikers to his feet and pushing him towards the bank leading back up to the vehicles.

Hugh's smile faded as fast as it appeared. He needed to find out who was behind that ambush. Until he knew, his life would never be his own.

Twenty-five

'Any luck?' Hugh asked, walking into the station a few hours later. He'd gone home to arrange a tow truck to bring his bike back to the garage and to make a phone call to a contact in the force for some more information.

Nate gave Hugh an irritated glance as he pulled out a chair across the desk from him, but didn't make any comment about making himself at home. Technically this was police business, but Hugh was long past playing the civilian at this stage. He knew how it worked, and he knew that he wasn't about to get fobbed off while the cops made their by-the-book enquiries.

'The numbers on the phone we retrieved were traced to a clubhouse in western Sydney. You were right.'

Hugh didn't take any comfort in the knowledge. The club knew they were up here and, if they didn't hear from them soon, they'd come looking.

'They wouldn't talk during questioning,' Nate added.

'No shit,' Hugh muttered. 'You think they're intimidated by a bunch of country cops?'

'Country cops who don't have to keep you in the loop in this investigation, I might add,' Nate snarled.

'Yeah, all right. I wasn't trying to hurt your feelings,' Hugh said sarcastically. 'I'm pointing out a fact. These guys are hardened criminals. They're conditioned not to talk.' Memories of the lengths the Rabble went to in order to extract information in the past was horrific and, even though Hugh had always prided himself on having a tough stomach, there were times when even he'd flinched. It wasn't for the faint of heart. 'You won't get shit outta them.'

'We've contacted the gangs squad and they're going to get some eyes on the clubhouse and report back any activity.'

'If whoever sent them doesn't hear from them soon, they'll send a party out. We might not have much time.'

'Whoever sent them? You don't think this is club related?' Nate asked, his gaze zoning in on Hugh's.

'I don't know. Something doesn't add up. I'm not entirely convinced they're acting on club orders. There's no way those guys would venture out and risk being spotted—not when the club keeps them fairly well hidden. They're wanted for some pretty heavy stuff. That's what bugs me—why send these two out to find me? If this was club sanctioned, they'd have used some young probationer, one who wouldn't necessarily draw any attention.'

'The Rabble aren't the force they once were. Maybe they just don't have the manpower to send anyone else. Anyway, we should have enough time to get reinforcements from Armidale up here, just in case.

'Not necessarily. If I were that intent on tracking someone down, I wouldn't want my backup a day's road trip away from Sydney. I'd have them stashed somewhere closer. Too many men on bikes would attract a lot of attention, but leaving a few of them somewhere out of town would be safer.' Hugh sent Nate a level look. 'We may not have much time before they get here.'

Lucy looked up as the office door opened and she let out a small sigh of relief as Hugh walked in.

For a few moments neither of them spoke, and she watched quietly as he moved stiffly across the room.

'You're hurt,' Lucy said, standing and circling around the desk.

'I'm okay.'

The initial relief she'd felt upon seeing him was quickly replaced by anger as she remembered the tow truck arriving with a scratched and crumpled bike on board. Her stomach had lurched, even though only a few seconds later she'd seen Hugh hobble up to the driver and direct him as to where to unload it. She'd almost sunk to the ground in silent gratitude, but had somehow managed to hold herself upright long enough to retreat back into the office and slump into her chair. She hadn't been able to face Hugh just then. She was too vulnerable. Part of her had wanted to throw herself into his arms and hold him tight. The other part had remembered she no longer had the right to do that.

'I need you to do me a favour.' From his tone, Lucy knew it wasn't going to be something she would like.

'I need you to lock up here and go home.'

'Why?'

'Because I don't know what might happen, and I don't want you here if something does.'

'But I thought you got those men, the ones Ross was talking about . . .'

'There's a fair chance there will be others coming.'

Lucy stared at Hugh and felt a cold sweat break out across her back. He was serious. 'This is insane. What the hell is happening? Why are they doing this?'

'It's too long and complicated to get into now. I just need to make sure . . .' He let out a long, tired sigh. 'I just need you to do this for me, okay?'

She hated seeing him like this—it didn't matter what their relationship status was now, she still cared about him. 'I'll lock up and then go and get Belle.'

'School's probably the safest place Belle could be right now. Nate was pretty adamant he didn't want to create widespread panic, and I agree. They're probably not stupid enough to do anything in the middle of town, but if they know I own this place, then I'd rather keep everyone here safe by closing for the day. I don't want to give them any more targets than absolutely necessary.'

'But, I don't—'

'Lucy, I know that given what you've found out lately you don't have a great deal of confidence in me right now, but you have to trust me on this. I'm going to make this all okay, I promise.'

'How are you going to fix it? You're lucky you weren't killed, pulling a stunt like you did earlier. What were you thinking?' Her voice rose a notch as she glared at him.

'It's complicated.'

'No kidding,' she snapped. 'Everything about you is complicated, but that doesn't mean you get to just push us all away.' This morning, watching him ride away to face those men had shaken her . . . badly. The very real risk Hugh could be killed had sat like a heavy weight in her stomach as she'd waited anxiously for news. When she'd caught sight of the bike on the back of the tow truck, it had put everything into perspective. *What if she had lost him?* Nothing else mattered.

She *knew* Hugh hadn't had anything to do with the drugs coming into town—she'd known it even before she'd uncovered Stringybark's dark secret. She also knew Hugh had only acted the way he had that night out of self-defence. He'd been hurt to think she could believe even for a split second that he'd been involved. Wounded pride and maybe a little defensiveness from a past he wasn't proud of had created a perfect storm of emotions and led to them both saying things they now regretted.

'I know I hurt your feelings the other night,' she said softly, taking a step closer to him. 'But you have to believe that *I did know* you couldn't be behind the drugs. It just somehow got blown all out of proportion.'

He seemed surprised by her admission and for a moment the tightness in his face eased. 'You had every right to doubt me. Given my past connections, it would be natural to at least consider the possibility. I acted like a jealous dick.'

Lucy smiled a little at that. 'You have no reason to be jealous of Nate. There's only one guy who has ever managed to drive me to the brink of insanity on a daily basis.'

Hugh's expression softened slightly at her words. 'Whoever that guy is, he sounds like more trouble than he's worth.'

Lucy gave a small shrug, 'I've never done anything the easy way. Why would I start now?'

'I need to take care of this before I can offer you a future,' he said, brushing the side of her face gently with his fingers. 'Do you understand?'

Lucy shook her head. 'No, I don't. I don't understand why you have to deal with these people. I'm really scared for you, Hugh.'

'They won't stop until I meet with them. I can't have a life here, or anywhere, until I do. And I want a life, Luce. With you and Belle. But I won't put you in danger to have it. I need to clear my name once and for all. You just have to trust me on this.'

'I know about the money that went missing,' she blurted, and saw a shadow of wariness cross his face. 'I don't want any more secrets between us. I *know* you had nothing to do with it, okay?' she said, hoping that he could read the sincerity in her words. Whatever happened she couldn't let him go off wondering whether she believed in him or not.

'I've got a lot to sit down and tell you after all this, and I promise I'll fill you in on everything this time, but I still want you to get home and stay there. I need to know you're safe.'

Lucy reached out and touched the side of his face gently. 'Just don't do anything stupid.' She paused. 'Make that *more stupid* than taking on a bunch of bikers. I need you back in one piece, okay?'

'I'll do my best. I have a lot to get back here for.' He placed his hand on top of hers, taking it away from his cheek and squeezing it gently, before stepping away. 'But I have to find a way to end this for good.'

He let her hand go and turned away, leaving her to stare at his back as he left the building.

An uneasy feeling settled inside her at his quiet words. If it didn't end here today . . . *when* would it end? And more to the point, how?

Hugh found Nate inside the station, talking to a constable, when he walked inside a few minutes later. Nate gave him a nod of acknowledgment and finished up with the younger man quickly before heading across to him.

'I need to talk to you. My office.'

Hugh frowned at the brisk order, something about the tone of the cop's voice alerting him to the fact he had some news . . . and it wasn't necessarily good.

'What's going on?' Hugh asked as soon as Nate pulled the door shut behind them.

'There was another number on that phone we took off your old mate this morning. I had a search done on it.'

'And?'

'It belongs to a Detective Mulligan. Why would a wanted felon like Terrier Williams be calling a narcotics detective?'

Hugh's fist clenched involuntarily by his side. 'Son of a . . .' his words trailed off as pieces of the puzzle fell into place.

'Listen. I broke protocol to let you in on this, but you gotta fill me in on the details.'

'Mulligan was one of the detectives working on the bust I was acquitted over. Never did trust the guy, but I couldn't find anything to connect him to the Rabble. But he had opportunity, and he knew enough about the bust to tip off someone and plan an ambush in order to get hold of the money.'

'If that's true, he took a big risk. The detectives on the case would have considered him a suspect as well,' Nate said.

Hugh gave a dismissive grunt, 'They didn't need to, not when I was set up so convincingly.' Hugh saw the police officer chewing over this information silently. 'Look, I get that it goes against the grain to believe one of your own could be corrupt . . . and I get that *my job*, hanging around scum, instantly makes me a suspect,' he added, 'but I'm tellin' you, this guy is crooked and I think you know it too.'

'I admit it's suspicious that he'd be a contact on a guy like Terrier's phone,' Nate sighed, rubbing his hands across his face in frustration. 'Yeah, okay, I've got a bad feeling about it all but, if it's true, we'll handle this via official channels. I'll have to pass this info on to my superiors.'

'If you do that, it'll get covered up and I'll guarantee you'll get a sudden transfer to some inner city hellhole. I'm tellin' you, I've seen how these guys work. You pass the info on to your superior, who has to then pass it on to his, and eventually it's going to hit someone's desk and it'll all disappear. Then they'll make sure you and everyone else connected to it stays quiet somehow.'

'So what do you suggest we do with this information?'

'Just sit on it for now. I've got an idea. If we can get Terrier and Chainsaw to implicate Mulligan, then those phone records will be useful evidence.'

'You think they'll just blurt out everything we want to know?'

'They might if we provide a little bit of encouragement.'

Hugh ignored Nate's confused frown, as his idea gathered momentum. 'We need to lure Mulligan up here.'

'And just how do you suppose we do that?'

'I'll let him know I have Terrier and Chainsaw. He won't want those two spilling their guts, and I'm willing to bet he'll show up to make sure he ties up all his loose ends this time around.'

'You really are crazy,' Nate said, shaking his head.

'The way I see it, we don't have much choice. We need to make sure we've got this thing airtight before we hand it over to anyone.'

'We? Last time I looked you were out of the force.'

'Yeah, well, I'm mixed up in this now, and I don't intend to sit back and let anyone else control what happens.'

Nate studied Hugh silently for a few minutes, seemingly weighing up his options before he spoke. 'I'll keep the phone records under wraps . . . for now. But eventually we have to find someone we trust to hand them over to. When that time comes, I'm the one who will make the decision about who that person is.'

'Fair enough. Providing, of course, we're both still alive after the Rabble get to town,' Hugh added.

'I've been thinking about our options,' Nate said, his gaze focused out the window thoughtfully. 'We need to head them off before they reach town. I don't want any of this spilling over around here.'

'I was thinking the same thing,' Hugh said. 'I think I know a place.'

Twenty-six

'You sure they'll go for this?' Nate asked sceptically, eyeing the notes he'd jotted down as they'd hashed out a rough plan.

'They've gone to a lot of trouble to track me down. I'm guessing they won't want to waste time asking questions.'

'If it were me, I'd be assuming it was a prime place for an ambush. What makes you think they'll put themselves at risk?'

'Working with the cops would be the last thing they'd think I was doing.'

'Why would they think that?'

'Because they think I'm mixed up with Ken's drug lab. At least, that's the info I had planted through reliable channels. They'll check on any gossip going around and they won't doubt it if it comes from the kind of sources I've contacted.'

Hugh gave a bitter twist of his lips at the cop's doubtful look. 'If it's one thing I know well, it's how the underground works. Trust me, I had a lot of favours to call in.'

'So you'll wear a wire?'

'Only if I want to get shot in the head. No,' he said, with exaggerated calmness, 'but we'll need some kind of way to plant a bug somewhere nearby. Something that'll pick up any conversation at a distance.'

Nate's eyes lit up immediately. 'I can help with that. Let me give Larry Meyers a call.'

'Who?'

'He's with National Parks and Wildlife. They've been monitoring wildlife around the area, using these digital field recorders to record endangered species calls.' Nate waved his hand briskly.' I don't know much about it, I just remember Larry raving on about how it feeds back to a computer or something, so I'm thinking that might be a secure way for us to get the evidence.'

'It might work. How fast do you think we can get it organised?'

Nate was already reaching for the phone. 'Dunno. I'll find out. But considering the office isn't too far away, I can probably get him to meet us out there.'

National parks bordered most of the area around Bundah, which contributed to its isolation but also to its attraction for people wanting a bush escape. The two men pored over a map of the large national park and decided on an easily accessed picnic spot. 'There won't be too many tourists up that way now as it's been closed for maintenance for the past few weeks. There's a decent track in, which means we can get people up there to block it off and make sure no one wanders into the area unexpectedly. It's also not too far off the main road.'

'So Harleys could manage the terrain?'

'Yeah, I reckon so. It's paved pretty much the whole way.'

'They'd hate getting their stainless steel dusty,' Hugh muttered.

While Nate got on to Larry Meyers, Hugh took a deep, calming breath and hit Basio's name on the phone they'd taken from Terrier earlier.

'Terrier, where the fuck have you been? I've been callin' you for hours. What's going on?'

'Long time no hear,' Hugh said, the sound of the voice on the end of the phone sending him spiralling back in time.

'Who's this?'

'I'm crushed. Surely you haven't forgotten me so soon?'

'Well, I'll be stuffed.'

'You *do* remember me.'

'Where's Terrier and Chainsaw?'

'They're here. They're kinda tied up at the moment, though.'

'You know that we're coming for you, don't ya?'

'I kinda hoped you'd forgotten about me, actually.'

'You betrayed your brothers, and you stole my money. Not so easy to forget something like that. Let's not make this difficult. Give yourself up.'

'I'll meet you, but on my terms.'

'I think you might be forgetting who you're talking to.'

'Not at all. But the way I see it, I have some information you might be very interested in, and that gives me the upper hand here.'

'What kind of information?'

'It's about your missing money. And if you're not interested, then I know for a fact the cops will be. So it's up to you. Agree to my terms or I'll tell the police everything I know.'

'What terms?'

'I don't want you in town. I like this place. I don't want anyone getting mixed up in this.'

'Where then?'

'I'll text you the directions.'

Hugh disconnected the call and put the phone down on the desk. He felt sick. God, he wished he never had to hear that voice again, to get mixed up in that world once more, but here he was about to walk straight back into the nightmare.

'Think he'll agree?' Nate asked.

'Yeah. He doesn't care where it happens, as long as it happens. He's been waiting for this day for a long time.'

'You need to wear a vest,' Nate said, walking towards a storage room.

'No.'

'Don't be stupid. You have to. You can't just walk into the middle of the bush without some kind of protection.'

'You know, you're kinda sounding like you're beginning to care about me, Nate. I gotta say, I'm flattered and all, but you're really not my type.'

'They're going to kill you. You know that, right?' Nate said, ignoring Hugh's attempt at lightening the situation.

'I know that.'

'And you're just going to let them?'

'No. I don't have a death wish. I'm kinda hoping you and your guys will do your job and stop that from happening,' he said. 'But they already don't trust me, so if they suspect I'm working with the cops, they'll shoot first and we won't get anything out of them.'

'If you wear a vest and they shoot first you'll at least stand a chance of not ending up dead.'

'And we won't have anything to implicate Mulligan. I need to clear my name once and for all because, after this, that's all I'll have.'

'A reputation isn't worth getting yourself killed over.'

'Only someone who's never had theirs questioned could say that. I'm not wearing a vest.' Hugh turned away and left the office.

Hell, yes, he was scared stupid of walking into a meeting with Basio without any kind of protection, but it wasn't as though he'd never done that before. His entire undercover life had been one gamble with death after another. He didn't want to die today. He wanted the life he had been dreaming about. The life of the owner of a pub in a small country town, with the woman he loved by his side. Living the simple life—that's all he wanted. And deep down he knew it was only a dream. He was never going to have that life. Damn, he hated that he'd had a taste of it. Now it would hurt that much more to lose the dream so close after holding it in his hands.

Hugh couldn't look at the pub as he rode out of town for the second time. He couldn't think of everything he was about to give up. He just had to concentrate on the task at hand and try not to die.

When Hugh turned off the car engine, the picnic area was quiet save for the sound of the whip birds. He walked across to where Nate was talking to a guy in a National Parks uniform and the younger cop stood guard over two men sitting tied to a tree nearby. They glared at him as he passed, and the old expression, if looks could kill, had never been more apt.

'We need blindfolds on this pair as well,' he told the younger constable. 'I don't want any kind of tip-off to Basio that something's going on.'

'This is Terry,' Nate introduced the other man briefly. 'He's just set up the recorder.'

Hugh searched the area and eventually spotted a dull green box tucked up under a large fern nearby. At first glance you might pass by it unnoticed. Unless you were looking for something, he doubted anyone would see it, but then again these guys were notoriously paranoid and he couldn't be certain they wouldn't spot it, but it was the best they could do in the time frame they had to work with.

'And it'll pick up from a decent range?'

'It'll be fine for what you need here. It'll upload to the laptop and be saved wherever you want it sent.'

'All right then. You guys better get out of here.'

'I still don't like this.'

'They're not exactly favourable conditions, but we don't have a lot of choice. Let's just hope your backup gets here in time.'

'ETA was forty minutes. I'll go and wait for them at the fire trail and bring them back on foot.'

Hugh watched the two officers melt into the bushland. There was something incredibly peaceful about the silence of the bush. Although it wasn't really silent, once you listened hard enough there was a chorus of insects humming and birds calling out high up in the treetops, leaves rustling in the wind and branches scraping against tree trunks. But the absence of man-made sound was like a balm to the soul. If he had to die today, at least he could take this moment of calm with him.

A rumble sounded in the distance and Hugh's skin began to prickle. The sound grew louder, a slow, steady roar that grew in strength as it came closer. Bikes, and lots of them, were heading his way. He shook off any lingering thoughts and focused on the task ahead.

Flashes of blinding chrome and steel and a deafening roar of motors signalled their arrival as the posse approached slowly in single file along the paved road and into the clearing of the picnic area. It was intimidating to see the ten bikes arrange themselves into formation, parking in a tidy line which seemed out of place here in the bush.

Hugh kept his eyes on the big man who sat on the front bike, sizing him up with a steely glint. Basio was a man used to being obeyed and he did not take betrayal lightly. He was here to kill Hugh. It was as simple as that. But it wouldn't be done clean and fast. He'd make sure Hugh was quite aware of how much he hated narks and being made to look like a fool.

The biker looked across at his two men tied to the tree and raised an eyebrow at Hugh. 'Bit much?'

'Not when they won't shut the hell up. Besides, I don't think you're going to care too much about their welfare once you hear what I've got to say.' All Hugh had was a strong hunch about what went down that night—but he knew he had to play the card—it was all he had.

'Really? And what could you possibly tell me that would make me turn on two of my own?'

'These two were working for a detective named Mulligan. I saw them that night with the money, just before the Jokers arrived. Mulligan arranged the Jokers' hit so he could get the money out before the official raid. Mulligan sent them up here to kill me.'

Hugh saw the biker's eyes harden and his mouth tighten in a hard line.

'I didn't steal your money,' Hugh said.

'You're still a cop,' Basio spat.

'Not any more. I was doing my job, that's all. Now I just want to be left alone. I'll give you your guys back without bringing the cops into it, and you can go deal with Mulligan and get your money back . . . In exchange I just want to be left alone.'

Basio eyed Hugh silently. 'Not going to happen. You betrayed us. That's worse than stealing from us. Bikers' code demands retribution.'

'Bullshit. Drugs, gun running and crime were never what the bikers' code was all about and you know it. The Rabble don't stand for anything any more. Bikers' code means nothing now.'

'Who the hell are you to tell us what we stand for? You're the worse kind of scum—lyin' and cheatin' and wormin' your way into people's lives, only to go reportin' back to your copper mates. And even they can't stand ya, can they?'

'I couldn't give a shit who likes me or not. I was just doin' a job to make sure criminals get put away where they belong.'

'Funny how that line gets a bit blurred, though, isn't it? Nice how you can wash your hands clean of the part you played in everything over the years. But it don't make you any less guilty, though, does it?' Basio said.

A nearby shout immediately sent everyone into high alert. Hugh felt his stomach drop to his knees, hoping like hell the police ambush hadn't been discovered and they weren't all about to die.

A small group of Basio's men who had obviously been left as lookouts appeared. 'Boss, we've got visitors,' a stocky Rabble soldier announced as he and a half-dozen other Rabble members frogmarched a disgruntled-looking

Mulligan and six equally unimpressed men wearing Joker patches into the centre of the clearing.

'Who the hell is this?' Basio demanded, eyeing the detective ferociously.

'This is the man who stole your money,' Hugh said.

'Seems you neglected to mention we'd have company when you invited me up here for a catch-up, Thompson,' Mulligan said, shaking his arm free of the biker who had hold of him.

'What is this?' Basio snarled, his gaze pinning Hugh darkly.

'You wanted to find out who stole your money, so I got him up here.'

The detective's appearance clearly unsettled Basio and his men. As far as plans went, it wasn't the safest option, but it served its purpose: create chaos and throw the players off guard. The bikers were shuffling uneasily. One wrong move could send this whole thing into an instant bloodbath.

'This is Detective Mulligan from narcotics. He stole your money and planned the ambush that killed your men.'

Basio's expression hardened into granite as he glared at the detective.

'You brought us all up here just to throw around these same old worn-out accusations?' Mulligan said, shifting his gaze sideways to Hugh.

'Interesting company you brought along with you, Mulligan.' Hugh glared at the men beside the detective, who were all well-known members of the Joker bike club.

'Makes it a little harder to believe you had nothing to do with it when you're best buddies with the enemy.'

Hugh saw the detective's gaze dart around the circle of men and could almost hear the cogs in his brain as he searched for a viable way out of the situation. After what seemed like an eternity, Mulligan must have finally realised there wasn't going to be any point in denying it.

'It was an opportunity too good to pass up,' he shrugged.

Hugh tried not to let his expression give away his surprise. Mulligan was guilty as sin, but he hadn't really expected him to actually admit it out loud.

Hugh looked across at Basio and saw he'd stilled, his attention zeroed in on the detective but Mulligan had quickly recovered his cornered rat instincts.

'Only it wasn't my idea. I was approached by those two,' he said pointing at Terrier and Chainsaw. 'They planned it all.'

Basio turned a disbelieving gaze upon his two most loyal members, who were both expressing muffled outrage behind their gags.

'I wanna hear their side of the story before we go any further,' Basio said, his tone heavy with suspicion.

Hugh couldn't let that happen. The moment those gags came off, they'd warn everyone of the police trap. Whatever else they might be, Terrier and Chainsaw were Rabble brothers first and foremost—especially since Mulligan was now selling them out to save his own hide.

'Look, clearly we've both been conned and brought up here under false pretences. We can stand here and bitch about past grievances and then kill each other, or we can forget all these dramatics and I can give you a way to get your money back,' Mulligan cut in.

Hugh sent a brief glance around the clearing, trying to gauge the mood. Basio's men were on edge, looking to their leader for further instruction.

Basio said nothing. His trademark blank stare could unnerve the toughest of bikers, and, for all Mulligan's bravado, Hugh could see a line of sweat beading at his temple and knew the detective wasn't as unaffected as he'd like everyone to believe.

'I can get you in on a deal I have going down in a few days,' Mulligan said. 'Double what you lost in that last bungle. As a show of faith, I'll give you the whole lot. I'm starting my own crew.' He nodded towards the Jokers. 'These men work for me now. With my connections, you would be in a position to claim the Jokers' territory for your own business expansion. You'd control the largest territory on the entire east coast. You could make the Rabble a formidable club once more.'

Hugh could see a glimmer of interest brewing in Basio's eyes and knew he had to step in fast. 'You're going to trust this guy? He's a *cop* . . . in narcotics. It's a set-up.'

'If it were a set-up, why would I be here with these guys?' Mulligan threw back, indicating the members of the Joker gang.

Hugh's gaze narrowed on the detective. Did they have enough on the recording to convict Mulligan once and for all? He wasn't sure. He'd never get another opportunity to try—he had to make sure they got this guy once and for all. 'So it wasn't enough that you turned Basio's men against him,' Hugh said, pointing at Terrier and Chainsaw, 'you had to try and implicate *me* in the whole mess?'

Mulligan sent Hugh an irritated glance. 'You were always going to be the scapegoat. No one working UC for that long could be squeaky clean. But these two were supposed to plant the evidence I gave them on you and they didn't. They panicked after they dumped you on the side of the road.' His irritation turned to sarcasm. 'And you got off. It was your lucky day, wasn't it. Shame your luck has just run out, hey.'

'Enough of this. Untie Chainsaw and Terrier,' Basio ordered, tossing his head at two of his men. 'I want to hear it from my men.'

It was becoming clear to Hugh that the detective was quickly losing his audience. Basio didn't seem inclined to believe him, and this whole thing was turning into a three-ring circus.

Then, before anyone could move, a hoarse cry of warning came from the tree where the men were tied. 'It's a trap! Get outta here! He's got the cops waiting.'

Hugh realised too late that Terrier had managed to work his gag free during the stand-off.

Hugh turned to head for cover, knowing the looming crossfire between the police and two rival gangs would not differentiate between targets; besides, he was wanted dead by pretty much everyone standing in this clearing.

He heard the sharp, clear bang of fired bullets, and as he dove for cover he felt a burning sensation hit the back of his thigh. An endless blanket of gunfire echoed through the once peaceful bushland, before becoming spasmodic as the last few shooters managed to get off a few more rounds.

Then it was over. In the distance, Hugh heard men's voices issuing orders, followed by a flurry of radio activity. Hugh sat up slowly and looked around at the carnage. Men lay scattered like broken, discarded toys on a playroom floor. A few groaned and made noises as police in vests carefully checked for vitals and began first aid on those who had not been killed outright.

Hugh grabbed hold of a nearby trunk in an attempt to pull himself to his feet.

'Don't even think about it,' a voice said nearby and Hugh looked over to find Nate heading towards him with a first-aid box.

'It's just a flesh wound,' he said, waving Nate off.

'That's an awful lot of blood for a flesh wound. Sit back down.'

'Did it record?'

'Yep, got it all. Thanks to you, we've got quite a bit of evidence to go on. Mulligan got away, but he won't get far; he was wounded and there's no way he'll be able to talk his way out of this.'

'I just want my name cleared.'

'Pretty sure we've done that,' Nate assured him.

'What about Basio?'

'Dead.'

Hugh quashed the moment of regret he felt over the news. Basio was a criminal, and as bad as they came, but part of Hugh's job had meant getting close to these people and, like it or not, he had. Basio had said he'd washed his hands of the things he'd seen and done, but that wasn't true. He could never do that; some things he would have to live with for the rest of his life.

'Listen,' Nate said as he finished wrapping Hugh's leg. 'What Basio said earlier . . . about undercover cops. Not everyone thinks that. It takes guts to do what you guys do.'

Hugh swallowed back his surprise at the other man's comments; it was almost as though he'd been reading his thoughts.

Nate held his hand out and Hugh blinked in surprise, hesitating only briefly before clasping his hand and giving it a firm shake, caught off guard by the rush of emotion the words provoked in him.

A flash of movement caught Hugh's eye as Mulligan staggered from the tree line behind Nate, gun raised and hatred spewing from his eyes. Hugh didn't stop to think about what he was doing. He pushed Nate aside moments before he heard a deafening volley of gunshots. The last thing he felt was the white-hot burn of light as his body convulsed.

Twenty-seven

'Here, drink this,' Nicole said, forcing a glass of amber liquid into Lucy's cold hands. 'You need something to settle your nerves.'

'You really think it's appropriate for a doctor's wife to be prescribing alcohol for nerves?'

Lucy took a sip then put the glass down on the coffee table and laced her fingers together tightly as she looked out the window and thought about Hugh.

'He'll be okay,' Nicole said, sitting down beside her and placing a comforting arm around her shoulders.

Lucy hadn't told Nicole everything about Hugh, but enough for her to know that Hugh was caught up in the middle of something extremely dangerous.

'I can't believe that scumbag Ken,' Nicole said after a moment of silence. 'You think you know someone.'

Lucy tipped her head back and closed her eyes. A knock at the door had them opening again and sitting up straighter as Nicole jumped up to answer it. For a moment Lucy held her breath, hoping to hear that familiar deep voice, but had to force a smile when Russell stuck his head around the door. 'There she is! Our little survivor,' he said, moving past Nicole to engulf Lucy in a tight hug.

'We heard all about your horrible experience. It sounds just like something out of *Underbelly*. I said to Steve, "Nothing like this ever happened to us back in the city." It's all rather exciting, isn't it?' he said, pulling away to look down into Lucy's face.

'Russell, let the poor girl breathe.' Steve rolled his eyes. 'Are you all right, Luce?' He looked at her with gentle concern.

Lucy smiled. 'I'm fine. Just a bit of a bump on the head,' she said, lightly touching her temple, which was turning a delightful shade of blue and purple.

'We wanted to drop by and make sure you were okay,' Russell said, giving her one final tight squeeze before stepping away.

Another knock at the door sounded and Nicole retraced her steps to go and see who it was, coming back a few moments later with a raised eyebrow, followed by Mavis carrying a white casserole dish.

'We didn't think you'd be up to cooking, so we brought you over a few meals,' she said, placing the dish on the table and looking over her shoulder at the two other women who bustled in behind her with a collection of small white eskies.

'You didn't have to go to all this trouble, Mavis,' Lucy said, touched by the gesture.

'Nonsense, you've been through a terrible experience. That Ken Baxter's just lucky I'm not able to get my hands on him.' Her lips flattened into a grim line and her eyes narrowed. 'He won't want to be showing his face around this place again if he knows what's good for him.'

Lucy didn't doubt for a minute that Mavis meant every word. She still managed to scare Lucy, even when she was being nice.

'Well, we'd better be off. Although something must be happening around town; it's deathly quiet and there's an awful lot of police about,' Russell said.

'Probably still dealing with all the red tape and paperwork Ken and Ross have made for them,' Nicole suggested, walking the two café owners to the front door.

'Bye, Lucy. Hope you're feeling better soon,' Steve called.

Lucy blinked back a sting in her eye, touched by the fact so many people cared about her. She really was lucky to have these people in her life.

'Well, I guess I should be off too. The CWA has been asked to cater for a meeting at the police station later today. I'll let you off, Lucy dear. But Nicole,' she said, turning her hawk-like gaze on the tall blonde, 'I'll expect to see you at the CWA rooms later to help make sandwiches.' She moved across the room and out the front door without waiting for a reply.

'I'll expect to see you at the CWA rooms,' Nicole mimicked behind the door as it shut. 'Well, maybe I just won't turn up. She can't make me.'

Lucy chuckled despite herself. 'I *dare* you not to show up.'

'She doesn't scare me,' Nicole said with a delicate sniff.

'So in other words, you'll be there then,' Lucy said smugly.

'Yes,' Nicole said on a deflated sigh. 'I really detest that woman, you know.'

'You know as well as I do she'd be there to help you out in heartbeat if you needed it.'

'I guess so. But why does she have to be so . . . bossy. Seriously, she's worse than my mother.'

Lucy picked up a book, before putting it back down again, too distracted to concentrate. She flicked the TV on and clicked through the channels, finding nothing there to take her mind off things.

The sound of a helicopter flying low over town a few minutes later sent a shiver of dread through her. The distant scream of sirens turned her blood to ice. She knew they somehow involved Hugh and whatever he had gone to take care of.

A long time later, after Nicole had gone to do her sandwich duty, there was a knock at the front door. Lucy got up to answer it with an eerie kind of calm. She knew it wouldn't be Hugh she found there.

It was Nate.

'Where's Hugh?' She couldn't recall seeing Nate look quite so sombre before and fear clutched firmly at her heart. 'Is he all right?' she whispered.

'He's pretty bad.'

'How bad?'

'He has multiple gunshot wounds to the abdomen, leg and head.'

'Head?' Lucy gasped, her hand gripping the door handle tightly.

'Hugh is alive, Lucy. But he's in a critical condition. He's in surgery right now.'

'I need to see him.' She dropped her hand from the doorknob, ready to reach for the car keys hanging beside the front door.

'You can't.' Nate's words made her pause. 'They've taken him by chopper to Sydney.'

'Then I'll drive there. Which hospital?'

'Lucy.'

She turned her gaze onto Nate and noticed the look on his face. Her blood ran cold.

'They don't think he's going to make it,' he said softly.

Lucy opened her mouth to deny what she was hearing but closed it again abruptly. *He had to make it.* Things weren't settled between them. He couldn't . . . She couldn't even bring herself to think the word. 'I need to see him. To be there when he wakes up.'

She looked away from Nate's sympathetic expression as her eyes began to water. She wasn't going to cry.

A phone started to ring and Nate reached for his mobile. 'Sergeant Pearce,' he said briskly, then paused, listening to the caller on the other end, before thanking them.

It was the tone of his farewell that brought Lucy's gaze back to Nate's face. He'd sounded . . . gutted. In the space of a heartbeat she knew. He didn't need to say a word, and she hoped that he wouldn't, but he opened his mouth then quickly clamped it shut again and shook his head slowly.

'No,' Lucy said defiantly. 'Call someone. It's a mistake. Get on your phone and call someone else,' she demanded roughly, taking Nate's phone from his limp hold and pushing it against his chest. 'Do it, Nate!'

'Lucy, I'm sorry. He didn't make it through the surgery.'

She couldn't breathe. She couldn't speak. She couldn't cry. Her hands shook as she lifted them in front of her to warn off Nate as he took a step closer to hold her. He ignored her protest and gathered her close, holding her tightly as her world fell apart.

Twenty-eight

18 months later

Lucy tapped in the last few digits and gave a small sigh of relief when the total came up in the positives instead of negative.

She sat back in her chair and closed her eyes briefly. She was a business owner. It wasn't glamorous, but she was now the sole owner of Bundah Petroleum and Auto Parts. A week after her kidnap and the following shootout, the police had caught up with Ken as he was about to board a plane for Indonesia. So once again Bundah had been in the news, with reporters heading into town by the truckload as they covered the aftermath of the biggest bikie–police shootout in decades. Mulligan had been wounded but survived his injuries and the trial was big news; a narcotics cop stealing three million dollars in drug money had made headline news all around the country.

Lucy had only appeared once in court when she had given testimony against Ken and Ross. She had had no desire to sit in court each day; she'd had no wish to hear anything about that day or the events that followed. Her pain had been too raw.

The thing that helped her get through it all was coming to work each day. Had it not been for Marg Baxter, she wasn't sure she'd have managed to leave the house at all.

It had been a week after Ken Baxter's arrest that she'd received a phone call from Marg, her small bird-like voice sounding more confident than she could ever remember hearing it before.

'I'm so sorry, Marg,' she'd said, feeling for the old woman whose only living relative looked like going to prison for quite a long time. 'Are you all right? Is there anything you need?'

'Dear, I'm fine. Don't you worry about me. It's you I'm worried about. I heard what happened . . . what Kenneth did. Words cannot express how terrible I feel.'

Lucy sighed. It was still sometimes hard to believe herself. 'I'm all right. And you have no reason to feel terrible.'

'Oh, but I do. I always knew Kenneth had a mean streak. No one ever believed me, of course. I tried to tell people, but he was always a charmer. He could charm his way out of anything.'

Lucy felt a small stab of guilt over Marg's words. She'd never liked the way Ken had treated his sister, but he'd always managed to make her believe Marg was more than a little demanding and exhausting to be around too long.

'What will you do, Marg? Will you be all right down there?' She knew Ken sent her money and took care of all her bills. Who would do that now he was in prison?

'Well, that's what I'm calling about, dear. You know that I'm very fond of you. I want to thank you for all the birthday and Christmas cards and presents you sent on behalf of Kenneth. I know they were never his idea.'

Lucy automatically opened her mouth to protest, but closed it quickly. She didn't have to defend her ex-boss, but she hadn't really done it for Ken's sake. She'd done it because she knew how much it would mean to his lonely older sister to receive a gift from her brother.

'You're a good girl, Lucy, and you didn't deserve what my brother did to you.'

Again Lucy opened her mouth to protest, but Marg continued before she could get a word in. 'I want to give you something.'

'Marg, please, you don't have to give me anything. I'm fine. It's all over now.' She smiled sadly at the lovely gesture, but she doubted very much Marg would have anything to give even if she agreed to accept it.

'I want you to have the business.'

'Excuse me?'

'The service station, dear. I want you to have it.'

'Well, that's very kind of you, Marg,' Lucy said slowly, 'but I'm pretty sure the police will have frozen all of Ken's assets and the business won't belong to him any more.' Oh, the poor woman, what was going to happen to her now? Lucy felt terrible; Marg probably assumed that Ken's assets would somehow pass on to her, being his next of kin.

'I'm sure the police *have* frozen all his assets, dear,' she agreed almost cheerfully on the other end of the line. 'However, Ken didn't own the service station. Or the real estate . . . or the rental properties in his portfolio. He transferred them all across to me a few years ago.'

'What?'

'The businesses belong to me. I'm calling to offer you the option of buying the service station—at a very reasonable price.'

Lucy was struggling to keep up. Marg went on to tell her the price she was asking and left it with her to think over. The price was a steal, and despite the fact she was still in shock, Lucy had already done a rough calculation in her head and realised she might actually be able to afford it. She spent a long night tossing and turning, before calling her father the next morning and running the idea past him.

Three weeks later she'd had a copy of the contract in front of her solicitor and had been given the go-ahead to purchase. It seemed Marg had had the last laugh on her brother after all. She had sold up property left right and centre, and had handed to the police prosecutor a list of hidden accounts where Ken had been keeping his drug money. It obviously didn't pay to misjudge your sister for so many years.

Lucy still smiled when she thought of Marg. She hadn't needed to worry about who would take care of her. Marg Baxter was more than capable of taking care of herself.

The phone rang and Lucy picked it up, giving a distracted, 'Bundah Petroleum and Auto Parts.'

'What are your plans for the weekend?'

Lucy smiled as she heard Nicole's voice on the other end of the line. 'Overly ambitious as usual. I thought I might tackle painting the inside of the house. Why?'

'I'm thinking about heading down to the city for the weekend. Wanna come?'

'Aren't you supposed to be accompanying your husband to some kind of reunion this weekend?'

Nicole gave a tortured cry on the other end of the phone. 'Not if you come with me. We can go shopping and eat out, and he can do the reunion.'

'Oh no. I'm not going to be the reason you break your husband's heart,' she said with a chuckle. 'I heard him the other day, and he was so excited you were going to be going with him to this thing.'

'But I don't wanna go,' she pouted.

'Suck it up, princess. I know for a fact you made him suffer through that art expo a few months ago. You owe him. Big time.' She also knew that her friend was exaggerating slightly in order to make Lucy feel as though she would be doing Nicole a favour by getting away from town for a few days. This was Nicole's way of keeping an eye on her. Lucy had lost Hugh, and then Belle had left home, and she knew Nicole worried that she'd had too much to deal with at once. She loved her friend for caring about her, but she didn't mind having time alone. Sometimes it was nice not to have to fake a smile for everyone just to reassure them that she was fine.

Belle had moved to Brisbane and was enjoying university, but she called home at least three times a day. Lucy had to smile at that: she'd always thought it would be her calling Belle, not the other way around. It had been a big adjustment at first. She'd missed Belle terribly, but this was a new experience for her. It was the first time in her life she didn't have anyone else to take care of. It was actually kind of liberating. At least that's what she told herself, and most days she believed it.

Thank goodness for the servo. At least it felt familiar. Bundah itself had a different feel about it now—not necessarily bad, just . . . different. There were new faces around town—people who had continued to make the move up to the highlands from the city. At least some good had come from all of the horror. Ken's campaign had paid off, and the town being thrown into the spotlight hadn't done any harm, in fact it had done the opposite. Bundah was on the map now. It had attracted interest from a trout hatchery which had begun operating on the outskirts of town, creating the first decent employment opportunities in the area for many years, with plans for more growth in the future.

The town was once more full of life. There were always people chatting in small groups, bustling in and out of shops. The only downside was the beautifully restored top pub sat quiet and empty. It had closed while, presumably, Hugh's estate was sorted out. And not even Bundah's gossip mill could track down any solid information about when, or even if, it would ever reopen. It was a sad reminder every time Lucy drove past. She still couldn't look at the building—it was too hard. She hated seeing all Hugh's work going to waste. It was a constant, painful reminder of the man she'd loved and lost.

No, life hadn't ever gone back to normal; it had changed forever. It was still difficult to contemplate the amount of carnage which had resulted from that day. Locals could never understand the betrayal by two of their own. A lot of people were ashamed of their part in the angry meetings and fiery threats against the newcomers over the drug allegations. In some ways, though, it had made them more tolerant of the new people moving to Bundah. It was as though the town had learned a painful but important lesson.

Lucy's friendship with Nate had also taken a turn. He'd been her rock after Hugh's death, and part of her suspected that he carried a lot of guilt over the fact that Hugh had ultimately sacrificed himself in order to save Nate's life. They'd gotten close over the subsequent months, but he'd never pushed her for more while she mourned, and he'd given her ample room to grieve. Then he'd come to her and told her he'd been offered a promotion and things had finally came to a head. He'd turn down the offer if she wanted him to stay, if she thought there was a future for them.

In her heart, Lucy had known she could never give Nate the love he truly deserved. He was a good man and he needed a woman who would love him with all of her heart, not someone who was still in love with the memory of another man. She missed his friendship since he'd left town, but she hoped he'd find what he was looking for in a new place and make a fresh start.

The sound of a motor driving into the station roused Lucy and she gave a tired sigh as she got to her feet. No rest for the wicked.

A big silver bike glided to a smooth stop beside a bowser and for a moment Lucy's breath caught as she watched the rider sit back and remove his gloves. Then came the rush of disappointment. It happened now and again. Something familiar would make her think of Hugh before it would be brutally ripped away as reality hit her squarely in the chest.

He was gone.

She forced her grief back into its box where she kept it firmly under lock and key. 'Hi there,' she said as she approached the rider.

He slowly dismounted his powerful bike, and she reached for the pump but stopped when the rider grabbed it first.

'We offer full driveway service,' she said with a frown, until the memory of her saying that in another place and time made her hand shake with the force of it. *Get a grip,* she scolded herself silently. What on earth was wrong with her? Everything was sparking memories of Hugh today and she wasn't sure she had the energy to deal with tears. She hated that grief could sneak up on you. Some days life seemed to be getting back on track, and then out of the blue she'd have a day where all she did was cry. She took the nozzle from the man's hand and inserted it in the tank, turning to watch the bowser tick over.

'How much do you want?' she asked without looking at him.

'Fill it up,' he said, his voice a little husky, deep and low, muffled by his helmet.

Lucy lifted her gaze, her confused expression reflecting like a mirror on the tinted visor. Her eyes followed his movement as he released the buckle on the helmet, slowly taking it off.

When he lifted his head to look at her, the breath rushed from her body, She held his gaze, searching the familiar depths of his eyes, recognition hitting her like a splash of cold water. 'Oh my God.'

His eyes crinkled in the corners, and she covered her mouth, dropping the pump as a rough sob tried to escape.

'It's you,' she whispered.

In two steps Hugh was by her side and Lucy was wrapped in strong arms. Her shock turned to confusion, quickly followed by anger. 'You let me think you were dead!' she yelled.

She saw Hugh look sideways before taking her hand and dragging her back into the office, locking the door behind them. 'I'm sorry, Luce. It was out of my control.'

'What the hell are you talking about? What happened to you? They told me you were dead. Nate said . . .' Her eyes widened. 'Did *Nate* know about this?' She knew she was firing questions at him too fast, but she couldn't help it. None of this made any sense. Hugh was dead; she'd been living with the nightmare for almost two years.

'No one knew about it,' he told her, letting go of her arms as she shook him off and moved away. 'As far as Nate knew, I died on the operating table. And I did . . . twice in fact,' he said with a bitter twist of his lips. 'My old boss stepped in and made the decision that I was going into witness protection. I found out a few days after I came out of ICU.' She saw his eyes darken as though he were remembering it again. He stepped towards her and Lucy flinched involuntarily, making him stop and sigh. He ran a hand through his long hair in frustration. 'I couldn't put you or Belle in danger.'

'In danger? How was not being dead going to put us in danger?' she demanded.

'If Mulligan knew I was alive, he'd have used you somehow, either as payback or something worse before the trial. You don't know these people, Lucy. They don't stop and they don't care who they hurt.'

Lucy couldn't believe this was happening. She stared at him, fearing that this was all a dream and when her alarm started beeping she'd wake up with the same emptiness inside she'd been living with all this time. Her eyes stung and she had to blink fast and hard to keep the tears at bay.

'I spent months in physio and it gave me time to think about stuff. I was offered witness protection, a new identity. A new life on the other side of the country. I took it to keep you and Belle safe.'

'Then what are you doing back here?

'I got a phone call to tell me Mulligan's dead. A dirty cop makes a lot of enemies in jail. Guess he doublecrossed the wrong guys. But at least I don't have to worry about him coming after the people I love any more.'

Lucy tried to digest everything he was telling her.

'I figured it would be easier for you if I just stayed away . . . stayed dead,' he amended with a wince. 'Only, I couldn't do it, Luce. I needed to see you again. I love you.'

Lucy sucked in a startled breath. Pain and heartache had been her constant companions for such a long time now that the miracle before her was almost overruled by her sad heart. But wasn't this what she'd prayed for? If she could just see him one more time . . . hold him one more time?

She looked deep into those blue eyes and saw his own pain and the suffering and knew that her outrage wasn't any greater than the horror he'd had to endure. She took a step towards him and then another, coming to a stop in front of him. She lifted one hand and placed it cautiously against his cheek, all the while holding the gaze of the man she thought she'd lost forever. She shook her head softly. 'It's too much,' she whispered.

She saw a flash of disappointment cross his face before he gave a small nod. 'I understand. I didn't know how else to break it to you. I wanted to do it face to face. But I get that this is a bit of a shock.'

'A bucket of cold water thrown over you is a bit of a shock,' she told him angrily. 'This is . . . people don't just reappear after being dead. You can't expect me to just . . .' She stopped, her emotions tripping over themselves as anger, frustration and relief all battled it out for control.

'I'm going to be staying at the pub,' he said, 'when you're ready . . .'

'Staying? For how long?'

'There's nothing keeping me away now. Mulligan gone changes everything,' Hugh shrugged. 'Convicting him cleared my name, and everyone in the Rabble is either dead or has drifted off after the club was disbanded. I don't think I'll have any more trouble.'

Lucy was reassured by the earnest look in his eyes, and relief rushed through her, taking what little self-control she'd managed to hold on to. The tears came too fast to wipe away and she saw his face crumple into anguish at the sight, then he pulled her tightly against his chest, his arms closing around her in an embrace that promised her a haven of safety.

'I'm so sorry I put you through all this,' he whispered as though the words were being ripped from his chest.

'I thought I'd lost you forever.' God, it hurt to remember all those endless, empty nights alone in bed huddled in a ball of misery.

'I'm here now. I promise I won't leave you ever again.'

Her hands grabbed the back of his shirt tightly, as though she would never let him ago. She wasn't sure how long they stood there, holding each other, but the ringing of the bell on the counter was a harsh intruder and Lucy pushed gently against his chest, wiping her face and trying to regain her composure.

'I have a customer,' she sniffed. 'You'd better go.'

'Will you be okay?' he asked, watching her with a concerned frown.

'I'll be fine. I just need some time to . . .' What? Adjust? Get used to the idea of him not being dead? She was too scared to think that maybe this was just a horribly cruel trick of her imagination.

He paused in the doorway. 'I'll be waiting . . . when you're ready.'

Lucy swallowed a painful lump in her throat as she watched him leave the office, then heard the roar of his bike fade away.

After she served the customer, she sat for the longest time staring at her paperwork without seeing anything. Slowly, the shock began to wear off and something quite different replaced it. *Hugh was alive. He was in Bundah . . . and she was . . .* She blinked and looked around. *Sitting at her desk?* In an instant she was on her feet and, grabbing her keys, she turned the *Closed* sign over and locked the door. She didn't head to her ute, she didn't have time; she ran instead. Past the new takeaway shop, past Madam Latoy's, past the café, ignoring Russell calling out to her as she went. She didn't stop until she reached the pub, running around the back and lifting her hand to bang on the back door.

The door opened before her fist connected with the timber and she was pulled into the tightest hug she'd ever felt in her entire life. Lifting her head she saw Hugh staring down at her, relief seeping out of his every pore, before their lips met in a hungry soul-searching kiss.

'Thank God, Lucy. I wasn't sure if I'd hurt you too much to trust me again.'

'I missed you so much,' she said, trying to catch her breath. 'But you better listen to me. From now on, I don't care if you think you're protecting me, you will *never* leave me behind again. Do you hear me? I never want to go through anything like that ever again.'

'I promise. Never again.'

Later, as they lay in each other's arms in the dark bedroom, Hugh stroked her arm gently. 'Would you come with me if I asked you to leave Bundah?'

Lucy lifted her head off his chest to look at him, still marvelling at the miracle of him. 'I could never leave Belle without telling her where I was, but if you thought you'd be safer somewhere else, then, yes, I'd follow you anywhere you needed to be,' she said, holding his intense gaze. She'd hate to leave Bundah—all her friends, her business, her memories—but knowing how much she'd lost when she'd contemplated a life without Hugh, she knew she'd do it in a heartbeat.

'You were the only thing that kept me going through some dark days, Luce. Knowing I had to get back to you one day was what kept me alive. Without you, I wouldn't have fought so hard to recover.'

'But you didn't come back,' she said softly.

He didn't answer straight away and Lucy waited patiently, reassured by the strong solid strength of his body next to her own.

'Once I regained my strength, I realised you were safer without me. I couldn't risk anything happening to you.'

'What if Mulligan hadn't died?'

'I'm not sure if I could have stayed away forever. I thought about coming back to check on you—I half expected you to have moved on . . . with Nate Pearce.'

Lucy gave a small shake of her head. 'It was never like that. I couldn't bear to think of being with anyone else.' They lay quietly for a few moments, both lost in the peace that had fallen around them. 'So, is it back to the three-year plan then?'

'I have a feeling it's going to be a bit longer than three years. I'm thinking it's turned into more of a lifetime plan. Think you can put up with me that long?'

Lucy gave a wobbly smile. 'I think I could manage that.' She searched his face, still unable to believe he was there. 'I love you, Hugh,' she whispered, and sighed as he gently wiped the few stray tears that ran down her face.

'Marry me,' he said quietly.

She nodded, wishing she could stop the happy tears from falling. This was not how she'd pictured accepting a marriage proposal—naked, with red-rimmed eyes and a runny nose—but right now, at this very point in time, she couldn't imagine anything more perfect.

It wasn't only Hugh who had got a shot at a better life by coming here. Bundah really was her second chance town too.

Acknowledgements

Thank you to Mark from Faunatech for valuable information about recording devices used in the research of wildlife. To Greg Coombes for help with sorting out police hierarchy. To Cindy Gosewisch Eichmann and Kristy Watson being my go-to readers, and to Catherine Finnegan for the title! To all my Facebook friends who continue to be an invaluable source of information, inspiration and friendship—thank you!

And many thanks to all the amazing people at Allen & Unwin, who work so hard to make my books the best they can be.

A huge thank you to my family. To my parents who have always supported and believed in me. To my husband who lets me rant about frustrating plot points and characters who won't behave, even though he has absolutely no idea what I'm talking about most of the time. To my children of whom I'm so proud. And to all my friends and family who constantly go out of their way to promote my books and convert non-Karly Lane readers all across the country!

ALSO FROM ALLEN & UNWIN

Tallowood Bound

KARLY LANE

When Erin Macalister leaves the city to take care of her beloved grandmother, she's relieved to be escaping the remnants of her broken marriage.

Arriving in the small rural community she grew up in, Erin finds nothing much has changed—including Jamie McBride, who is still as ridiculously good looking as he was when they were seventeen and madly in love.

Leafing through old photo albums evokes vivid memories for her grandmother of a soldier she once loved. Erin's curiosity about this mysterious soldier deepens when she finds an engagement ring he once gave her grandmother.

Meanwhile, Jamie McBride seems intent on rekindling his relationship with Erin, even though she's not at all sure she wants to risk heartache again.

From the bestselling author of *Poppy's Dilemma*, this poignant, heartfelt story of old loves and new possibilities is both inspirational and entertaining.

ISBN 978 1 74331 727 3

Gemma's Bluff

KARLY LANE

Smart and reliable, Gemma Northcote has always done what's expected of her. So it's not surprising that after uni she defers to her father's wish that she join the family business.

Gemma's best friend, Jasmine, is a different personality altogether. She thrives on spontaneity, is unpredictable and has generally pursued her own path.

When Gemma and Jasmine decide to spend a working holiday on a large rural property, their friends and family are surprised. Neither has any experience of country life (unless you count Jasmine's love of *McLeod's Daughters*) and they're not exactly farming types.

Away from her family, Gemma feels liberated. The longer she's away the more she questions what she really wants to do with her future. Ultimately, she realises she needs to choose between duty and what's right for her in life—and love.

From the bestselling author of *Bridie's Choice* and *Poppy's Dilemma*, this inspirational novel is sure to appeal to anyone who's questioned the direction they should take for true happiness.

ISBN 978 1 76029 041 2

Poppy's Dilemma

KARLY LANE

Poppy Abbott seems to have it all. Bright, successful and attractive, she lives in a beautiful apartment with sweeping views of Sydney. However, since the recent death of her beloved grandmother, she's been struggling to come to terms with her grief.

Feeling nostalgic one evening, Poppy decides to sort through her grandmother's belongings, which she hasn't been able to face before. She's hardly started when she comes across an old leather diary with the name 'Maggie Abbott' written in the front. It's not long before she's drawn into Maggie's life and her fears for her soldier boyfriend during the First World War.

As her interest in Maggie's diary intensifies, Poppy decides to spend some time at her grandmother's house in the country. Away from the city, Poppy begins to wonder if all the things she's always valued so much are what she really wants out of life. And then love intervenes.

From the bestselling author of *Bridie's Choice*, this is the story of a woman leaving a fast-paced existence in the city for a calmer, more meaningful life in the country, where she finds herself re-evaluating just about everything.

ISBN 978 1 76011 133 5